Life's
PERFECT
PLAN

by

Sarah Goodman

Cover Design by Wicked by Design

2nd edition edited by Raelene Green of word·play by 77peaches,
a division of 77peaches enterprises, LLC. www.77peaches.com

Formatting by Integrity Formatting

Dedication

To my handsome little men....

This book is dedicated to my three sons. You three are proof that you can't plan out life. Life gives you the ultimate plan, and boy did it ever for me! My wish for you is to live each day to the fullest and enjoy every moment life hands you. Find the positive in every negative situation. You are my sunshine and I love you to the moon and back.

Table of Contents

Chapter 1

One More Time

August

"Beth, I don't think we should do another round."
I am sitting at our kitchen table going over work
when my husband just blurts this out. A ghostly look
crosses my face, and my jaw hits the floor. "Seriously
Beth, with the last two failing it's a sign."

"What is a sign, Grant?" I reply in a vulgar tone.

"The signs that we are going broke, that we had to
sell my car for the last go around. This is not
conventional. I am so tired of everything being
planned out by dates, time, and temperatures. I am
so God Damn tired of that plastic cup! This is not
what I signed up for!" He says with such anger and
frustration. His fists are on his hips and his head is
hung low. I don't need to listen to the rage he is
spewing. I see defeat and aggravation all over his
face.

He's never once implied that he didn't want this.
Now all of a sudden he doesn't think we should.
Grant and I have been married for four years. We
did all the things married couples do when you are
first married; we built our dream home, we traveled
to many different locations, including our most recent

Hawaii trip over Labor Day weekend. His father made him a partner in his firm, so now the practice is called "Thomas and Thomas Law Associates."

For our first anniversary I bought him a Harley motorcycle. He loved to ride his Ducati speed bike, and it scared me with how fast he could go on that, so I bought him a V-Rod Muscle Harley, encouraging him that I wanted to go on more trips with him. Even though, that is the last thing I want to ride on. Those things scare me. I've dealt with too many cases involving motorcycles. Grant reassures me that he takes all the precautions necessary to ride the thing.

Two years ago I approached him saying I think it was time to start a family. My best friend since childhood, Kate, was pregnant with her first pregnancy. My other best friend Ella and her husband were trying for their second. I wanted to get on the band wagon with my BFF's, and experience and enjoy this time with them. Well, I missed the wagon when it came to getting pregnant. I couldn't get pregnant without help outside the bedroom. We tried artificial insemination six times, and that failed. We tried IVF twice, and that failed. Now here we are two years later sitting in our kitchen nook discussing how I might never be a mom.

Just then Grant slams the refrigerator door and brings me back to the present. "Beth, I want us to go back to how things were before all this madness. I can't handle how excited you get to just get knocked back down again. The procedures are painful, the medicine makes you become a raging lunatic, and normal sex has gone out the window. I can't remember the last time we just made love. I am so tired of the planning. Maybe if we let it go, it will happen naturally?"

"Do you think for one second this is what I signed up for? You think I like taking drugs that make my skin crawl, where I feel I am going to jump out of my body because I have so many hormones going through me? You think I signed up for the painful retrievals of eggs? Where in your right mind do you think I want this? I wanted to make babies the normal way just like everyone else, but for some reason that isn't our plan."

I sit in the kitchen chair, as I place my head in my hands, and try to take in deep breaths. I look up to watch him pull his hands through his hair. "Grant are you serious, you just want to stop? You don't see a future with a child? I want a baby, Grant. I want to be a mother. It kills me to see pregnant women. It tore my heart out to plan both of my friend's baby showers when I couldn't get pregnant. It shredded my dreams when I held their babies. I grieved when Kate had two babies, I couldn't get one. Now you come home from work and somewhere between us leaving the office and coming home you have an epiphany that we shouldn't be parents. "

He pulls the other kitchen chair out and sits next to me. He grabs my hands and pulls them into his lap. "Sweetheart, I never said we should never be parents. I said we should give IVF a break. I want to be a dad, but maybe this way of doing it isn't what nature intended us to do. Maybe….let's… look into adoption? You know we have handled many cases that the families were in our shoes. They get their baby, and go on to live a normal life. All I am saying is let's take a break at least till the New Year, and look into other options. That's all."

I pull my hands out of his, push the chair back to where it slams into the bay window behind me. I grab my pen and throw it across the room. "Grant, I want a baby that grows inside of me! Part you and part me. I have done those cases, and it is just as God damn hard as what we are going through now. I don't want to wait months upon years for a baby that might be ours or might not! A baby that enters our lives that can easily be taken from us. You and I know the laws. I refuse to go that route." I'm shaking. I have never gotten so angry with Grant in all the years we've been together. I don't understand why this is happening.

I go into the family room, and sit on the cream linen love seat. I grab the denim blue pillow, hold it to my chest. I feel that at any second my chest is going to open, and my heart is going to fall out. I am so desperate for a baby! I see that it's changing our marriage. It's changing us, not only as a couple, but as individuals.

"I'm scared Grant, I don't want us to be alone forever. I'm approaching thirty. I know my window for babies is only open for a little longer. I want us to have children, grandchildren, and great-grandchildren. I envision us sitting in that formal living room with our children opening Christmas presents. We even built this huge house for a future family. It scares me that it will be just you and me in this house. It scares me even more that you will get bored with just me, and leave me for someone who can give you a child."

Grant walks over and scoops me into his lap. I rest my head on his firm chest. I breathe him in. I wrap my arms around him brushing his long dark brown hair off his shoulders. I kiss his neck, I dart my tongue out and lick the sensitive spot on his neck. He tastes salty, and starts to shiver.

"Beth, look at me sweetheart." I push my arms out and grab his shoulder as I look into his deep brown eyes. He uses his thumb to wipe away the tears on my cheek. "Sweetheart, I'm not going anywhere. Whether we have a baby or not I will be by your side till the day I die. I can't fathom a life without you. We've been together since we were twenty one, and we will be together till we are one hundred and one."

I give him a smile and a little chuckle. "That's a long time with me, you sure about that?" I snicker.

"It's not long enough, I will need longer with you."

I wrap myself back into him and grab his face and kiss him with everything I have. He tells me to hold onto him. He stands up, and carries me into our room. He gently places me in the center of the bed. He lies to my side, grabs a hold of my chin with his thumb and forefinger. He stares at me as if he is remembering every detail of my face. "Sweetheart, I love you so damn much. We will have a family one way or another. Just take a break for a while, for me. Please."

I put my arms around his neck and bring him to my lips. We kiss long and hard. He puts his hand under my blouse and rubs my stomach. My hands are in his hair trying to pull him closer into me. I need us to be even closer. He yanks my blouse up and over my head, along with my bra. Grant kisses my neck, then gives me gentle kisses along my collarbone, down my chest to my breast where he starts to suck and tug my nipples. With his right hand he fondles my left breast; he tugs and pinches my nipple with his finger and thumb. Shocks of electricity go straight to my core. "Grant, please I need you…please make love to me." Pushing himself up, he sits back on his heels, licks his lips. He scoots back from sitting between my thighs. He removes my belt, opens the button on my slacks, pulls my slacks off and throws them on the floor. He puts his thumbs in the waist of my black lace panties and leisurely pulls them down. He just gazes at me, full of love in his eyes. I love this man more than anything, I love him more than any future children we may or may not have. I look into those coffee colored eyes and appreciate he is my family. I get lost in the taste of his mouth, the slide and thrust of his tongue, and the sensation of his hands on my body. He stands up and gets completely naked in front of me. Leaning back down on top of me I feel his arousal pressed against my thigh. I whimper and plead. I need him. "Please Grant…I need you."

He fills me in one hard, yet gentle thrust. I moan into his neck, the intense feeling was surreal. In that moment I felt alive, and normal. We made love. The type of love that we haven't made in a long time. The type of love that has brought us back to where we should be.

The next morning we wake up entangled with each other. "Good Morning, my sweetness. How did you sleep?" Grant says is his morning voice.

"I was thinking, about what we talked about."

"Beth, can we give it a rest for a few days? We just talked not even ten hours ago about this."

"Love, just listen and then I won't bring this up for a long time." I roll completely onto him, and place his head in between my hands. "Listen...One more time. All I ask is we give IVF one more time and then we will look into other sources if it doesn't work out. Just, one more time and who knows maybe by the end of the year we will be pregnant?"

He places his hands on either side of my cheeks. Licking his lips, "Sweetheart, I would do this over and over, but it is you that I worry about. Your body and mind go through so much stress. I just want a break from it all. I am all for one more time, as long as you promise we are done for a while. We can practice more on the old fashion way of getting pregnant." He says while wiggling his eyebrows at me.

"I promise, this is our last time...for a while."

Chapter 2

Deja Vu

October

It's Tuesday morning and I'm standing against the kitchen counter waiting for the coffee to brew. I am looking through my phone calendar of my day's itinerary. I have to go in for blood work. After our talk in August, Grant agreed to one more procedure. I've been on Lupron to get my ovulation on track. I have a good feeling about this round. I feel better, Grant and I couldn't be happier in our marriage. He even seems happier this round. I hear Grant coming down the hall. He approaches me, grabs my waist and pulls me into him with a long and sensual kiss. He tastes of mint toothpaste.

"Last night was amazing, sweetheart. Maybe we can have a repeat?" He wiggles his eyebrows at me. I push him back because I want to look up at him. I'm only 5'4, whereas he is 6 ft. "Not tonight, love, my period has visited. I wouldn't mind messing around with you though." I whisper to him as I slowly lick the side of his neck.

"We are getting close to the wire, huh?" Grant says, as he kisses my forehead.

"It's getting there, maybe another two weeks and I'll be having the transfer. Hopefully in a month we will find out that we are parents."

"Sweetheart, one step at a time here, let's get through today and worry about tomorrow when it arrives." Grant reassures me to stay focused on the present and not worry about the future. I notice that he takes out his phone and starts looking at it. I watch as he pulls his top lip in and bites it. This is his thinking expression.

"What's wrong?" I ask him as I pour creamer in my coffee. "Nothing, I'm just counting down the days and all this will be happening around the time I go to Daytona. I just need to figure out what to do. I don't want to let you down or the guys."

We live in Central Florida. Every year Grant, his best friend Sean, and a few others go to Daytona for Bike Week and Biketoberfest for the weekend. I've never been. I don't see the fuss over a bunch of people riding their bikes around a crowded city. Plus, it gives him his break, and some guy time. With my insecurities, I can't be around some of those biker babes. Grant has always been my "bad boy" man. He sure has the looks for it. He's tall, lean, dark shoulder length hair, dark eyes, always has a five o'clock shadow, tattoos, and lives every day as an adventure. He is equipped for speed, always has to go, and go fast. These are the only fears I have when he is gone, because I know what he likes to do, and what he is capable of doing. He might be thirty, but once a bike is between his legs he acts like a stupid eighteen year old.

I walk towards him, bringing his cup of coffee to him. "You sir, need to take your own advice." I sarcastically say to him as I kiss him on the cheek. Walking back to the fridge I tell him not to worry. "Keep your plans for your motorcycle trip, I am sure everything will work out around the transfer and if you aren't there. I have Ella or Kate who can take me. I've done this before; it's not that big of a deal."

Within two strides Grant has his arms around my waist and facing me. "Dammit, Beth it is a big deal. This is our last time and I want to be there for you. We do this together all the way through. I don't care about the stupid bike trip. I love you and this is more important." He leans down and kisses me. He picks me up and places me on the counter. Standing between my legs, he has me wrapped in his lean arms. Our kiss is intense and the hold he has on me is even more powerful. We stay embraced and kiss for what seems like minutes. He pulls away and his chocolate colored eyes look into mine. He stares, thinking of what to say. "Sweetheart, I love you and don't ever think that just because I don't have a physical part in this baby making process that I don't think it's a big deal. It's a huge deal, we are making a baby. Our lives will be forever changed. I'm by your side through all of it." He kisses me again and pulls me off the counter.

I grab my things and head for the door. "Now, let's get to work before the boss kicks my ass!" I say with a giggle to him.

"There is a lot more that I would like to do with that ass then kick it, sweetheart!" Grant snorts.

I put in a few hours at work, before I head to the doctor's office. I have blood work taken and was given an ultrasound. I wait to hear back from the doctor and go on from there with the drugs. After my appointment I return to my office to see a huge, beautiful bouquet of pink roses, blue hydrangeas, and baby's breath. There is a card leaning against the crystal vase. Seeing that it is in Grant's handwriting, I open the card and read it.

> Just know that I love you. I have been thinking about you. You will be an excellent mother and our baby will be as lucky as I am having you in my life.
>
> I love you!

That man is the sweetest and caring man ever.

Friday morning comes and I get a call from Dr. Wilson's office.

He has been the one that has been handling our IVF procedures. When our insurances changed last year, my best friend Ella referred me to Dr. Alexander. Ella is an OB/GYN nurse in his office. She said he is great, and has great contacts with doctors in the infertility field. Dr. Alexander referred us to Dr. Wilson. Dr. Wilson is a wonderful older gentleman. He has been doing this for decades with a lot of success! He has a great reputation of getting

85% of his patients pregnant. I hope I am not the other 15%. I just pray that third time is a charm! My desk phone starts to ring and I pick it up, "This is Elizabeth how may I help you?"

"Hi Elizabeth, this is Lucy from Dr. Wilson's office. I have your test results. Everything came back great and Dr. Wilson wants to start you on Clomid. Can you come in this afternoon?" Looking at my calendar I see that I am free. "Yes, Lucy, put me down I will be there this afternoon." I hang up the call and walk towards Grant's office.

His door is open which means for me to enter, but he is busy typing away on his computer. Working with him has been the best decision I could have ever made. I really enjoy the closeness of being with him all the time. I couldn't imagine working eight to ten hours away from him. Here I have the leisure to go and see him whenever I want, unless he is in court.

I tap on the door, he looks up to me with those puppy dogs eyes and gives me the best smile. "Hey good looking, what's up?"

Walking to his chair, he scoots away from his desk to make room for me to sit on his lap. Sitting down he gives me a kiss. "I just got a call from Dr. Wilson's office. All my tests came back, and everything is good. I go in this afternoon to get my Clomid shots."

"Are you okay will all this?" He gives me such a worried look.

"It's just a Déjà Vu moment. That we've been here and done this and I'm scared we will fail again. We can't fail, again."

With his thumbs he wipes away the tears that are slowly falling down my face. "Sweetheart, we have talked about this a thousand times. Just because we have done this song and dance before, doesn't mean it's going to go down like it did before. Have faith, sweetness. I promise you, you will be a mom!"

"Thank you, love. I know this will be different. Nerves just got the best of me." With that I lean in and give him a kiss. "I'm leaving here around 3:00 p.m. Do you want to come, then we can catch dinner, or are you busy?" I quietly say as I nuzzle into his neck.

"Never too busy for you sweetheart, I'll be there." I get up from his lap and try to finish my work for the remaining of the day.

Chapter 3

Third Time's a Charm

On Monday I went back to the doctor. I've been on two injections of Clomid two times a day for the last ten days now. I went in for my hCG shot. Today, it is Wednesday; the sun hasn't even risen yet. I sit at the kitchen table drinking my coffee and silently praying for a great and blessed day. I listen to our dogs snore away as they are spread out on the sofas. I feel my heart is in rhythm with the kitchen clock. I'm so nervous and so scared. Just thinking that this is the final step to becoming parents' scares the hell out of me. I can't, and won't go through adoption. Not, that I wouldn't love a non-biological child any less, I just don't want to jump through all those hoops. I feel if I wasn't a lawyer and didn't deal with Family Law and see what these clients go through, than I would have jumped head first into adoption. Sitting at the table and slowly sipping my coffee, I hear Grant walking into the kitchen.

"Good Morning, Beth. Why are you up so early?" He kisses the top of my head as he walks towards the coffee maker. Watching him lean against the counters in his black boxer briefs and his bed head, I know that I am extremely blessed to just have this man in my life. He pulls the chair out next to me, and slides the chair closer; leaning into me he kisses my bare shoulder. "Sweetheart, talk to me." He whispers against my skin.

"It's just nerves Grant, I'll be okay when this is all said and done." I stand up and walk to the kitchen to place my cup in the sink when I walk back to the table I stop in front of him. "Want to take a shower with me?" I say as I slowly start to pull my tank top over my head.

"Hell yeah!" I run towards our room laughing and squealing because I know if he catches me I am in trouble. Before I even make it to our bedroom door he has scooped me up and lifted me over his shoulders. I laugh the whole way into the shower.

We are sitting in Dr. Wilson's office where we both have appointments. I with the egg retrievals and Grant with his intimate moment with a plastic cup. He can't stand this part, and I knew he was going to be tense. I wanted him to go in relaxed so the outcome would be a good one. Last night while he was in the shower I decided to take some naked pictures of myself.

Once he went back into the room at the doctor's office I surprised him with pictures of me naked, close ups of my tits and pussy. He texted me back while I was sitting in the waiting room.

Grant: Thank you! Seeing your sweet pussy is so much better than the trash they have in here. I will be out in no time. I love you!

Me: You're quite welcome! Third time's a charm, baby!

After his speedy appointment I am called in for my retrieval. Dr. Wilson retrieved 8 eggs. A couple hours after the procedure Grant and I go home where we cuddle up in bed and sleep the rest of the day away.

It's Thursday, tonight I want to make Grant a nice dinner. I know he has been in court all day, and I know he will be exhausted. So I make him his favorite, Chicken Marsala with mashed garlic potatoes and Caesar salad. I am mashing the potatoes when I hear his bike pull into the garage. I grab a beer from the fridge and meet him at the door. His eyebrows are pushed together, so I know he is pissed. "Everything alright?" I quietly ask as he puts his briefcase on the washing machine in the laundry room and grabs the beer out of my hand. He pulls me in for a kiss on the lips, and then brushes his lips across my forehead.

"Everything is just fucking great. I had a case with Judge Myers, damn I can't stand that asshole. Anyway, I'm thinking the feelings are mutual because he gave me hell about everything I tried to present. Court ended up being dismissed for the day and will resume on Tuesday. So now my client has to sit in jail even longer. It's just one of those days, sweetheart."

"Mine was ok, tons of paperwork on my end, but the best part was I didn't have to get out of my pajamas. At least you will have a stress free weekend. Go do your manly things, ride your Harley, and enjoy yourself" I say as I walk up behind him as he is over the stove looking what is in the pot. I wrap my arms around him and kiss his back.

"That is what I am looking forward to. You can still come if you want to. Jack is bringing his girlfriend. You would have a female to shop with or hang out on the beach."

"No, you go ahead. Dr. Wilson said that they wouldn't even do implantation until Monday. I'm just going to take it easy until then. Kate and Ella are coming over tomorrow night and on Saturday I am getting a much needed haircut. I have so much work to catch up on since our many doctor appointments. "What are you going to do to your hair? Don't cut it too short. I love your hair this long. It's so beautiful!"

He's always made me feel beautiful even though I stick out like a sore thumb. I have light auburn red hair that is long and wavy. My skin is pale, which sucks living in Florida. Year round, my lotion of choice is sun screen. My eyes are too big for my face; they are green with flecks of gold. Grant tells me they look like emeralds. He loves my eyes and hair color, which makes me feel damn good. All women want to be reminded how beautiful they are and Grant always does that for me. Like I said, I am 5'4, but unlike Ella or Kate I am stout and curvy. I'm not fat, I'm a size 6, but let me tell you I have some hips and a butt. I just wish I had more volume in the boob department. I'm not too small, but I don't fill out my size C cups as much as I would like. I kiss the person who invented the miracle bra, those have been my saving grace in the cleavage department.

"I'm going to get it all cut off!"

His jaw just hit the floor. "You're wh-what?" He tries to sputter out of his mouth.

"Grant chill, I'm messing with you. I'm just getting a trim, maybe layers and possibly thinking of going for bangs, again."

He smacks my ass, "Woman! Don't scare me like that. I love your hair. It makes you glow, like an angel."

I look up to him and smile. "Geez, I need to make more threats to get compliments like this from you. You made my night. It was worth the meal I made for you."

"I see mashed potatoes, what else did you make?" He steps to the side and pulls open the oven door. He shuts it, turns around, and grabs me to one with his body. "You are the best wife ever! You made me Chicken Marsala. If I wasn't starving I would take you to our room right now and have my way with you .....but I'm hungry, let's eat!"

Friday morning Grant gets up early. He is meeting Sean for breakfast before they head to Daytona. "Are you sure you don't want to come and get breakfast?" he asks as he throws some clothes into a duffle bag.

"I'm sure. I'm meeting a client for brunch anyway."

I pull myself out of bed, walk by him, and slap his adorable ass on my way down stairs to make coffee. As I pour the water into the coffee machine I look up to see him standing and staring at me. "What's wrong?"

"Nothing, I'm just watching my beautiful wife making coffee. I'm going to miss you. Are you going to miss me?"

"Grant, of course, I'm going to miss you. Have a lot of fun, and get it all out of your system, because you are mine when you get back." I say this as I walk over to meet him, hold him close to me, and grab his ass.

"Careful sweetheart, my ass has to sit on a bike seat for the next two days."

I kiss him long and hard. He sucks on my tongue and then bites my lower lip. I can feel his cock stir in his jeans. I pull him closer to me and I'm literally fucking his mouth with my tongue. I don't want to stop, but he grabs my face with his hands. He stares down into my eyes while rubbing his thumbs across my jaw. "Beth, you continue to kiss me like this I'm going to throw you on the floor, strip you naked, spread you wide, and have my way with you."

I smile and blush while I take my hand and rub his twitching cock. I quietly whisper to him, "Please throw me on the floor."

He gives me that laugh, and then I start to laugh. "Sweetheart when I return home I will have the pleasure of having my way with you on the floor. I really need to get going. Sean is waiting." He grabs my hand and walks me to the garage. He gives me a brief kiss on the lips, and then moves to leave a kiss on my forehead.

"I love you, sweetheart."

"I love you, too. Please be safe and let me know when you get there."

He hops on his bike, walks it out backwards. He starts it up. Before he leaves the driveway, he turns around and blows me a kiss. Before closing the garage door I stare at him as he leaves the cul de sac. All of a sudden I don't feel too great. I close the door, and head to the shower to get ready for work.

As I am about to head into the shower I hear my cell phone ring. Wrapping a towel around me I run to retrieve my phone. I answer it. It's Lucy from Dr. Wilson's office.

"Hi Elizabeth, this is Lucy. Your embryos are ready to be implanted. We need to do it quickly because four didn't make it. Can you come at 9:30a.m.?"

Shit! I sit here, thinking this isn't going to be a 'third time's a charm' if those eggs are looking not worthy in a petri dish. "Umm…yeah I can be there. I will make it work. See you soon."

I call Cole, my father in law, and let him know that an emergency appointment came up. I don't go into details because that is just too bizarre, but he does know it has to deal with me trying to get pregnant. I ask him if he can get Indira to go on my brunch meeting. Indira is another associate with the practice. I relay the details of my meeting to him. I let him know I'll be at home if he needs me, otherwise I'll see him on Monday.

Then I call Ella, I need her to go with me. I can't call Grant. He's been looking forward to this since summer. I hope to catch her before she goes into work.

"Hola Chica!"

"Ella, I need a huge favor. Dr. Wilson's office just called. They have to do implantation this morning. My embryos aren't looking good. This is my last go around. Can you please get the morning off and take me?"

"Beth, let me see what I can do, but I am sure I can. Let me get into work and see who can cover my shift. What time is your appointment?"

"It's at 9:30. I can drive myself there. We can just get my car tomorrow."

"You sure about this Beth, do you want me to call Grant?"

"Ella, he just left for his bike trip for the weekend. I've done this before. I just need a ride home."

"Alright, I'll call you back."

I hop in the shower and take my time since I know I won't be going to work. As I am drying my hair Ella returns my call, and tells me that she will come here to get me. She got someone to come in and cover her shift for the morning.

I finish getting ready, throw on a pair of black yoga pants and purple V-neck shirt, grab a pair of black flip flops, and pull my hair up in a ponytail.

I go let our dogs, Pebbles and Bamm-Bamm, out. Our first born babies, they're chocolate labs, brother and sister. As I watch them run around the backyard I remember when Grant came home with them. It was after our fourth insemination failed. He put Pebbles in a hot pink crystal studded collar and Bamm-Bamm in a faux black leather collar. As we were trying to come up with names a Flintstone Vitamin commercial came on. We looked at each other and laughed. We knew what each other was thinking. We shrugged our shoulders, and declared that they would be Pebbles and Bamm-Bamm. I close the sliding door and go into the laundry room where I fill up their food bowls. I hear Ella honking her horn. I go and let the dogs in, kiss their heads, and tell them to be a good boy and girl.

I walk out to Ella's swanky white BMW sport utility vehicle. I hop into the front seat, lean over and give her a kiss on the cheek. She returns the favor, giving me kisses on both cheeks. Ella is gorgeous. She is a several inches taller than me. She is part Argentinean and Italian, so she has the silky dark brown hair, big beautiful brown eyes with those envious long lashes of hers. Her olive skin tone complexion is always glowing. She has the fullest lips, lips that would put Angelina Jolie to shame. As I buckle myself in I say, "Hey there pretty mama. How has your week been? How are the girls, Nina, and Chris?"

"Honey, we don't have enough time to talk about my Mama drama. Alexis had a meltdown in ballet class. She didn't want to do what the other girls were doing, so she took off her slippers and threw them at the teacher. Then took off her tutu and put it on one of the girl's heads that was dancing next to her. We are potty training Brooke. She decided that she doesn't want to poop in the potty or even wear a poopie diaper. She just wants to paint with it. Last night after she had her bath and was tucked her in she decided to become Monet and paint her crib and wall with shit! Oh, and mama has cut holes in Chris's underwear. She says they are too tight, and she wants a grandson ASAP. Little does she know that I am on birth control. There are no more babies coming out of my hoohah anytime soon. Chris is over her, and threatens to put arsenic in her tea. Yes, welcome to my life."

"Oh!"

I don't know what else to say because it does sound like a lot of draining motherhood crap, but at the same time I want to have those daily crises with my child.

I can tell she is tense and probably nervous for me. I'm sure she feels bad for me. She wants this to work just as bad as I do, so I can then be a part of the mommy club. It is very difficult to go through life's milestones, then I come to a barricade, while my two best friends continue on with their life plan. *"Please God; please let this work this time."*

Ella has two beautiful girls. Alexis is five and in Kindergarten. She has a spit fire personality like her momma. Brooke is almost two, and the energizer bunny in the family. I would love to have an eighth of that toddler's energy.

Ella married her high school sweetheart Chris. Chris and Ella were the whole afterschool special couple. Head cheerleader and the quarterback, prom king and queen, the most beautiful and most likely to succeed couple, blah, blah, blah. I met Ella as a freshman in college. We were dorm roommates. Then two years later we moved into an apartment, along with Kate. Kate is my childhood friend, who I have known since we were six.

Chris became a Pharmacist and works many long hours at the local drug store. When Ella became pregnant with Brooke, it became difficult to juggle everything. They asked Nina, Ella's mom, to move in to help out. I'm sure every mother has these daily scenarios, it's just life handing you lemons, and you finding a way to make lemonade, or some bullshit like that.

I just hope Ella realizes how lucky she really has it. She is living the American girl dream. If I get pregnant, I don't have my family close by. They live outside of Asheville, NC. My brother Ethan followed his girlfriend there, and opened his own mechanic shop. Dad lost his job here. Ethan offered him a partnership, so Mom and Dad packed up and moved there. I don't have the luxury of having my mother live over the garage. It will be hard, and I know that, but I want this baby so badly.

Minutes later we pull into the doctor office. She walks with me into the waiting room. I sign myself in. She plays on her phone as I nervously tap my foot on the floor. She puts her hand on my knee. "Honey, it's going to be OK. Have faith and hope." Why is that so much easier said than done? I love her to death, but she has no fucking clue what is going through my head. She looks at Chris wrong and BOOM she is pregnant. I hate this feeling of not having any control over my own damn body, especially when there isn't a damn thing I can do.

"Elizabeth Thomas" I hear my name called by the nurse. Ella gives me a hug and I walk back. I change into a gown, and get in position on the table. I'm given a sedative to relax me. Dr. Wilson comes in, "Hi Elizabeth. Sorry to make you rush, but I thought it would be best to implant today. Do you want to do the usual two embryos?" I look at him and panic. If I do two then the other two that aren't that viable are disposed, but what if they have a chance inside of me. I sit and stare at the table that holds my embryos ….my babies.

"Dr. Wilson, can we do all of them today? This is our last attempt at IVF, and I want to put them all in."

"You do realize that there is a chance for multiples if we do this? I mean more than twins, more than triplets." Well, of course, I know there has always been a chance of multiples because we always implanted two. Since two might not make it I have two backups. So if anything I just might get pregnant with one, or at the most twins. We can handle twins, we were hoping for twins.

"Yes, I understand and want all my eggs implanted." Before the sedative kicks in. I fill out some last minute paper work. I lay there for twenty or so minutes as he implants my eggs into my uterus. I lie and wonder if Grant has made it to Daytona. I picture babies around the Christmas tree next year. I think to myself that I might not tell Grant about this implantation today, that maybe if everything goes well I will just surprise him with pink and blue cupcakes saying DADDY on the icing. I would have to look into Pinterest for fun ideas to surprise him with.

Another elephant would be released off his chest if I got pregnant.

Dr. Wilson is done. He left me there to relax and be still for over an hour. The nurse comes in and lets me know that I can slowly get up and get dressed. I'm sore and completely loopy. My body and mind are in a tranquil state. The nurse helps me get into my panties and pants. She helps me walk out to the waiting room, where Ella is on the phone. She ends her phone call and helps me to the door. "How are you doing, Beth?"

"I'm doing good, very relaxed." She helps me into the car and buckles me in. My foggy brain is slowly coming back to life. We sit in silence for a while. "Ella, I think we need to postpone girl's night till Saturday. Is that ok with you? Do you think you could call Kate, tell her what happened, and see if we are on for Saturday night?"

"Sure."

"Ella, don't be mad." I want to tell her….I need to tell her because I can't tell Grant or he will lose his marbles.

"What would I be mad about?"

"El, I put all my embryos in me."

"That was the plan, right?" she slowly ask me.

"No El, not two, but all four. I put four embryos in this time. I only had four left. I couldn't sit there and choose which ones to put in and which ones to throw away. Those are mine. I swore to Grant that this was our last go around, no more IVF for us. I couldn't pick and throw away." I rush to explain.

"BETH! Grant is going to shit his pants if you end up pregnant with four babies. Did you think what happens if all four take?"

"No, I didn't think. El, I had about a 60 second time frame to let the doctor know what I wanted. I don't think all four will take. At the most two will. That is a big IF!"

"If this is what you want then I support you. You know I have your back in any decision you make. Well, I'm hoping for a boy, at least one. We need a little boy in our gang. We need some balance, especially when my girls and Kate's go through puberty. Our poor husbands will vanish once a month. Can you see Chris and Keith dealing with periods, bras, tampons, and boyfriends?" She laughs so hard that she starts to snort.

I start to laugh and whack her hard in the shoulder. "Cut it out, I can't laugh!"

I hear my ring tone for Grant go off in my purse. I answer my phone.

"Hey sweetheart, how is your day going so far? Are you at your meeting?"

"Hi handsome. Yes, I am at my meeting. Did you make it to Daytona?"

"Yep, we are checking in now at the hotel. Then we are going to go cruise around the loop. I'll call you tonight when I get back to the hotel. Are you and the girls going to hang out tomorrow?"

"No. Kate is having a babysitter issue, so we are just going to do it Saturday."

"Well then maybe tonight you can send me some of your sexy pictures."

"Ha, we will see! Have fun and please be safe."

"You know I will. I love you, sweetheart."

"I love you too, bye."

"Bye sweets."

"You aren't going to tell him, are you?" Ella cautiously says to me.

"Not now. He is about to have a fun weekend with his buddies. Hopefully by this time next week I will be able to tell him that he is going to be a daddy. I want to do this the normal way for once. Please say you support me on this."

Ella puts her hand on my leg and rubs her hand on my thigh. "Beth, I love you, and I am here for you and have been. You know that! I am just nervous for you. I want this to work for you so bad. I talked to Kate. We're on for Saturday. "

"Thanks." It's all I can muster up, I feel so torn, scared and lonely. I wish I had girlfriends who wouldn't give me that look of pity all the time and stutter with words because they don't know what to say like I am glass and going to break. I get enough of it from my husband. I guess I just want this time to be as normal as possible. I wish I didn't feel so alone right now. I wish Grant was here to hold me. Three more nights and he will be in my arms naked on the family room floor. I have to focus on that.

We pull into the driveway. Ella walks me in and lets the dogs out for me. "Beth, I hate to do this to you, but I have to get to work. Kate said she will stop by on her lunch break. Do you need anything before I leave?" I walk to my bedroom, strip off my pants, and curl up under the covers. I grab Grant's pillow that smells of him and wrap my arms around it.

"No, I'm good El, thank you so much for your help this morning. I am just going to go to sleep and let my embryos settle in." She tucks me in as if I was a child, kisses my head and walks out.

"I'll call you tonight and check on you….love you."

"OK, love you too!" I shout back not knowing if she heard me or not. I know she let the dogs in because they run in and jump up on the bed with me. I slowly drift off to sleep.

I awaken when the dogs are going crazy prancing on my bed. Kate is here. I look at the clock and see it is one o'clock.

"Bethy-baby, how are you feeling?" Kate is a nut, she's been calling me Bethy-baby since I was six years old when she moved next door to me. She was so excited to be older than me by six months so her nick name for me has always been Bethy-baby.

I croak out, "I'm real good, just tired."

"Well I got you a turkey and spinach wrap and a raspberry and strawberry smoothie for lunch. You hungry?"

"Yes, I'm starving. Thank you so much." I prop myself up on the bed to a sitting position as she places the bag and smoothie on the night stand. She walks out to let the dogs out in the backyard.

"I brought them these bones to chew on so they should be content for a while" she says as she prances into the room. She lies down on the bed next to me and closes her eyes.

"Are you going to take a nap?" I ask as I have the straw in my mouth and trying to suck the smoothie up.

"I'm just closing my eyes. I'm so tired Beth."

"Be my guest and sleep. I'm going to eat this delicious lunch and then join you." Katie Bear, as I used to call her as my nickname for her, has been my "sister from another mister." She is my everything. She has been with me through all of my life plans.

Kate is a gorgeous blond bombshell. She has shoulder length blond hair, a hint of freckles on her nose, sapphire blue eyes, and is a little taller than me, but not as tall as Ella. She has killer legs, and a body like Malibu Barbie. The real shocker is looking at her you would never know that she pushed two babies out of that body at one time. She went home from the hospital in pre-baby clothes. GAG! I know, I hate her too. She is a Veterinarian …yep this hot chick next to me just became a doctor a few months ago. She is an equestrian and big animal doctor. She has always had a love for horses, but she takes in all animals.

Her granddaddy is a Veterinarian and has his own practice. When he retires next year the practice will be all hers. Kate spends her days tackling animals, then goes home to her hubby Keith and two year old twin girls, Nicole and Julia. Kate met Keith three years ago at a bar. They hit it off great, their developing relationship went fast. She got pregnant two months into their relationship. Once she found out they were expecting twins they got married at the court house. A few months later they were a family of four.

I know I have been so caught up in my fight to get pregnant that we haven't talked much. Something is going on, and she doesn't want to bother me with her life issues, but she is my best friend. I wish she would open up. I stare at her. She is softly snoring, I know she is exhausted. She is practically a working, single mom. Keith is a police officer and works crazy shifts, shifts that don't work around the 9-5, five days a week job and daycare hours.

I finish my lunch. I get up to go pee, then let my babies in from the back yard. Pebbles and Bamm-Bamm seem very content with devouring their treat from Kate. I go back to bed. She is sitting up trying to comb through her hair with her fingers.

"Sorry I was such miserable company. I can't believe I fell asleep when I should be taking care of you."

"Girlfriend, I'm good. Obviously you needed the sleep, so I don't mind. You can go back to sleep, that is what I'm doing."

"No, I got to head back to the office, then I promised the girls I would get them early and take them for frozen yogurt."

"Where's Keith?" I ask, knowing we are going into dangerous territory.

"Who knows Beth, he is never home. He says he is working night shift, then working doubles, then working overtime. I get the same run around. I have a gut feeling he is having an affair. Right now I am so busy with the girls and work that I haven't done any digging or even asked. I guess right now I just don't care."

"Katie Bear, I'm so sorry. Why didn't you come and talk to me about this? You know I am here for you?"

"I know, but this is just embarrassing and a situation I never thought I would be in. I know our relationship happened so fast, but I thought we were truly in love. I thought he loved me as much as I loved him. Oh well, shit happens!"

She gets up, walks around my side of the bed, tucks me in, and kisses me on the cheeks. "Do you need anything else?"

"Nope, I'm good. Thank you for bringing me lunch."

"No problem, we will talk Saturday. My parents are taking the girls, so I can stay as long as you need me. Love you."

"Love you too!"

I roll over and sleep.

I am awakened by a baby crying. I roll over and nudge Grant to go get the baby. My hand rubs over the bed where the sheets lay cold. I sit up quickly to see a hall light on. I get out of bed and grab the baby swaddled in a yellow blanket. I hold the baby against my shoulder, slowly rock while saying 'Shh'. I hear Pebbles and Bamm-Bamm whining. I call out to Grant, but I hear nothing. "Grant, where are you?" Nothing! I go into the garage and see Grant slouched on the motorcycle. There is blood dripping all over the garage floor. I run to him, screaming 'GRANT'! The baby is screaming, I am crying. Grant slowly turns his head to me, while blood is all over his face. He mutters, "Put the baby down and help me!" I just hold onto the baby and walk backwards. "I can't put the baby down." He yells to me "it's me or the baby"... I stumble and the baby falls...

I awaken out of my sleep, sweat dripping off of me. I'm shaking and cold. *"What the hell was that nightmare about?"* I ask myself. I walk to the kitchen where I see my dogs laying on the couch. Opening the sliding door I let them out. It is 7:20 p.m. I go to the kitchen counter, pick up the phone and call Grant.

"Hey sweetheart, how are you?"

"Grant, I can barely hear you, where are you?"

"We are at some bar eating. Hold on a sec and let me go outside."

"Grant, please tell me you are not drinking. I worry so much when you are on that thing. Plus I just woke up from a nightmare from hell."

"Beth, I am having one beer. We're not planning on leaving anytime soon. Plus out hotel is less than a mile away. What was your nightmare about?"

"I had a dream that you were bleeding to death on your motorcycle. You were asking me to help you." I bite my bottom lip and try to suppress the tears that are forming behind my eyes.

"Sweetheart, are you okay, do you want me to come home? I can be there in two hours. I don't like how you are sounding."

I inhale a deep breath. Don't want to worry Grant. I am sure he can hear the fear in my voice from the terrible nightmare I just woke from.

"I'm good, just a bad dream and a long day. I just miss you and worry. No, stay with Sean and finish out your weekend. Sunday will be here soon enough."

"Alright, Love. I love you so very much. Call me if you need me. You know I will come home if you need me to."

"I know handsome. I love you! Please be safe! Goodnight."

"Goodnight, my sweets."

Chapter 4

Can't Breathe

Opening the door to the pizza guy, I give him the money and tell him to keep the change. After walking to the kitchen with the take out boxes, I get out the plates and wine glasses for Kate and Ella, and pull out a bottle water for myself. "Bridesmaids" is in the DVD player. I look at the clock and see that it is 6p.m. They will be here any minute.

I put the dogs outside, as the ladies are walking into my house. I love how we are so casual with each other. They come in through the garage since they know my garage code.

Kate finally looks like her old self; she is smiling and holds up her bottle of wine. "Let's get this night started, ladies!" Kate shouts while raising the wine bottle.

"Kate pour me a glass; I need to use the restroom." Ella says as she sashays to the bathroom.

"Bitch, this whole bottle is mine …..find your own" Kate shouts down the hall to Ella. I look into the wine cabinet and look for a bottle that I know Ella will like. Hopefully I won't need any of these bottles anytime soon. Ella comes back from the restroom and puts her iPhone on the base charger on the kitchen counter. She turns on *LMFAO* "*I'm sexy and I know it*". Ella starts to get all Latin on us and out does us by shaking her hips and rubbing her ass against Kate. I sit on the bar stool just laughing at the two most important girls to me. These ladies are my world, and even though these moments are becoming few and far between, I cherish these moments tremendously.

The girls are done shaking their hips. I take the pizza out of the oven. Kate hugs her wine bottle to her chest like a baby. Ella grabs the salad and their wine glasses off the counter. We sit at the table and talk. I adore the girl talk with my girls.

Kate finally has enough wine in her to spill her guts out. She tells us that she caught a text message from a strange number multiple times on Keith's phone. That one text said "that she wanted to suck him off." She said that she's moved him to the downstairs guest room. They haven't had sex in three months. Kate starts to tear up at the mention of getting divorced. She can't live like this and be treated like shit.

Ella slurs "I sorry mi amore. You want me to kick him in the balls for you?"

"Be my guest, if you can find him? Can you believe that asshole hasn't been home in three days, nor has he called to say hello to his daughters. Who the hell gives up like that on being a parent? I didn't plan for a baby, let alone two, but those girls are my world and I can't fathom going a day without hearing their sweet voices. It literally breaks my heart to see what my babies will go through."

Me being the only sober one, I start to cry. Cry for my best friend and for her daughters. For a life that is about to flip upside down for her and her daughters. I wipe my cheeks and start to clear the table.

I tell Ella to go turn the movie on. As we settle into the couch when the doorbell rings. "Who the hell is that?" Kate slurs as she gets up off the couch and walks to the door. She opens the door and mutters, "What the hell are you doing here?" She opens the door a little more as I see Keith walk into the foyer.

I notice right away that he is not here for Kate, his gaze is on me and he isn't losing focus. "Keith, what's going on?" I say as I unexpectedly feel nauseas. Keith is white as a ghost and barely can look at me.

"B ...Beth umm, I heard on the radio that there was lane closures on A1A south bound. There is a massive fatality accident involving 8 motorcycles and three vehicles. I called it in to get the drivers names, knowing that Grant was out that way." He pauses then continues, "Umm ...Beth."

My heart is in my chest, and I am staring at the girls and they are white. The blood has drained from my face and my ears are pulsating. "Spit it out Keith, is Grant hurt?"

"Beth, he was one of the riders. He was rushed to the hospital and left the scene in critical condition. "

"Keith, you've got to take us there!" Kate voices to her husband. "We can't drive. We have been drinking and Beth is in no condition to drive the trip out there."

I run into the laundry room to grab my purse and flip flops. Glancing at the clock above the flat screen TV. It's 7:20p.m. I fold over and vomit. I collapse to the floor trying to catch my breath. I feel like my lungs are shrinking up in my chest cavity. I can't breathe.

Ella rushes over to me, "Beth let's go! Get up and walk to the car now! We need to go, you can't do anything sitting on the floor and you don't know anything till we get there." She sternly speaks her words into my ear. I walk to the door, seeing Kate talk to Keith.

Keith looks at me with tears in his eyes. "Beth once we are close by, I'll call the hospital and see if they can give us a report on him."

I get into the back seat of his police cruiser with Ella. She is holding me and telling me to not freak out. She keeps grabbing my wrist and counting my heartbeats. "Beth, think of the baby, the one that is trying to grow inside of you. You have got to calm down and think of that right now" as she places her hand on my lower stomach "that is all you can control right now." She holds me and chants, "breathe in and breathe out, breathe in and breathe out." This is all she says the whole way while rubbing her palm over my belly.

All I can think of is that terrible nightmare, seeing Grant's face covered in blood. *"Oh please God let me be able to identify him, let him live, let him be alright."* I silently repeat this over and over. I can't lose him,

Grant is my world. What seems like hours we finally pull into the ER. Ella helps me out and she is by my side the whole time.

I rush to the check in desk. "Grant Thomas, please he was in a motorcycle accident." I rush all my words together so quickly that I hear Ella repeat it to her just slower.

"Are you family?" She snidely says.

"Yes, he's my husband, this is his sister." I tell her, knowing full well they wouldn't let Ella back there, but she is a nurse and she can help Grant and me. Glimpsing away from her computer and discloses that he's in room eight.

I turn around to see Kate crying in Keith's arms. I babble something about I will call her and to go home.

She says she is staying and to let her know what is going on. I don't fight her, so I turn on my heels and shove my way through the double doors.

It was like walking into another dimension. It is so earsplitting and people are frantic and yelling. We come around the bend in the hallway and I hear hollering "CODE BLUE!" I'm not an idiot, I know what that means. I walk a little faster holding onto Ella's elbow. I see the number 8 above the doorway where everyone is shouting. A young man runs in with a crash cart. I'm unable to see because the tears are blurring my vision. Ella tries to hold me back, but I push through.

I run to his bed side and scream at the top of my lungs, "GRANT COME BACK!!! I'm here….come back!!!!" I feel arms wrapped around my waist and I am pulled to the end of the bed. I grab the end of the bed. I'm not leaving this cubicle! I see an older man in a white coat with the electric paddles held high above his head. He yells '*CLEAR*' and everyone jumps back. My husband looks peaceful, like he does when he is asleep. I see him jerk on the table. Nothing happens. The alarm is beeping in one piercing tone. I want them to turn it off. The noise is deafening to my ears. The doctor yells out numbers and then shouts 'CLEAR' again. Grant jerks again.

Ella is to my side with her arms around my waist holding onto me. I start shrieking, "NO ....NO ...NO" over and over again.

Sweat trickles down the doctor's forehead, a look of defeat on his white pale face. The doctor stares at me and mouths, "I'm sorry." He turns the ear-piercing monitor off and glances to the nurse, and calls the time of death.

Pushing away from Ella I run to Grant's side screaming to him, "Don't you dare leave me Grant, and wake up now, WAKE UP DAMMIT! You are not allowed to leave me, you are not DEAD, wake the hell up." I start to smack him on his chest telling him to wake up. My cries are brutal. It takes everything I can to inhale. My heart aches. I feel that at any second it is going to stop beating. All I see is Grant. I hear voices and I can feel movement around the room, but none of that has my attention. I just stare at my beautiful husband, wanting to wake up from this horrendous nightmare.

"Grant, wake up please." I whimper softly to him. By now my head is on his chest and I have wrapped my arms around his neck. For being in an accident there is little blood. His face appears perfectly fine. I guess he was safe and wore his helmet. He has bruises all over his chest and abdomen. Rough looking scratches and bloody marks on his arms, but he just seams banged up….not DEAD! "Grant, please don't leave me. There is so much we still need to do, so much to share, and grow with each other. I needed to tell you that you might be a daddy. I might be pregnant. Please, you have to be by my side for all of this. I can't do this alone, I can't fucking do this alone!"

I lie on his chest for what feels like forever, until I feel myself go cold. I feel him go cold. Ella is by my side and tells me that we need to go, that I need to rest, and to think of the baby. I wish I could see his eyes behold me one last time. All he had to do was look at me and I knew what he was feeling. I lean down to give his eyelids a kiss. I brush his hair away from his face, and kiss his lips one last time. I rub my fingers against his stubble, then down his neck, across his collarbone, down his pecks, and trail them down his abdomen. I'm straining to grasp all of him in just a few more touches. I grab his left hand and entwine our fingers together. Taking my thumb and rubbing his wedding band. I kiss his hand and ring.

Ella is trying, without success, to pull me away from my husband and I can't let go of him. "Ella, please I can't let go of him, ELLA PLEASE!!" I scream bloody murder at her. Ella separates our hands and places his hand on his stomach.

"Beth, please honey ... come with me." Ella cries to me.

I watch the nurse come over to his other side and drape a sheet over Grant's beautiful body. "Don't you dare cover him up!" I shout out to the nurse, "Don't you dare!" I hear silence as everyone is looking at me. The next thing I know I feel a pinch on my arm and another set of hands wrap around my shoulders. As I try to turn my head to see who is behind me, my body starts to feel like liquid. Then everything goes black.

Chapter 5

Jacob
- Sleeping Beauty -

My cell phone won't stop ringing. I just got off a shift at the hospital. All I want to do is go home, have a beer, and relax. I keep getting this unknown number and it is really pissing me off. On the third call, I answer. "Dr. Alexander, can I help you?"

"Uh, Jacob right?"

"May I ask who is calling?"

"Ella Hudson told me to call you. My name is Kate, and our friend Beth is in trouble. Ella asked me if you could come down and help her out."

I'm irritated. I just left the hospital. Placing my car keys back in my jeans, I am walking back into the hospital.

"Where is Ella and what is going on?" I ask inquisitively.

"Ella is with Beth in the ER. Beth just had implantation done a couple days ago. Ella, is scared she will miscarry with the news that was just given to her."

I hear Kate is starting to cry, *Jesus Christ, what the hell is going on?* "Okay, I am coming back into the hospital right now, what can I do to help Beth?" I am starting to run through the hospital. The ER entrance is on the other side of the hospital.

"Beth's husband was in a motorcycle accident, it doesn't look too good for him. Beth has had IVF three times and this was her last time. She can't lose the baby Jacob; you have got to help her." This girl is sobbing and I feel my body's adrenaline starting to kick in. Ella has been such a great co-worker, nurse, and also a friend. I can only imagine what she is going through with her best friend. I have heard so much about Ella's best friends, Beth and Kate. I know they mean the world to her, she has a picture of the three of them in a hot pink frame that says "GIRLS RULE" on her desk next her family pictures. I don't know which is which, but they all are pretty women.

"Kate, I will get there in a few minutes. I need to hang up and get with a nurse from the ER. I will let you know what happens."

She sobs a goodbye on the phone and I quickly call the ER. I get with Ruth, a nurse, who briefly tells me what is going on with Beth's husband. I tell her what I need and that I need a room ASAP for my patient. As I approach the ER wing I slow my run down to try and catch my breath. I swipe my badge in front of the doors and walk to the nurses' station. As I walk, I hear the cries of a woman and my heart breaks. Hoping that this isn't Beth, I'm in search for Ruth. Asking one of the nurses at the station she points me to her. I walk past room number 8 and I see Ella with her hands over her mouth and I see a petite red head leaning over a man on a gurney. I quickly walk by knowing that was Beth. As I approach Ruth, I feel a hand pulling my bicep. It's Ella. "Jacob, you've got to help her! Her husband just died and she is a mess. Please, give her something to calm her down."

I grab Ella and pull her in for a hug. "I'm working on it now."

"Thank You." is all she tearfully says and walks back to room eight. I arrive to Ruth's side and introduce myself, show her my badge and tell her I need what I asked for. She takes me to the cabinet that she placed the medicine in. Once it is in my hands, I fill the syringe up and head towards Beth. I hear the dreadful screams from her voice, I hear Ella's begging pleas to move. I have never been in the position before, and right now I have no fucking clue how to approach this. I go the easy route. As soon as I see Ella, hold Beth in her arms, I walk behind Ella and prick Beth with the sedation. She is in such a state of shock that by the time she turns around to see me, her big beautiful greens eyes close.

I drop the syringe and jump in front of Ella to grab Beth. I scoop her up in my arms like a baby and we walk to the elevators. "Jacob....thank you....she can't lose the baby, on top of what she just lost in there." Ella wipes her face with the sleeve of her shirt, and tries to slowly take in some breaths.

"I'll do what I can, Ella...I'll do what I can." Is all I can say as I stare at this beautiful woman in my arms. She looks so peaceful, almost angelic like.

Even with the mascara smudges, and her face is tear stained from crying, she is still the most beautiful woman I have laid eyes on. We finally get to the Perinatal High risk floor. Walking into her room, I gently place her on the bed. I lay her head against the pillow and fan out her red hair. I pull off her shoes, and pull down the covers. I walk to the end of the bed and just stare at this beauty that is sleeping peacefully. "I'll let you get her undressed. I'm going to the nurse's station to get her file started." I say to Ella as I slowly walk out the room. I close the door to a woman that has captivated me. I haven't heard her say my name and I haven't had the privilege of those beautiful green eyes looking at me, but that woman in that room will be life changing for me. I don't know what it is about her, but I have to get to know her.

Once I come back to the room, Ella has placed her in a gown and covered her up. The night nurse is starting an IV. I've prescribed a muscle relaxer, and I think with the state her body is in, she will just sleep. I don't know if she is pregnant, but I want to treat her as if she is. "How long will she be out?" Ella asks as she gets a pillow for herself.

"Not sure, it could be a day or a week, it just depends on how her body takes in the medication. She was hit with a huge blow." I say as I stare at Beth. I watch her breathe, and look at her pink lips that are just barely apart. I turn around and see Ella get cozy in a recliner chair. "Ella, what are you doing? Go home to your family."

"Jacob she is my family. I can't leave her, what if she wakes up?"

I walk to the recliner and squat so she and I are eye to eye. "I understand that, but you need to be with your family, and you need to let Kate know what has happened. I will stay here with her. I have no one to go home to. I promise, to take care of her. Go, home to Chris... please."

With her eyebrows scrunched on her forehead and eyes narrowed onto mine, she softly says, "Why would you do that? You don't even know her?"

"I know she means the world to you and that you can't be in two places at once. So I will take care of her."

She leans over and starts to cry. I pat her back, and whisper to her that things will work out. She stands up and grabs her purse. She walks over to Beth and kisses her forehead. "Thank you Jacob. I'm going to go call her parents and Kate. I will be by tomorrow."

"Take your time Ella. Good Night."

I walk behind her and close the door. I turn off the main light and turn on the bathroom light and leaving the door ajar. I sit in the recliner and stare at the beautiful angel that lies before me. My mother died twenty four years ago, and there are times where I silently talk to her. *Please mom, embrace Beth's husband with open arms up in heaven. Mom, help me get through this with her. Let me be the man and friend that she needs me to be to get her through this difficult time.* Within the hour my eyelids are heavy and sleep consumes me.

It isn't until morning that the day nurse walks in. I walk over to the bed, and check her monitor noticing that she is still in a deep sleep. I ask her nurse to bring me a breakfast tray and to change her medication. I spend Sunday sitting in the recliner and watching Beth. That night her parents come by along with Kate and Ella. I meet her parents, Grace and Evan. I inform them what we are doing to her, and just hoping that we have given her embryos a chance for survival. I let them know that I can do an hCG count by the end of the week, but that it is still too early to know if she is really pregnant.

Monday I go back to work. I give Ella the week off so she can spend her days with Beth. I swing by when I am done with the office and I frequently visit with her when I am on call with the hospital. By Thursday I do blood work to see if her hCG levels are elevated. That afternoon I give Ella the results that indeed her hCG levels are elevated, but not enough to clarify that she is truly pregnant. I let her know though that at the rate her hCG levels are going that she will be truly pregnant by mid next week. Ella screams in cheers. She jumps up and down laughing hysterical.

That night I decreased her medication and hoping within the next twenty four hours she will wake up. Ella has run to the cafeteria for a late dinner and I sit at the edge of her bed, just looking at her. She is truly beautiful and already glowing. There is some kind of pull towards her and I don't know what it is, but I need to get to know her. I want to be here for her, she has had the worst thing imaginable happened to her, yet she hasn't even walked in hell yet. I want to ease her ache, the gut wrenching ache that will shatter her heart. I want to be the person she relies on to get her through this whether she is pregnant or not. I can't explain the feelings that have consumed me, but I need to have her.

Chapter 6

Pregnant

There is light all around me as I slowly awake. I'm lying in a bed. The sun is pouring through the window, this is not my room, and that is not my window. Ella is sleeping in a chair. *"Holy shit! I'm in a hospital room, what the hell happened to me? Oh God tell me I didn't miscarry."* I pull the sheets back, lift my hips up and pull my panties back looking to see if there is blood, or if I'm wearing one of those huge pads. There is nothing there. I am attached to an IV so I pull a pillow around that was behind my back and throw it in Ella's lap. "Ella, wake up." I sternly say to her.

She wakes up rubbing the sleep away from her face. Shit, she looks bad, what the hell has happened? As she is pulling herself up and stretching I remember, Grant …accident …DEAD! "Ella, please tell me it was a nightmare, please tell me he isn't dead. Why the hell am I in this bed?"

"Beth, I am so sorry" is all she says as she crawls into bed with me and holds me. I start to cry, pulling her to me as I sob into her neck. "Shhh, Beth please don't get upset. I have news to tell you. You have to promise me you won't get upset. It's not good for you."

"Oh God, what is wrong? You're scaring the shit out of me."

"Beth," she looks at me smiles with tears in her eyes, "you're pregnant!"

"I ...what?" What the hell is she talking about? I am sitting here, thinking. There is no way. I just had implantation done three days ago. It's what ....Sunday morning?

"Beth, you're pregnant. They did a blood test last night. Your hCG levels are elevated for just having implantation."

"Ella what is today? There is no way to find out this early."

"Beth, its Friday."

"What the fuck? How the hell is it Friday? My husband just died on Saturday night. What the hell happened to me?"

"Beth please don't be mad, and know what I did, I did with the best intentions of keeping you pregnant. I didn't want you to have another loss. I knew this was your last attempt to getting pregnant, especially with what has happened to Grant." I start to cry for my husband, and then for the total clusterfuck that is going on in my head.

"Ella what happened?" I say quietly.

"Beth, I texted Kate when we were watching the whole mess with Grant. I told her to call Dr. Alexander. Knowing he had a shift at the hospital and tell him to get his ass here. She told him what was going on and that you might be pregnant. Once you started to panic and freak out, he gave you a heavy dose sedative to knock you out. We've kept you in the hospital, kept you hydrated, and rested. We needed to give your baby a chance to develop. Yesterday afternoon, Dr. Alexander came in wanted to get blood work done. Well, it shows that you are indeed pregnant. It's a start to a healthy pregnancy, based on where your numbers are at. He will want more blood work today to make sure they are going up the way they need to."

My jaw has hit the floor. I have so many emotions running through me, the loss of my husband, but the gain of a baby. I'm highly pissed with the universe, how the hell does this happen to someone? Grant was thirty. We were trying to start a family and live this next chapter of our lives together.

"El, what happened to Grant, do Cole and Anna know what is going on since I have been out ….oh my god my dogs…El?"

"Honey, Kate has the dogs at her place. They are fine and the least of your worries. Cole and Anna knew what happened right after he passed. Keith had his partner go and pick them up to bring them to the hospital. They saw him minutes after you were asleep. They started to plan his memorial, if it's ok with you they would like to do it tomorrow night? Ethan and your parents are here. They are staying at your house. They came in Sunday morning, and have been by to check on you."

"Grant and the others were killed by a drunk driver on a motorcycle. Apparently, the rider swerved into the other lane, making a car weave in and out of the lane. Grant was traveling down the road with a pack of seven motorcyclists. The car swerved and hit the back riders, who were killed instantly. The front three were cut off by the second car that was traveling behind the first that tried to move out of the way for the drunk driver. Grant was part of the three riders. The front three bikers were thrown from their bikes and landed a long way from their bikes. Grant went flying into a group of outside tables and chairs. He shattered his pelvis, broke both legs, and his lower back. He ruptured his spleen and his right kidney. He had massive internal bleeding and a collapsed lung. He ended up going into cardiac arrest. He crashed in the ambulance. They brought him back, but once he got here there was nothing the doctors could do."

"Oh my god" is all I can say over and over.

"Honey, one more thing." I take in a breath and give her the look to keep on going. "All the bikers in that group have died. They were all friends of Grant's, including Sean and Jack."

"Oh my God, El! So you are telling me that Kelly's husband is dead. This is horrifying. Those men were lawyers, accountants, husbands, and fathers. Kelly had a baby girl six months ago." I lay my head back in an awkward position and realize that I am not the only person living this awful nightmare. Kelly's child will never know her father....*Just like mine.* I weep. I don't sob because I know that will get me going and isn't good for the baby, but I let the tears run down my face.

"Beth, what do you want to do now that you are awake and you know what is going on?"

"I need to see Cole and Anna. I need to be with them. I need to tell them some clear and hopeful news. Grant was their only child. I need to give them hope during all this. Then I need to call Kelly. I want to go home, El. I need to go home. I have to prepare to say goodbye to my husband."

A couple hours later I was released by the doctor on duty. He gave me medications and a list of instructions and release papers to sign. I was able to leave with Ella.

My parents, Grace and Evan, and my brother, Ethan, welcomed me home with open arms and more tears. With the little strength in me, I push them away and tell them I need to lie down. I walk into our room, it is so cold. Looking around the room it is foreign to me. It was just nine nights ago we made love in that bed. I can't believe he has been gone for six days. I can't believe that I have been sleeping away while everyone is grieving the loss of our loved one. I think of Cole and Anna, and that they lost their only child. I pick up the bed side table phone and start to dial their number. I need to see them. We need to talk.

"Hello." Cole answers the phone is a raspy voice. I know he has been crying.

I start to cry. "Cole, hi it's Beth. Umm I need to see you and Anna as soon as possible."

"Well, Anna is sleeping right now. Her doctor gave her Xanax to cope. How about I wake her in a couple of hours and we can come by around seven tonight?"

"Okay, I'll see you around seven." I hang up the phone in pure pain, my heart is beating so fast, my palms are wet; my pulse in my temples is bulging out. The phone call to my in-laws was pure hell. We have never talked, or ended a phone call like that, in all the years we've known each other. *What's going to happen to our relationship now?*

I get up to go to the bathroom. As I walk I pass his closest, I stand in the doorway, and stare at all his clothes and belongings. I charge right through and grab as much clothing as I can, plastering my face into his shirts. They smell of him. I take in his scent and the feel of his shirts against my face. I sob into the material and clench tighter to the clothing, hoping that the hangers and the shelving unit will hold my weight. Slowly I sink to the carpet pulling what clothes I can hold onto. I curl up and bawl my eyes out. Time stood still, I have no idea what to do, where to go, how to cope or move. I feel as if I am in some Twilight Zone episode, that this experience is just some horrible experiment. Grant will walk through that door at any minute pick me up and tell me that I had passed the worst experience of pain in my life.

I slowly start to drift off to sleep when I feel my body rise off the ground. When I open my burning eyes I see Ethan carrying me to my bed. "Ethan put me back, I need to smell him, that closest is all I have of him."

"Shhh, Elizabeth, you are in no condition to sleep on the floor. Let me lie next to you until you fall back to sleep." I don't argue. I am way too weak to argue or say anything. He lays me on Grant's side of the bed, and I take in his pillows. They still smell of him. I feel Ethan brush the hair away from my face and slowly brush my hair with his fingertips.

It's been a couple of hours but seems like minutes, I awaken by Anna rubbing her hands against my back telling me she is here. I roll over onto my back. Open my eyes and see a woman that has no life in her eyes. Her face is gray, she has dark circles under eyes, and the lines in her face are drooping down. Her once beautiful silver hair seems lifeless and just gray. I sit up as she sits down on the bed. We just hold each other. We don't say a word. I don't know how long we sit like this, but we finally separate when Cole walks into the room. I look at him and gasp. I've never really seen the similarities in Grant and Cole, but they look so much alike. Cole has short hair sprinkled with the salt and pepper look. I stand up to go and hug him and he puts his head on my shoulder and just cries. I feel Anna's arms come around me. The three of us stand and cry.

Once the crying has turned to sniffles and we feel there are no more tears to make, we all sit down on the bed. "Beth, you said you needed to see us right away, what's wrong dear?" She murmurs to me.

"First, I want to say I am sorry for not being there for you when Grant passed at the hospital. Ella felt I needed to be sedated because of my situation. I wanted to help you plan his memorial. I'm happy that you went along with Grant's wishes for him to be cremated. I was given two unexpected blows of emotions to me and I felt that you two needed to be a part of both." I take in a few cleansing breath for what I have to tell them.

"Last week, we did one more implantation. The only thing is that Grant didn't know about it. I had it done Friday morning due to the embryos not looking viable. They rushed me in for the procedure. I didn't want to tell him because I knew he would drop everything and come home. I knew how much he looked forward to the trip. I didn't want to ruin it with all of this that we have been through a few times." I start to shake, because I realize if I had just told him, he would have been home, none of this would have happened. He would be here with me; we would be celebrating the arrival of our baby. I start to cry hard, "Oh God, it's my fault I should have told him, he would be here!!" Anna shushes me and says it's the drunk drivers fault. Cole asks me to continue.

"At the hospital I saw the doctors trying to revive Grant. I lost it and broke down. Ella was with me. She knew that I had the procedure done forty eight hours prior. Somewhere between my break down and sobbing fit she had a doctor give me a sedative to knock me out. She knew I needed to be calm for the implantation to go smoothly. Somewhere between the days I slept they did blood work on me....and I found out that I....I...I'm pregnant." I sputter the words out as if someone was holding my tongue. It is such a hard blow to me that I finally got pregnant when Grant is dead. Felt like an eye for an eye for me to get a baby I had to lose my husband. It felt so wrong.

Anna just holds onto me and cries. What came next I never thought would happen. I feel heat and prickly pain across my cheek. "You selfish, selfish, selfish bitch!" Anna stands up and screams at me. I hold my cheek and cry. Not knowing what to say or do. Cole grabs Anna and hugs her tight, telling her to calm down. "Cole let me go! I will not calm down when she decided to put her needs first before thinking of our son."

Cole grabs Anna and tries to push her out of the room. She swings around and points her finger in my face. "Let me tell you something ...I know my son wanted a baby just as desperately as you did. You know he would have wanted to be with you rather than on a stupid bike. You only thought of yourself and didn't give him a chance to experience this with you. I hope to God he takes this baby from you. You don't deserve to have any part of Grant!"

"ANNA enough!" Cole shouts to her. He grabs her by the elbow and tugs her away from me and pushes her through the door.

I wrap my arms around my stomach and rock back and forth on the bed. "Oh God ...Oh God!!" I get mad and scream. I get so mad that I throw the pillows off the bed; I swing and knock the lamp off the table. I throw the remote across the room. Then I pick up the picture of Grant and I standing underneath the waterfalls in Hawaii and I throw it across the room where glass splinters into tiny pieces all over the place.

"AAAAGGGGGGHHHHH!!" I scream at the top of my lungs while I thrash my hands through my hair. Ethan runs into the room and stops me from doing any more damage. I clench my fist and start to pound into his back. Tears and tears pour out of my eyes as gut wrenching screams come out of my quivering mouth. "Ethan, it's my fault…it's my fault he is dead! Ethan, oh God, help me! Ethan, I'm dying here! I need Grant …I need Grant. WHY!!!!" Ethan just stands there, holding me as my mother comes in with a glass of water and a tiny white pill.

"Elizabeth, please take this. Ella told me to give this to you if you start to freak out." My mother stands there with a little white pill in the palm of her hand.

"Freak out mother ….of course I am freaking out, my husband is DEAD! Some stupid fucker thought it was okay to get onto a motorcycle while drunk and drive down on the wrong side of the road. Some stupid fucker made a car hit my husband so hard that he went air born 37 feet and landed on iron wrought tables and chairs. Some stupid fucker not only killed my husband, his best friend, but five others and himself. So excuse me if I am freaking out, but I feel I have a fucking right to freak out!" I grab the water and pill out of her hands. The water feels great going down my dry and scratchy throat, making the pill slide down with ease. Grabbing Grant's pillow, I go back to lie on the bed and pray for some peace as I try to sleep.

Chapter 7

Goodbye

Saturday, evening comes way too quickly. Luckily I spent most of the day sleeping. Ella has been a saint with the pills. *I wonder if I could just keep taking the pills the rest of my life as it does make some of the pain go away?* Getting dressed hurts. Starting to button up my dark grey, short sleeved, blouse I stare at myself in the mirror and I see a woman I don't even recognize. I'm just a shell of a person. I tuck the blouse into my black slacks, slip my feet into black ballet flats, I brush my hair and place a black headband on my head. Not going to do anything fancy, for God sakes I'm saying goodbye to my husband today. My only make up that I struggle to apply is lip gloss. My hands can't stop shaking. One last look in the mirror before I head out the door, to a day I never saw coming. We were supposed to have sixty plus years together.

As I grab my purse and phone off my dresser, Ethan walks in with a DVD case. "Now is not the time to watch a movie, little brother." I sarcastically gripe to him.

"Elizabeth, I made something for you and Grant's parents. I told them and they think it's a great idea, but I wanted to tell you so you weren't surprised."

"What?" Is all I can say?

"While you were in the hospital I got pictures from Anna and grabbed pictures around the house of Grant. I made a video montage of his life. Something for you to keep. Something to show the baby when he or she is older, and something to show at the memorial. It's a celebration of his life. I know this is a grieving time for you, but I know Grant would want you to be happy. Happy that you both finally got what you wanted. That no matter what your baby will be watched out from up above. He loved you so much Elizabeth, all he wanted was for you to be happy no matter what."

"Wow, Ethan, when did you get all Hallmark on me? How can I be happy when my other half is burnt to ashes in some damn ceramic box? I know you are trying to be helpful and say sweet shit, but I can't hear it right now. Thank you very much for the DVD, and yes, I guess it will be fine to watch at the memorial." *I am such a bitch!* I know it. I know what just spewed out of my mouth was immature and hateful. Ethan walks out of the room with his shoulders hunched forward and his head turned down. As I am walking to the kitchen bar to grab my things, he grabs his keys, walks through the front door and slams it shut as he walks out. My parents look at me and know not to say a word to me.

The hotel reception room that my in-laws reserved for the memorial sight is beautiful. Grant and I didn't belong to a church and we knew the crematorium wouldn't house the many people we were expecting. The only option was to hold his memorial at a hotel. There are chairs all lined up in rows, with Grant's memorial program on each chair. There is a podium up front with baskets of flowers around it. There is a small table to the left that has an 8x10 head shot of Grant from our wedding. His ceramic black box of his ashes with candles lit around it. There are tables and chairs in the back, for the small reception we'll have later of coffee and desserts. By the back of the wall are long tables and lining the tables are awards, plaques and pictures of Grant some with family and friends, but mostly him. I can tell many were from Anna's house. There was a huge glass bowl and note cards where people could write memories with Grant and place them in the bowl. I'm told that once we spread Grant's ashes on the beach, we are to read these slips of paper. I feel my mother in law is making this more of a party than a quiet good-bye.

Cole's brother, who is an ordained minister, will be doing the memorial service. Family, friends, and people I have never met come to me and give me hugs, kisses and their condolences. I'm engulfed with arms that give me a tight hug. Peeking over my shoulder I see it is Ella. "How are you holding up?" She whispers in my ear.

"Besides this being the shittiest day of my life, I'm just great!" She cocks her head to the side and gives me a kiss on the cheek.

"Come on and let's go sit. James is about to start the service."

"Ugh, Ella I can't do this. I should just leave. Anna hasn't even looked at me, I feel like a stranger around all these people."

"Let's go, you can do this!" She says as she wraps her arm around my waist and guides me to the left side of chairs. She places me next to my mother as she sits to my left. James starts the service by talking about Grant, who his parents are, when he was born, how he was as a child, him in high school playing football, at college, law school, meeting me, our wedding, and him as a damn good lawyer.

"Elizabeth's brother has made a video of Grant's life. You can see firsthand what a wonderful life Grant had. It was way too short for him, but he made every day count and lived it to the fullest. Let's watch." James says as he walks to go sit next to Cole.

I start to shake, my heart beats are doubling in rhythm. I can feel sweat starting to drip down my back. Closing my eyes because I don't think I can watch this. I listen as I start to hear *Josh Groban's* song *Awake* come to life. The first picture to appear is Anna in the hospital holding Grant, there are pictures of him as he ages every year. Mostly his birthday and Christmas pictures through the years. Many football pictures, his high school graduation picture, college graduation. I finally see a picture of him and me in our caps and gowns, one of us looking at the camera and the other kissing, then there are pictures of him in law school, us on dates, us on the beach, and us at Disney World with Mickey Mouse. These pictures seem like they are such a distant memory, but at the same they seem like they just happened yesterday.

Hearing the lyric*s*, *"just keep me awake, so I can memorize you ..."* It is the most touching song I have ever heard and so true. I can't cry for the loss I have.

I watch these pictures memorize Grant and our memories. I see our engagement pictures appear, then our wedding. Watching our wedding I feel like someone had punched me in the gut. Our wedding was the most magical day I have ever experienced. I couldn't breathe. I had finally cracked! I have died on the inside.

Ella slides over to hug me, whispering me to breathe. She keeps saying, "it's okay." I want to smack her and say it's not okay. This is a cruel, sick joke that life vomited in my face.

I wipe my tears to watch the last few pictures are of him lying in our backyard with our dogs, then our family picture of him and me sitting in the grass with Pebbles and Bamm-Bamm. Kate took those pictures during the Labor Day Barbeque at our house. I was going to use them for our Christmas card pictures this year. Then the final two are of him on his bike, and then the close up of him on the bike in the same pose. He was so damn handsome; I wish I would have taken more pictures of his face. He was so photogenic. I just stare at those beautiful brown eyes, as if he is staring at me through the camera lens. Feeling more tears slowly side down my cheek, because I know I will never see those eyes look at me again.

Ella hugs me to her. I turn around and kiss her cheek. Needing to get up, I walk over to Ethan, sit on his lap and just hug him. I whisper in his ear, "Ethan thank you for giving me something so special. I am so sorry for what I said earlier. I'm sorry for being such a bitch. You know I didn't mean it. I love you and thank you so much." I kiss his cheek as I get up and walk over to Cole and Anna.

Cole rises as he sees what I am doing. He embraces my hug and squeezes me, "Beth, you know Anna didn't mean anything she said yesterday. She's hurting. We all are hurting. Most of all we love you as our own. We couldn't be happier about our grandchild. We just hope you will keep us in his or her life."

I push away with my hands on his chest. I gaze into those same beautiful brown eyes as Grant's and say, "I could never keep the both of you away from this baby. I hope that he or she brings you as much joy and happiness as Grant brought to you both. I am truly sorry for what I did. I will live with this guilt the rest of my life, please know that. He should have been there."

Anna stands up and puts her arms my waist and hugs me. "Please forgive me Beth. I'm so sorry and I want this baby just as much as you. This baby is all I have left of Grant." I nod my head in agreement. I kiss her on the cheek and start to make my rounds to family and friends.

Chapter 8

Birthday Surprise

November

Today is my 30th birthday. To me though it is just another day where I struggle to get through every hour and every day. Grant has been gone a month, it has been the loneliest, scariest month of my life. It kills my soul to think this is how my life is going to be.

Rolling out of bed today, I feel cramps, my abdomen is very sore. I appear very swollen. I have been having all day sickness. Why on earth they call it morning sickness beats me. I become really concerned because I just saw Dr. Wilson last week. Where he confirmed my pregnancy and saw the heartbeat of the baby. I call Ella and explain to her what I am experiencing. She tells me to call the office to fit me in. She sounds very concerned and I do not like her tone. Once I am off the phone with her I call the office. They can fit me in to see Dr. Alexander at 9:45. I agree to the appointment and feel even better since I only have to wait less than two hours. Stripping off my clothes realizing my boobs are extremely sore. One glimpse in the mirror I notice they are huge. *Holy Shit!* I walk hunched over to the shower, I just let the warmth of the water run all over me. I do deep breathing, because I refuse to have another sudden blow happen to me. I rub my swollen belly and talk to my baby. *We are going to be okay, you and me. Just hang on in there.* I don't bother with make up or my hair. I throw on some yoga pants and one of Grant's football shirts. I leave my hair combed and wet. I'll roll the windows down and let my hair dry that way. Once I am dressed and ready, I grab my car keys and hop into my sporty Camaro.

Thirty minutes later I am in the office. Ella comes around the counter to give me a big hug. "Happy Birthday, Beth!"

Squeezing her shoulders into me, I mutter, "Thanks Ella!"

She drags me to the back and tells me to hop on the scale. I'm afraid that she is going to get mad, because I feel I might have lost weight. I haven't really been eating. I can't stomach to eat or even smell the food. Smoothies have become my food of choice.

"Beth you've gained four pounds." She is so shitting me, on my birthday of all days. I turn around to look, and see my weight tinkered up four more pounds.

"How is that possible? If I continue at this rate of not eating and gaining four pounds I will pop out a butterball turkey."

"Let's wait and see what Dr. Alexander says." With that remark I pick up my purse and head to the room. I get undressed below the waist and sit on the table with a thin sheet over me.

The knock on the door jolts me out of my daydream of me looking like the Michelin Man by summer. A very tall, gorgeous man walks in with a manila folder in his hands. He is wearing a white jacket, with Dr. Alexander embroidered on it, but he is not the Dr. Alexander I saw before I got pregnant. I pull the sheet up a little farther, because I know I am blushing, hell I didn't even trim down there and this God of a man is going to look down there. *Holy shit, please let the floor open up and swallow me whole.* I glance to Ella who just winks at me. I am so going to murder her. *Oh my God, he stares at me and he has blue-green eyes, they are almost a turquoise color.* "Good Morning, Mrs. Thomas and Happy Birthday by the way. What brings in you today?"

"Well, thank you. I am getting concerned because lately I have been having consistent pain, almost like cramping, I am always nauseous and I feel swollen for only being around seven weeks pregnant. By the way, you aren't the Dr. Alexander I saw a couple years ago. So who are you, if you don't mind me asking?"

"I am Dr. Alexander; you must have seen my father Dr. Jeff Alexander. I am Dr. Jacob Alexander. My father only does GYN visits. I see you conceived by IVF, with Dr. Wilson. Implantation date is around seven weeks. Let's get an ultrasound done and see what is going on for your symptoms. As Ella gets the machine, I will be right back."

He walks out of the room as I grab Ella's wrist. "Mariella Adrianna Luciano Hudson, why in the hell did you not tell me about *that* Dr. Alexander?" I'm so embarrassed, that man is beautiful. He is so tall he must be around 6'2 and his shoulders are so broad, and those gorgeous eyes. "How in the hell, am I going to tolerate those eyes looking at me down *there*!"

Ella laughs; the bitch has the nerve to laugh at me. "Beth calm down, do you know how many woman blush, every time he walks in. You aren't the only one. Plus, he's gay, so don't worry about it. Pretend you are at the dentist; just open your legs and say '*ahhhh*'." I flip her off as she struts her ass out of the room. I jump off the table wrap the sheet around me and dig in my purse for my lotion. I rub it all over my legs, and stomach. I really don't give a shit if he is gay or not. I will not let those sexy eyes look at my dry legs. Not much I can do about trimming up my bikini area. *Note to self…store a razor in my purse for now on.*

Minutes go by before Ella, along with Dr. Dreamy, walk in with the machine. Ella is quietly giggling, because I am sure she can smell my sweet pea lotion all over me. Dr. Dreamy pulls out the stirrups and guides my feet into them. *Oh my God my feet. Note to self…get a damn pedicure!* He pulls the sheet up and over my knees so I won't be able to see him. He tells me to relax and he pushes my knees apart further. I throw my arm over my head as this is the most humiliating moment of my life.

He inserts his fingers in me. I feel I have been electrocuted in my vagina. I jolt off the table. He holds my hips down. "Elizabeth, sorry did I hurt you?"

"Uhh …No, sorry …I'm good." *Ugh!* I hear him pull the gloves off and tell me that my cervix looks great. He puts a condom on the trans-vaginal wand, and lubes it up with some gel. He turns the monitor so I can somewhat see. I notice he is very quiet and is having a hard time looking at me. I decide I am going to watch Ella's face since I can tell more by her reaction then the black and white on the screen. He's moving around and apologizes for the pressure. He keeps it still and pushes a bunch of buttons on the key board.

I look to Ella and I see tears in her eyes. *Oh shit, this isn't good. I'm miscarrying.* "Ella, what's wrong?" As my voice constricts the words out. She peeks to Dr. Alexander.

He turns the monitor; he says "I can tell you, it isn't bad. You are having growing pains at a rapid speed, because, Elizabeth, you are having triplets!" Ella plops down on me and cries and laughs at the same time. I am speechless and shocked. Dr. Alexander points to the three black holes on the screen and says that those are my babies. "Three babies, I am going to have three babies at one time?" I squeal. *Oh Shit!!*

He puts his hands behind my neck and I feel like he shocked me, that lighting has stricken my veins. I get hot all of a sudden as he helps me up into a sitting position. "Well congratulations Elizabeth. This is some birthday, 3 babies for turning 30! "

All I can do is smile and quietly say, "Yes, yes it is."

Dr. Alexander leans against the counter and is writing in my file. "Dr. Alexander, how come Dr. Wilson didn't tell me this news last week? He saw the heartbeat. Meaning one, not three. Why?" I barely catch my breath as the words run out of my mouth.

"Mrs. Thomas ..."

"Please call me Elizabeth."

"Alright, Elizabeth. Since I don't have your records as of yet from Dr. Wilson, I can only assume that either the babies were hiding behind one another or he didn't want to alarm you saying there were three. As soon as I have his notes, I can inform you why he didn't tell you. I assure you he did this with best intentions whatever the reason." He says with such grace and confidence. While placing his hands on his lean hips, he excuses Ella from the room.

"I'm going to leave you to get dressed. Once you are done, I would like to talk to you in my office about your pregnancy and I have information to give you.

Once I am dressed I open the door to see Ella leaning against the wall. "You okay?"

"I'm good, just so much to take in at once." I quietly say to her as I swing my purse on my shoulder.

"Dr. Alexander's Office is this way." She says as she grabs my arm. "You know, Beth, that this is the Dr. Alexander that took care of you that week in the hospital, he's the one that told me you were pregnant."

Nothing comes out of my mouth, I just nod at her. Once we are at his office the door is open and I see him at his desk. I give Ella a hug and tell her I will say good-bye before I leave.

Chapter 9

Jacob
- Friend of Mine -

I couldn't get out of that room fast enough. I'm sitting here trying to catch my breath and bring my nerves to a state of calm. Who would have thought that would be the worst exam on a patient in my career life. It tore me apart, to see her reaction towards me when I touched her. That is one thing I didn't want to do the first time I met her. I love what I do, and I know that many women dread the gynecologist office. So many women are nervous, embarrassed, and even bashful, but my profession is nothing different than any other doctor. I remember when I was in high school I admired my father. To take on the role of single father raising two teenagers and running a practice inspired me to be just like him. When I had concerns of going into a profession where I looked at vaginas all day, he was right there beside me saying. "Son, if you've seen one vagina you've seen them all …all the same and they serve two purposes …sex and birth."

Being a doctor for several years and looking at vaginas never bothered me until today, until Elizabeth was on my table. I have got to tell her I can't be her doctor. This is too awkward, and doesn't feel right. Now she's pregnant with triplets and that means more visits for her. *I just can't do this.* I'm on the computer printing out information for her on her pregnancy with multiples when I can see from my peripheral vision that she is standing by my office door with Ella. Damn!! She is stunning, even with the clothes she is wearing, hair not done and no makeup on she is beautiful.

A knock on the door diverts my attention to her standing nervously against the door jam. "Come in Elizabeth, please have a seat." I say as I keep clearing my voice. *Dammit, calm down, Jake!!* "I'm just printing off some information for you."

I watch her sit in the chair with her leg crossed over her knee. Her foot is shaking a mile a minute and she keeps rubbing her hands together. I can tell she is nervous around me. I wish I knew why I made her so nervous. She wants to tell me something, her eyes are focused on the back of my computer screen. The wheels in her head are spinning.

"Dr. Alexander …um, I want to say thank you for what you did the night my husband died. Ella told me it was you that sedated me so that my babies would have a chance for survival and obviously it worked. So, thank you." She says quietly and I see the tears start to trickle down her cheeks. *Shit!!* I don't want to see her cry.

Leaning over my chair I grab the tissue box from the shelf behind my desk. I hand them to her. "Here, please don't cry Elizabeth." She pulls the tissue out and dabs it under her eyes.

"Thank you, I'm sorry I don't mean to cry, it's just today of all days is very emotional."

"I completely understand." I say to her and truthfully I do understand the heartache she is going through. Maybe one day I can tell her that we are more alike than she thinks. I need to get to the point of why I brought her to my office before the nurses come banging on my door. Turning my chair around I pull the papers off the printer and pull the yellow folder of pamphlets, coupons and websites off the shelf. I place the yellow folder on my desk, leaning forward I open it up and show her what is inside. Then I hand her the papers I printed off. I advise her to have no caffeine, but if needed no more than one cup a day. I want her to limit her salts and greasy foods, up her fiber and water, and sleep eight to ten hours a night. Sleep when she is tired, and most importantly listen to her body.

"Any questions or concerns you call the office." I hand her another associate's business card. This moment is what I have been dreading; this is a moment that I have never had to do in my career. I want to see Elizabeth as she is, not as a patient. It morally isn't right for me to see my patients as any more than patients and I want more with her. I know it will take her time, but I feel it in the beat of my heart that she is the one for me. She is the one that I have been searching for the last twelve years.

"This is Dr. Weller. He is a great associate of mine and I think he will handle your multiple pregnancy better than I would. He's been delivering babies for as long as I have lived." She just stares at the business card. *Shit say something….anything.* After what seems like minutes, I ask her. "Elizabeth, are you okay?"

She examines me with those gorgeous green eyes of her, and the tears are just pooling in her eyes. *FUCK!!* "I don't understand? Why do I need to see a different doctor? Do you think something is wrong with my babies? I want you to be my doctor. Ella says you're the best and I trust her with everything I have, including my babies, which is all I have now. Why?"

She pulls more tissues out of the box. Dammit, this is not how I imagined things would go. "Elizabeth, first off there is nothing wrong with your babies. I just assumed you would want a more experienced doctor. Don't get me wrong I've done my share of multiple and high risk pregnancies...I just thought....shit...what I want to say is not coming out right." Watching her is breaking my heart. I just want her to smile; I want that glow to return that she had when she was sleeping. I want to take all this pain from her.

"I don't understand?" She says quietly and giving me a perplexed look.

I can't say what I want to say. It will scare the shit out of her. I will be the biggest ass if I say what is on my mind. Again, I am chicken shit and take the easy way out. "Elizabeth, I just wanted to give you an option in case you felt I wasn't the doctor you needed or wanted. Nevertheless, I want you to know that I am here for you no matter what." I walk around my desk and squat next to the chair she is sitting in. I take the tissues out of her hand and lay them on the floor. I grab both of her hands and hold them in my palms. "I was around a lot when you were in the hospital. Ella told me a lot about you, I feel like I know you, but then I look at you and I feel I know nothing about you. But I just feel... any friend of Ella's is a friend of mine." I hand her my business card and grab a pen off my desk. I write my cell number on the back of the card. "Here is my number in case you need something and can't reach me after hours. I want you to understand that I am here for you, pregnancy related or not. Just don't call me if you have a plumbing question, which is something to leave to the professionals." There it is! She smiles at my ridiculous joke. Her green eyes sparkle as she gawks at me. I pat her knee as I stand up.

Taking my card she places it in her purse. She stands up and puts her hand out for me to shake. "Thanks Dr. Alexander, for all this." As she holds up the folder and papers. "If you don't mind I would like to remain as your patient."

Letting go of her hand I tell her that I don't mind at all. I walk her to the reception area and tell her I will see her in two weeks. Before I go on to the next patient, I walk back to my office. It smells of her sweet pea scent. I pull out a bottle of Jack and take a few gulps. My nerves are still not calm, and I'm not sure if they ever will be having Elizabeth in my life now. Then I take a swig of water, from the bottle on my desk. As, I stand up to pull a piece of gum from my pocket, I watch from my office window. I watch her walk to her hot, red Camaro. I see that she is still crying, she has the phone to her ear. She throws her bag in, and steps into her car smoothly with ease. Within a few seconds she is gone from the parking lot. I leave my office, counting down the days until I see her again.

Chapter 10

Start of Something Good

December

It's hard to believe that December has arrived. The year has flown by; the year that started off so magical, and has ended with heartache, despair, and anxiety. I'm finally out of my first trimester. It's a week before Christmas. Do you think I have done any decorating for Christmas…Nope! I can't do it. I can't bring out all the memories that Grant and I have accumulated over 9 years. Also, I can't crawl up in the attic, so this year since it is just me. I am not decorating. I will be starting the New Year with seeing a realtor, I can't live in this house, knowing that this house was meant for Grant and me to raise our children. With him not here, it feels wrong and unwanted.

I have seen Dr. Alexander every week since my eight week visit. After that visit I saw Cole and Anna to give them a copy of the ultrasound. They were speechless to hear the news of having three grandchildren. Anna is over the moon and has offered her grandma-sitting services. I will happily oblige! Cole is excited, but hits him with a double-edge sword. Due to my high risk and carrying multiples, it was lectured to me by Dr. Alexander and

Ella to live a stress free life as much as possible, and relax as much as I can. I have got to keep them in me for as long as possible. So I let Cole know that I had to resign from the practice. One, it was for the pregnancy and two; I haven't been back since Grant had passed. I couldn't go into the office that he and I shared five days a week. I couldn't go into his office and see everything of his without him being there. One of our associates, Indira, packed up his and my personal items and shipped them to me. They are still in the garage. I can't go through it. I know what is in there. I can't go through the memories right now. Cole was great and assured me that once I was ready to come back that I will be accepted with open arms. I'm not sure if I ever want to go back.

Getting ready for my twelve week appointment I am nervous. It's that mark in any woman's pregnancy where it can go downhill or uphill. Where you wait for the twelve week mark to tell friends you are pregnant, but it's also that mark where it can go bad. Knowing that I could lose one or all still weighs heavily on my mind.

Kate is going to go with me. I haven't told her it is triplets. I want to surprise her with the ultrasound today! I was there when she found out she was having twins. I wanted to continue with tradition. Kate picks me up in her dark blue Ford F-150. I grab the oh shit bar to haul my butt up in the seat.

"Kate, how in the hell did you get the girls in the back seat?" I ask exasperated from pulling myself up.

"Girl, where in the hell do you think I got my guns from." As she is flexing her biceps to me. "Bethy-baby, just wait, you pick out this cute infant seat, but you don't realize that this seven pound baby does a lot of growing in its first year. Times that by two and you got yourself a continuous workout, but don't worry you can just snuggle your little wee one in that hot car of yours and be fine. I had to hoist up the girls in this truck. By their first year they were over twenty pounds plus the weight of the seat. UGH!! I don't miss those days. It's nice to tell the girls to jump in and then all I do is buckle"

I just smile, because she has no idea …I have no idea what I am in for.

Realization sinks in. I've got to sell my pride and joy. "Kate, did two seats fit in the truck okay, was there room for a third person to sit back there?"

She glances at me with her eyebrows scrunched together, "Umm, yeah there was room. When we went out as a family I sat in the middle to watch over them. Why do you ask?

"Oh, just wandering. By the way you didn't get those arms by lifting car seats, you got those arms by shoveling horse shit."

"Car seats …horse shit it's all manual labor, baby!"

We pull into the office. I warn her of how hot my doctor is. I tell her how we have made small talk during the last month. That when he touches me he makes me light up like a damn Christmas tree. We wait in the waiting room. Kate is fidgeting, she holds my hand, then her foot is tapping the coffee table a mile a minute, then she is rubbing my belly and talking to the babies. Kate has never been diagnosed, but just by being with her I can tell you, the woman is ADHD. She doesn't need caffeine, she has adrenaline running through her blood.

"Kate, you've got to stop, the women in here are probably thinking we are a lesbian couple."

"Who cares?" As she pulls my face to her face with her hands then gives me a quick kiss. I pull back and just laugh. As I turn around I see that Ella has witnessed the whole thing.

"Look at you two! I didn't know your relationship swung that way?" Ella says while trying to control her laughter. Since all these women are just staring at us.

"Kate, you are too much!"

"What? This place is so uptight, gotta loosen the vibe in here. Women are here to check on their baby, not to get their colonoscopy. Now that's an uptight waiting room!" She just cackles all the way to the examining room.

I am sitting on the table and waiting. Ella has left to go get the ultrasound machine. Kate is playing with the blood pressure cuff. "Kate, you are such a child, will you have a seat! GEEZ you would think you were pregnant?"

Kate laughs out loud. She sits down and places her elbows on her knees and head in her palms. "UH, No, you would have to be having sex to get pregnant and I haven't had sex in months. Beth, I need to get fucked."

Just as Kate had the F-bomb come out of her mouth Dr. Dreamy walks in. Kate looks up and then laughs to herself as she places her head back in her palms. "Talk about making an ass out of myself." She says quietly to herself.

Dr. Alexander walks over to the table, "How are you doing, Elizabeth?"

"I'm doing well. The nausea has somewhat stopped, just tired. This is Kate, she is my friend who doesn't think before she speaks."

Walking over to Kate, he puts his hand out to shake her. She obliges and sinks further into her chair. "Nice to meet you." As he walks to the table I peek at her as she is fanning herself. She mouths "Fuck me, please!" I just smile and gaze into those beautiful blue eyes. I bite my bottom lip to keep me from smiling so big.

"This is all good news I am hearing. Being tired is expected for your condition."

He measured my rapidly growing belly, then squeezed the gel over my belly. I hold Kate's hand as she leans into me. "This is so exciting!" She whispers into my ear.

"Oh just wait it gets better." I say as I turn and whisper into her ear. Ella just snickers and gives us both a wide toothy grin.

"Okay, let's see what is going on." Dr. Alexander mutters as he waves the wand over my belly. The images appear on the screen. He is doing his usual measuring and recording. He turns the screen towards us so we can see the whole screen. "Baby A is here, this is baby B and tucked over here is Baby C."

"HOLY SHIT!!! Beth you are having triplets!!" She just stares, her lips are moving, but nothing is coming out.

"Elizabeth, everything looks great. The babies are doing well. Hopefully in a month we will be able to tell you the sex if you want to know. Keep off your feet as much as possible. Let's keep your blood pressure in check, too. Did you decide on flying or driving to your parents?"

"I'm flying, is that alright?"

"Yes, your flight shouldn't be that long. You'll be fine."

"Okay." I say…man this guy has serious bedroom eyes. They literally change color with his clothing. This week he has on a grey collared shirt. His eyes are ice blue, last week they were green. *Wonder what they would look like when he's naked?* Seriously, these hormones need to taper back some.

I rub the gel off my stomach, and pull my shirt down. Dr. Alexander observes me, like he wants to say something, but not sure how.

"Uh…um…ah….Elizabeth, I know this is going to sound so unprofessional. I don't want you to think less of me as a doctor, but I want to ask you something."

"Okay" I say.

"My office doesn't do a Holiday Party, we do something entertaining every year. This year we have sky box seats to Chris Daughtry's Concert. I was wondering if you would like to go with us, Ella and her husband will be there if you feel uncomfortable."

Ella just smiles and nods her head yes. "I...it's...uh...I've just heard great things about you from Ella and I ...I just wanted to get to know you more. I think we have a lot in common."

I smirk and sarcastically say to him. "Oh do we? So you are carrying triplets, too?" He just gives me a beautiful smile.

"Come with us Beth, it will be fun. Look you get a concert and your doctor making sure you are okay?" Ella tells me as she pats my knee.

"Sure, I would love to go. I'm not much of a music fan, so I won't know most of his songs."

"Not a problem, I'll help you out. So are you free around five? I'll take you to dinner beforehand."

"Uh, dinner?"

"Yes, Elizabeth, dinner. Friends can go out to eat and have dinner. Is that okay?"

"So, it's not a date, because I'm not ready to date, plus you're my doctor."

He just chuckles. "Yes, I am your doctor and no, it's two friends having dinner before we meet with more friends. "

Deal!"

"Good, I'll pick you up at five, if that is alright?" He softly says to me while inspecting my file.

"I'll see you at five." I say as I bend down and pick up my purse from the chair. He opens the door for us, and we walk out.

"Thanks Elizabeth." Dr. Alexander says as I walk out of the office.

"Ella!" I call loudly for her. She gives me her shit eating grin smile. "He's not gay is he?"

"Whatever do you mean, Beth?" She replies in her sexy Spanish accent.

"At my first encounter with Dr. Dreamy, you told me he was gay!"

"Oh, well I just found out he's not." She bats her eyes to me.

"You are such a weasel Ella! I can't believe you...oh...wait...yes I can."

"Holy shit, Beth! Did I just witness that you are having three babies and that your doctor just invited you to a concert. Or am I totally dreaming this Jerry Springer episode?"

"Katie-bear you witnessed one crazy doctor appointment."

"Beth, that man is fucking-hot! Shit forget the damn Christmas tree. That man would light me up like Times Square. Makes me want to get knocked up just so I can see that man for nine months." She watches me as the tears trickling down my face. "Uh-oh, what's wrong?"

I get in the front seat and pull tissues out of my purse. "Kate, I feel like I am on the emotional roller coaster from hell. I lost Grant. I feel such sadness that he is not here, yet I am so completely horny. Then I see that man in there." Pointing to the doctor's office. "It's taking a toll on my sanity."

"Beth, you've been hit harder than most pregnant women. Not only are you carrying three babies, but you are also mourning your husband's death. Of course you are going to have so many emotions. It's normal and it's healthy. I would be worried if you didn't have them. Now on another note, I know why you asked about my truck. Babe, you gotta kiss that hot car of yours goodbye. No way are you going to get three babies in that car. Just look at it this way, Jillian Michaels will have nothing on you by the time those babies are one!" *God, I just love this girl!*

Friday night comes way too quickly. I am so nervous, my vomiting spells could happen any moment. I wear a pair of jeans, but due to my growing belly I use a rubber band to hold them up, wasn't expecting to shop for maternity clothes this soon. *Merry Christmas to me!* I throw on a hunter green sweater with a scoop neck and my black ballet flats. I curl the ends of my hair and put my makeup on.

To make the time pass, I grab two tennis balls and play fetch with the dogs. I hear the roaring of a truck come to a standstill. Wondering what semi just pulled up, the dogs and I walk into the house. I go, open the door, standing there in all of his hotness glory is Dr. Alexander. "Whoa, you look good....I mean different...but a good different." I stutter as I am trying to pick my jaw up off the floor. He is wearing a black long sleeved collared shirt, the sleeves rolled up to his mid-fore-arm, jeans, which hang just right on his lean hips, along with black boots.

"You don't look too bad yourself! You're beautiful, Elizabeth!"

"Well, thank you, Doctor."

"Please call me Jacob, or even Jake. Most of my friends call me Jake."

"You got a deal Jacob! You ready?"

We walk out. I shut and lock the door. Parked in the driveway is an all-black and chrome Dodge Ram truck. It's a hot truck with huge wheels. He helps me into the cab of the truck. I watch as he walks around the hood of the car. He opens the door and gets in with no issues. I guess when you have those long lean legs jumping into a truck is not a problem.

I buckle up as I sit back in the gray leather seat. "This is a really nice truck. I didn't picture you with a truck. I thought more of a Mercedes or Porsche kind of man."

"Nope, I have always been into trucks, plus you can't put a surfboard on a Mercedes, just doesn't seem right if you catch my drift."

"You surf?"

"Been surfing all my life, anything with water and I'm game. I have a jet ski, too. My father has a boat, he's into fishing. Fishing is too slow for my taste."

"Wow, umm I love the water, but I've never surfed."

"Really? Well, then I will have to teach you...obviously once you have the babies."

"I would like that. " I say shyly and mess with my hair. On our drive to a quiet mom and pop Mexican restaurant I learn that we have a lot in common. We ended up at the same high school, but him being seven years older than me; we kind of missed each other. He loves dogs, even has a Bullmastiff, but it spends most of the time at his father's house. He even showed me pictures of him on his phone like a proud father would. He's a cute dog, huge, but cute. He's all tan except his snout is black. I loved the picture of him with his dog cuddled on the couch. "What's your dog's name?"

"Scooby."

"You named your dog Scooby? Scooby was a Great Dane."

"Excuse me Miss who has dogs named after vitamins and cartoon characters, too."

"I know, but I would just assume if you have a dog named Scooby that he is a Great Dane. I like the name, it seems fitting.

"Again, another misconception of you." I say with a wink to him.

We each have one sibling, both of us being the babies in the family. We both love the outdoors and water. He's not a fan of motorcycles and starting this new chapter in life neither am I.

We park at the arena and it's a mob, Jacob grabs my hand and walks with me. I follow behind him, since I kept getting knocked around. We take the escalator up and walk into the sky box. I recognize the nurses and staff from his office. Smiling as we walk into the room, I see Ella and Chris. She comes up and hugs me, with Chris following behind her. I haven't seen Chris since the memorial service. "You look real good, Beth. Congrats!" I tilt my head and kiss him on the cheek. "Thanks, Chris!"

I'm escorted to a seat in between Ella and Jacob. The room's huge. I never knew that this is what was up here. They have flat screen TV's along the wall. The back wall has a table that has trays of food, and drinks. The chairs are really comfortable, too.

"Do you want anything to drink or eat?" Jacob asks.

"Oh, no I am good, thank you though."

"So, what is your favorite song of Chris Daughtry?" Jacob's question catches me off guard?

"Who?"

"Elizabeth, for real you don't know who Chris Daughtry is?"

"I know he was from American Idol, that's about it. I really don't watch TV or listen to music."

"How can you not listen to music? It's a staple into relaxing and entertainment. Don't you have an iPod or even listen to the radio in your car?"

I blush with embarrassment. "No, I don't own an iPod. I am always thinking and rethinking. It's a really bad fault of mine. If the radio is on I'm not paying attention." I blush harder with embarrassment. "I daydream a lot, it takes my focus away."

He grabs my hand, folding his fingers with mine. "I hope to one day hear about those dreams of yours. Maybe I could make some come true." He brings the hand he is holding and gives sweet gentle kisses on each finger. Then places my hand back in my lap. "Well, I hope you enjoy it, he sings rock. You okay with that?"

I try to control my breathing, why for the love of God do I have to endure fifty thousand emotions running through my body? I take in a deep breath and reply. "Yeah, as long as you think it's alright for the babies."

"It doesn't get as loud in here as it does down there. They should be fine. I'm here to protect." He says into my ear and places his right hand on the top of my belly. I just turn and smile at him.

The concert is awesome, I'm having a blast. Jacob is a huge fan of Chris Daughtry. Daughtry is starting to sing, "*Start of Something Good.*" I stare at the TV this time as he sings his heart out to this song. I listen to the words, they have so much meaning to what's in my life right now. The song is almost over when Jacob notices that this song is resonating with me. He grabs my hand again and threads his fingers through. Our fingers lock together like magnets. The electricity is so strong I feel like it will jolt my heart out of my chest. Jacob leans over and whispers in my ear, "Maybe this song will hold meaning to us both." I nod and smile at him. Daughtry sings a few more songs.

I really like him and need to go get his CD or an iPod, something to listen to his music. The stage is black, then Chris is standing at the microphone. There is little light on the stage. He tells the audience the importance of this song. I need to pee so badly, but Jacob tells me to wait if I can that I will like this song. Daughtry starts singing about how he can't wait to see their faces hold their hands, take them for walks and waiting for them. I realize he is singing about his babies. I watch the TV and you can just see the love that this man is singing for his children. I start to cry, for the beauty of this song and that my children's father will never be able to express his anticipation for the birth of his children.

As I wipe my eyes, Jacob leans over and places his other hand on my belly. "If your babies have half your beauty and love, they will be the most blessed children on this earth."

I try to gulp, but I can't. I feel like something is stuck in my throat. I say thank you and get up to go to the restroom. I hear steps approaching me in the hallway.

"Beth, wait up." I hear Ella shout out. "Ella, I just need to pee, seriously I am okay."

"I saw you crying, why?"

"Why do you think? My husband's ashes are probably still floating on the top of the ocean and here I am a couple months later at a concert and holding hands with my doctor. Do you hear how absurd this sounds, or is it just me? Because I feel like I am coming off the chain here. What in the hell kind of woman does this? Ella, I like him and I shouldn't. He makes me happy, we had a great time at dinner and he is helping me get through this pregnancy emotionally and professionally. Then hearing that song and knowing my babies will never know what their father thought of them, it j….just breaks my heart." I sob into the sleeve of my sweater. "Damn it, I didn't want to do this." I stomp my feet, lift my head up and wipe the running mascara away from my eyes. Ella puts both hands on my shoulder. Gives me her sweet, sympathetic smile.

"Beth, Jacob is a great man and you deserve a little greatness in your life right now. He likes you, and that is pretty awesome considering you are a single woman pregnant with three babies. Not a lot of men would go for that. Grant would want you to be happy. He would want his babies to have a happy mom. In time, those babies will know what a great man Grant was because you will be there to tell them. They will know all about him. Take it slow and see where this goes with Jacob. If anything at the end of all this, you will be saying thanks for his services as your doctor. Just breathe, honey, and take it nice and slow. You know better than anyone that life is way too short, so enjoy each day! I love you, now give me a hug!"

I hug her with all my strength, I am the luckiest woman to have this woman in my life. She is my anchor, rock, wall, and savior. I'm a soon to be mom with three babies because of her and her love for me. Once I finally pee, I am back upstairs sitting next to Jacob enjoying the encore of the concert.

After the concert he takes me home, and we talk some more. He really does put me at ease. Once he drops me off at my house he walks me up to my door.

"When do you leave for your parent's?"

"Christmas Eve, then I come back the day before New Year's Eve."

"How long is the flight?" "

"Just over an hour, it's not bad. I just hope the airport isn't a madhouse."

"Will you promise to call me, so I know you got there safe and sound?"

"Sure I will." I say with glee.

"Are you doing anything for New Years?"

"No, I'm really not in the state to drink and bring in the New Year."

"I'm not talking about drinking or partying. I was going to take my father's boat out. Along the coast many people light off the fireworks, plus it's quiet. I was wondering if you want to join me? I have to work Christmas, but not New Year's."

"Jacob, you know that I lost my husband two months ago."

"Beth, I completely understand what you are going through. I just thought you'd like to get out if you didn't have plans. I don't mean anything serious by it. I understand if you say no."

"Jacob let me think about it, okay?"

"Sounds good, Elizabeth. I had a great time tonight, thank you for coming along."

"Thank you Jacob, I had a great time, too! I will see you soon." With that he leans in and gives me a hug good-bye.

"Goodnight, Elizabeth."

"Goodnight."

Chapter 11

One, Two, Three

February

Valentine's Day is upon us. I loathe this holiday this year. Not a great day when you are a widow and extremely pregnant. I look like I could burst any day, and I still have the other half of my pregnancy.

Today is the day I find out the sex of my babies. Well at least I hope, last month they didn't cooperate at all. There is a possibility I am carrying at least one boy, the tech thought she saw a penis on Baby C. So we will see, crossing my fingers. Kate is going with me again. I want my girls to be with me for this special day, then we are going to lunch, after that SUV shopping. It is time to part ways with my hot, red Camaro, mainly because driving stick is getting way to uncomfortable and squatting this low I'm afraid a hand might fall out and motion me to stop!

Once I am at Kate's, I walk into the house, and it smells to high heaven of Menthol and Eucalyptus. "Why does it smell like a nursing home in here?"

"Beth, please help!!" I hear Kate, shout from upstairs.

"I'm a coming!!" As I wobble up the stairs. "What is this?" I fumble the words while my hand is covered in greasy goo from the banister.

"My lovely children decided to get into VICKS and massage themselves and the walls."

"Mommyyyyyy, my eyeballs are on fiiiiirrrrre!" Julia starts to scream.

"Good God Julia STOP rubbing your eyes, you have this shi…, I mean cream all in your hands. Nicole naked NOW, and get in the bath. Julia, please stop your eyes are starting to swell."

I feel like I am at a tennis match watching Kate bounce from kid to kid. She is running between bathtub and hallway. Walking into the bathroom I sit myself on the toilet to help Nicole get naked and into the bathtub. "Aunt Beppy how do the babies come out?" As she is taking her small greasy hand and rubbing my belly.

"UH…Nicole its magic the doctor says bippty boppity boo and they pop out. Now bippity boppity boo you need to get in that bath before your momma turns you into a mouse." She gives me her sweet smile, and bounces into the bathtub while pretending she is a mouse.

Kate brings me Julia to bathe, while she is scrubbing down the walls. "Juju look I'm a mouse." Nicole laughs as she is crawling around the bathtub.

"Beppy why is Nini a mouse?" Ugh I created monsters. Kate is just laughing.

"Hello!?" I hear Kate's mom call from down stairs.

"In you go Jules…saved by Gamma. Gamma is going to finish your bath." I kiss their heads and tell them I love them. I walk out of the bathroom a sweating and greasy mess.

"Thank God you are here, Mom. The girls just need to be scrubbed, their clothes are on their beds and you can thank them for being able to breathe better. Love you." She kisses her mom and runs into her room. I walk out to give Mary a hug and kiss.

We are finally out of the house and I take in some deep breaths as I felt my lungs were closing up in there.

"Okay, I need a drink. It's not even ten and my nerves are a mess!" Kate rushes her words to me. "So are you excited? You know we have to go shopping, it's a must once you find out the sex …pink or blue or both?"

"I'm nervous. I really hope we can see the turtle or hamburger."

"What the fuck is a turtle or hamburger?" Kate blanches out to me. I just laugh at her, this woman is a mother. I swear she did push out two babies; I was witness to that clusterfuck of labor.

"They say in the pregnancy book that the boy's penis looks like a turtle and the girl's vagina looks like a side view of a hamburger."

"Well, I have never heard of such a piece of shit analogy …hell I never read the damn books anyways. I waited for the doctor to say it's a ….girl and then another girl! Taa Daa, you don't need a book for that information. That is why you are seeing the hottie doctor, so he can tell you first hand. Please burn the damn books; I don't need to hear any more about reptiles and food analogies."

"I love you Kate! You seriously can make any situation into a comedy show!" I smart mouth back to her.

While sitting on the table waiting on Jacob to come in, Kate and I chit chat. "So how is it going with the doctor?"

"It's going well, Kate. He's a great guy, we talk on the phone, and since New Year's we've been hanging out. Nothing extravagant, I want to take this slow, my main focus is getting through this pregnancy, and he has been a huge help. "

Moments later he is walking in with the Ultrasound machine and Ella.

"Hi, Elizabeth, how are you?"

"I'm being swallowed by my children, but other than that, I'm good!"

He has the cutest laugh and a beautiful smile. "Well, let's add a gender to the children that are swallowing you, shall we?"

"Yes, Yes!" I'm so anxious to see. I lay on my back with help from Ella. I kink my neck so I can see the monitor. Once I see arms and legs on the screen, tears start pooling in my eyes. They are so beautiful to me no matter what, boy or girl. I am so in love with them, it terrifies me. I've never experienced this kind of love.

"Baby A is cooperating, and he is definitely a boy." Jacob says as he zooms on his penis.

Kate slaps my shoulder, "Girl you are crazy, but I can see why they call that thing a turtle. That is the cutest, tiniest penis I have ever seen."

"Kate, you are the sick one, who the hell calls a baby boy's penis cute?" Ella mutters to all of us.

"What?" Is all Kate can say?

"Okay, let's have you roll to your left for a minute, I will freeze the picture so you can see what you are having. Sorry for the pressure, but they are really snug in there ….There, got it! Roll back over and see what Baby B is."

I roll over and adjust my eyes; it looks the same as Baby A. "It's a boy? I have two boys so far."

"Yes, let's see what Baby C is, this time roll to your right." With more pressure by the wand, I have a clear view of the screen. Jacob is trying to get a good standstill picture, but I saw it already. It's another boy. I'm having triplet boys! *Holy shit!*

"Elizabeth, did you see what Baby C is?" I just nod, as tears are running down my cheeks.

"It's a boy, right?"

Kate shouts! "Hot dog, Elizabeth, you have three turtles in there. I'm going to name them for you, Donatello, Michelangelo, and Raphael."

"Why would she name them that? God Kate, what the hell was in your coffee this morning?" Ella disgustingly says to Kate.

"Oh my God, she talked the whole way here about how she hopes to see a turtle and hamburgers. She has turtles, so we are naming them after the Teenage Mutant Ninja Turtles. Well, at least I will have nicknames for them." She finishes with a mutter to all of us.

If I didn't have both of them on either side of me, I would have rolled off the table. I am just laughing hysterical. Hysterical from the fact that it is so real, I am really going to have three boys. Laughing that my nut of a friend wants me to name my children after cartoon characters, turtles no less. My friends help me off the table. I'm in another episode of the Twilight Zone.

Jacob hands me tissues, "Ladies do you mind if I speak to Elizabeth alone for a few minutes?"

The ladies leave. "Elizabeth, you okay? Are these happy tears or what?"

"Jacob, I am so happy. I've wanted these boys for a very long time. It is just so real right now. I'm scared; I don't know how to raise a boy, let alone three. They kind of need male role models. It's just awkward emotions that are running through me."

"Elizabeth, you know you are not alone in this. That I hope even after these babies are born that I am still a part of your and their lives. I really care for you, and I want to be there for you and the boys. Who am I going to teach to surf?"

I give a little chuckle of just the visualization of three little boys on a surfboard. "I hope you are a part of my life, too!"

"What are you doing tonight?" Jacob perks up and asks.

"Nothing, its Valentine's Day, where widows stay in and sulk."

"Well, what do you say you come over to my place and I cook you a good dinner, then we can sulk together?"

"Why would you sulk?"

"I told you that we have a lot more in common than you think, that I totally understand what you are going through. I'm….mm a widower myself." He quietly tells me this and I just stare at him dumbfounded.

"You are?"

"Yes, and see now we have a lot more to talk about, so what do you say to coming over? I don't live far from the hospital."

"Yes, that sounds like fun. I mean sulking together." I reply back.

"Seven pm, my house." He hands me a piece of paper with his address on it. He helps me off the table and leans in and kisses my hair. "Congratulations Elizabeth, those sons of yours are very lucky to have a mother like you."

"Thanks, Jacob. Really… thanks for everything. I will see you later on. Now I am off to trade in my sports car for a sports utility vehicle."

Driving to Jacob's house seems so surreal. I would have never thought in a million years since last Valentine's, with Grant that I would be having dinner with my OB Doctor. Pulling off the highway I realize he lives in a condo. That seems so odd for a doctor.

Sitting at the light, I think back on the day. Finding out that I am going to have three boys was the real kicker, and then lunch with Kate is always a riot. I traded in my Camaro for a Suburban. I was aiming for the Tahoe, but Kate pushed me for the bigger vehicle, her motto. "Go big or go home." I assume down the road it will be a perfect fit for my boys and me.

I pull up, grab my purse and Jacob's little Valentine gift. It's a small stuffed gorilla holding a bunch of bananas and wearing a shirt saying "I'm bananas for you." Cheesy, I know, but that is what this holiday is all about.

He answers the door in khaki cargo pants, a light blue shirt and he's bare foot. He has sexy feet. He is sexy from head to toes. "Welcome Elizabeth, Happy Valentine's Day."

"Hi, Jacob, how are you? It smells delicious in here." I slip my shoes off and my jacket. "Here this is for you, Happy Valentine's Day."

"Thanks, this is cute. Here is yours." He points to the dozen pink roses on the bar.

"Wow, Jacob these are beautiful. Thank you. So what are you cooking?"

"I hope you like Italian, I have lasagna, salad and garlic rolls. What would you like to drink? I have soda, PowerAde, and water. Sorry, I know you are limited to drink choices."

"No, water is just fine." I walk to sit down on his black leather sofa. His condo is very small. He has an open floor plan of a living room, kitchen, nook and then hallway with a bathroom and bedroom. "I was kind of shocked to see you live in a condo, another misconception of you. I pictured this huge beach style house."

"I would love to own a beach style house one day, but for now since it is just me it didn't see the value to have a home. Plus, living here is inexpensive. I feel like I live at the hospital, though."

"So how many days do you stay at the hospital?" I quizzically ask.

"Right now, it's about four nights. Another practice and I are looking into merging our practices together. I can't keep going at this rate. I never sleep when I'm at the hospital. I feel like I have no life." He laughs to himself embarrassingly. He brings me my water and sits next to me on the couch, holding his beer in both hands.

"Well, you should be proud of yourself, you have a rewarding profession. You bring miracles to women every day. You brought me mine today." I say as I pat his knee.

"God, Elizabeth you are gorgeous. You realize your eyes sparkle when you talk about your pregnancy."

"They do?" I blush so hard that I feel the heat on my face. I pile on the questions right away. "I know we have a physical attraction to each other, you are obviously very handsome with a great personality.

You think I am pretty, but why? Why do you want to start something with me, you do know that once these boys are born I am pretty busy for the next eighteen years. Why would you want that responsibility with me? I just don't get it, Jacob."

"Hold on." As he gets up, walks to the oven, and pulls out the lasagna and rolls. When he returns back to the sofa he sits, turning towards me where his knees are touching mine.

"Elizabeth, you are more than pretty, you are a beautiful woman. I look at you and I see everything about you inside and out. I knew of you before you came to me. Ella would rave about you to the girls. I ached when I saw you lost your husband. I know firsthand what kind of ache that is. I don't know what I felt, but I felt like I needed you, I needed to be a part of your life in more ways than one. Since that day in October I can't stop thinking about you. You have consumed me. Then there is this pull between us, I feel it every time we are close. Do you feel it?"

I stop twirling my hair, then fold my hands over my belly. "Yes, I feel it. But, don't most people feel an attraction to good looking people? I don't know if I can give you what you want. I spent the last ten years with a man that I thought I would have forever with. I can't change my feelings. I'm having my husband's children without him. The last four months have been emotionally hard for me."

"I know we both have had the loves of our lives, we both have loved deeply, but I have never felt this ache…ever. I will be honest with you. I want more, Elizabeth. But, I understand and will respect your feelings. I will wait for you. You are too precious to me to give up on."

He pulls me up and brings me to the table. Pulling me into him, taking his thumb and forefinger he lifts my chin to look up at him. "Elizabeth, I gaze into those green eyes and I just see you. Nothing else around me matters when I stare into those eyes. I touch your skin and I feel this." He picks up my hand and places it over his heart. "My heart beats for you. Do you feel this? It beats uncontrollably when I am around you. In this moment I feel like I can't breathe. You are a living dream. Whatever comes with you is a bonus for me, even three baby boys. They are a part of you and it makes me want to be in their lives even more."

I felt in that moment that I was going to pass out. Hearing his words were perfect, but the timing was not. "I don't know what to say?" With his hands on my shoulders, taking his left hand and brushing my hair behind my ears. I want to run for the door and never look back. My chest feels like it is caving in, my throat feels like it is squeezing to where I can't swallow, and my heart is pulsating so fast that I feel at any moment it will burst. Yet, I have this one feeling, this one feeling that keeps growing over time for him and I am not sure what to do with it. I adore this man. He has been the one male in my life that treats me as the same old Elizabeth, everyone else looks to me as if I am glass and if they say anything to me I will turn to dust. Losing your husband is agony, but it is also the loneliest I have ever been in my life. Jacob makes me feel like myself and that is one feeling I am not pushing away.

"Tell me you will give us a shot. Tell me you want to be in my life as much as I want to be in yours. Tell me you want to give this couple thing a try?"

"Jacob it feels right, but it also feels too soon. I feel like I am being dishonest to Grant for some reason."

He just nods and pulls out my chair. *Shit!* Now I feel like an ass and I still have to sit through dinner. He serves me dinner. We make small talk. We laugh at Kate and her actions from earlier. I tell him about my car shopping adventure with that crazy woman. I thought he was going to need the Heimlich maneuver done when I told him how Kate stole the golf cart and drove me around the car lot. When the salesman yelled at her for taking the golf cart she pulled on the charm, flirted, then gave the poor guy the wrong number. We sit for a while, talking about everything. Talking seems so natural for us. It doesn't feel forced or uncomfortable. He gets up to clear the table. "Elizabeth, remember how I told you that I am a widower, also."

I bring some plates to him, "Yes, but I understand if you aren't ready to talk about it."

"No, I want to talk about it. It's been thirteen years bottled up inside of me. Rebecca and I started dating our senior year in high school. We went to college together and our relationship continued. We graduated college together, she became an interior designer. I was on my way to medical school. She knew since she met me that I wanted to be a doctor, more so she knew that I wanted to be an OB/GYN. She knew that I wanted to give woman miracles, just like my father had. A year into medical school, we talked about marriage and were married nine months later. Had this big huge wedding, and bought our home. Things were going great. I was in school a lot but always made sure I made time for her. A year into our marriage, she ended up never being home. I knew she resented me and how I was never there for her.

One Friday night I come home from doing rounds and there is a note saying that she and her sister were going away for the weekend. I didn't think much of it because, they would normally do those kind of things. I was pissed she didn't tell me. The…next morning, I get a call from Natalie her sister that something was wrong with Rebecca, to come to the Marriott. I was pissed that she was at the hotel down the road from us. I get into the hotel room and find Rebecca unconscious and bleeding profusely from her vagina. Natalie is screaming at me, and then at her. Natalie called 911 and they came minutes after me and rushed her to the hospital. She was pronounced dead, by the time we got to the hospital. She lost so much blood. There was nothing we could have done."

I go behind Jacob and hug him from behind. I squeeze him and ask, "What happened to her?"

"I will never know the whole truth, but from what Natalie had told me. Rebecca went and had an abortion from a quack doctor. Apparently something went wrong and she bled out. Natalie took her for the procedure, but left her at the hotel overnight. When Rebecca didn't call Natalie, she freaked out and went back to the hotel. That's when she found her and called me.

"Was it your baby?" I softly whisper to him.

"I will never know, Natalie says that Rebecca didn't know who the father was, she cheated on me with her client. She didn't want to have the baby and then find out if it wasn't mine. Natalie said that Rebecca didn't want to even bring a baby into our marriage, whether it was mine or not, because I was never home. That she didn't sign up to be a single mother."

"Jacob I am so sorry, so sorry that you never got your answers or a goodbye."

"I'm more pissed, than hurt. I was so pissed when she died. That she went and had an abortion. Knowing that I was bringing babies into the world every day and she went and took mine away. It was mine no matter what, because it was a part of her and I loved her." He pounds the counter as he walks to the table to get the last of the glassware. "I'm so mad, that she was so selfish. That she thought the worst of me. She cheated on me, and never gave me a reason why. I loved her with everything I had, I would have fixed it. I would have fixed us." He says as he trails off his words. I can see the pain he still carries with him after all these years. He has unanswered questions. I just never got a goodbye. I can't imagine grieving for the answers.

He turns around and I place my hands on his hips, his hands are in my hair. "Don't you see Elizabeth? We both have had the same thing happen to us. Now fate, the universe, God, life, whatever you call it has brought us together. You aren't being dishonest to Grant by being with me. You are being dishonest to yourself. We are meant to be together. I like you, Elizabeth, and I want this new chapter of our life to have a happily ever after. Please ….please tell me you will give us a chance?"

I rested my forehead against his chest and closed my eyes as I pleaded with my heart rate to slow down. I inhale and deep breath, pull myself back, stare into his stunning eyes and say. "All, I can do is try, Jacob. I can't promise you anything, and we have to go slow. "

He places his hands around the nape of my neck and pulls me up to his mouth. "Can, I please kiss you, Elizabeth?" I stand on my tip toes to give him assurance that it is okay to kiss me. His lips are so soft. We kiss each other gently trying to explore each other's lips. Then I part my lips and I feel his tongue in my mouth. I taste his beer on him. Our kiss becomes more intense and stronger. He pulls away, and trails soft kisses along my jaw and down my neck. He stands up tall and looks down at me. Brushing the hair strands behind my ear, his thumb gently glides along my jaw. "God, woman, you make me feel things I never thought possible. You are so beautiful!"

"Thank you. I need to get going, do you want to walk me out and see my new mom mobile?"

"Would love to!"

He grabs my jacket and helps me put it on. He walks over and grabs my flowers for me and walks me out.

"Nice truck! What made you pick black?"

"I don't know, I recently met a great guy with a very sexy truck and thought that I could have a very sexy truck too, even though I will have car seats in it. Oh, and guess what, I have a luggage rack on top, so I can carry surfboards, too!" I said as I smile up at him. *God, he is really is good looking and tall!*

He gives me a kiss on the lips once I am buckled and ready to go. "Call me once you get home."

"I will." As I lean in for another kiss. "Thank you for today, I don't think I sulked once. Goodnight!"

"Goodnight, baby!" *Baby, oh my!!*

Chapter 12

Surfing

April

Being twenty eight weeks pregnant and carrying triplets is the equivalent to an elephant's pregnancy. I'm huge, strangers walk around me thinking a baby will drop out any minute. I get winded walking to the mailbox. I haven't seen my feet in weeks, maybe months. I thank God that I live in an environment where flip-flops are my norm. My skin itches everywhere, I feel like my ear lobes are stretching, and I practically live on a toilet since all I do is pee constantly. Pregnancy is some huge conspiracy against other women. You develop signs and symptoms that no one tells you about, not even your own mother.

With all this said and done, I feel great, I am blessed. Jacob assures me nightly that everything is going to plan, and the babies are doing great, including myself. My goal is thirty-four weeks. Anything after that is pure gold! I still go to his office weekly, but since Valentine's Day, I practically see him every day when he is not on call at the hospital. I look forward to our nightly talks where listening to his deep raspy voice puts me in a deep sleep until my son's use my bladder as a soccer ball.

Jacob has been extremely gentle in taking us slow. Over the last couple months, we talk constantly which reassures me that the feelings I am starting to have for him are normal and perfectly alright. No one can tell me what is right or wrong. I know I am in a state where I have to feel my way through all of this. Right now, I feel good. Real good, feelings of enjoyment and adoration for him and for us as a couple. Don't get me wrong, I think of Grant every single day. I ask him every night before bed for his approval. I guess in a way I am just trying to comfort myself that dating this soon after his death is alright. Only time can tell me what is right for me. Right now, time is telling me to just go with it. I find Jacob incredibly handsome, fun, sweet, and caring. I'm happy right now and that to me is all that matters.

It's Wednesday, Jacob has the day off, and so he says he has a surprise for me. I struggle to get ready, but lately my attire is maternity sundresses and flip-flops. Pulling my hair into a ponytail, lip gloss and mascara is all I do to get ready. Twenty minutes later and Jacob is at the door. He has a small box in his hand. I smile up at him as he bends down to give me a kiss. He's dressed for swimming. He has on black and white checkerboard swim shorts, black fitted t-shirt, and black flip-flops. He's so incredibly hot!

"Good morning, baby, this is for you."

"What did you get me?"

Walking to the dining room, I pull out a chair and sit. I open up the box. Once I pull out the tissue paper I see that he has bought me my very own iPod. "You got me an iPod, Jacob. This is so sweet of you.

But, you know you are going to have to show me how to download songs on to this thing."

"No worry, already done for you. I've downloaded a few of my favorite songs, songs about how I feel about you and us, and some songs that I know you might like."

"Are you for real? This is wonderful thank you so much, babe!"

Shit, did I just call him babe?

"Bring it with you. You can listen to it where we are going."

He helps me up from the chair. He runs into the kitchen to get my purse and phone. "Here you go" he says as I place the iPod in my purse. He puts his hand at the small of my back as we walk out to his truck. "Umm, Jacob I don't think I can climb in that."

"Sure you can, I'll help you up." He opens the door, I place my hand on the inside door handle and my other on the chair, I step up on the step bar, and as I hike my other leg up with Jacob holding my hips to help me up. In that brief moment a gust of wind comes blowing my way, and blows my dress up. *Oh fuck!*

I sit in the chair and turn around with my cheeks burning from blushing and watch Jacob smiling. "Wow, Elizabeth that was a nice surprise. Where are your panties?"

"I can't wear them anymore. They don't make them to fit in the butt or the stomach. One side is always tight and the other is too loose. Plus, it saves me from bending over about a million times a day to pee."

"Gotcha!"

"I'm so sorry, Jacob. I didn't mean to moon you there."

"Elizabeth, not to embarrass you more, but I have seen that part of your body before. It was just a nice surprise, I liked it. You drive me crazy! I've want to touch you so badly in an intimate way, not like I have to touch you in the office. I'm waiting till after the babies are born, so you will see me more as Jacob and not Dr. Alexander."

"I see you as Jacob more than I see you as my doctor. I think it is easy to say that we have developed past the doctor and patient to boyfriend and girlfriend. You just happen to be my boyfriend who will deliver my babies."

He walks around to his side of the truck, climbs in, and fires it up. Its hemi engine really gets your adrenaline going. I feel like I should be at a Monster Jam rally in this thing. "So, I see you in a bathing suit and your surfboard is in the truck bed. I'm assuming we are heading to the beach?"

He grabs my hand and entwines our fingers. "We are going to the beach. I want to go surfing. I thought I would bring you with me. Then we can get lunch somewhere along the beach, if you want?"

"Ummm...Jacob have you noticed, I am not cut out for the ocean. I will scare the sharks away."

He just gives me this panty dropping smile. "Will you knock it off with the negative remarks? You are stunning. You are a walking miracle with three babies in you. Yes you are bigger than most twenty eight week woman, but you have triple the work going on with you. No more with your negative remarks, I think you are beautiful and amazing."

"Fine, no more remarks, but I can't go swimming. My doctor told me I can't." I smile back at him.

He rubs his thumbs along my knuckle. He pulls my hand up to kiss it. "I'm proud of you that you listen to your doctor. No, you shouldn't go swimming. I brought a chair and umbrella for you, plus your iPod. It can be very relaxing. I won't surf long. I wouldn't want you in this heat too long anyways. I don't think your doctor would approve, we don't want you dehydrated."

We talk for our forty minute drive to the beach. I ask him a lot of questions about the pregnancy. "Jacob, I'm really nervous about having a C-section. How bad does it hurt and how long am I going to be out of commission? I need to be there for my babies."

"Elizabeth, I'm not going to lie, it will hurt after the surgery. The sooner you are able to get up and move around the better it will feel. I will give you pain meds that won't bother your breast milk. You won't be alone, you'll have help. I will be there through it all."

"How many multiple births have you done? Will you be able to talk to me through it all? Will I see the babies before they are taken from me? What happens if they come before thirty two weeks? What if…"

I'm cut off by him putting his fingers over my lips. Gazing into those blue eyes of his and looking for the answer in his eyes. I see peace in his eyes, his eyes are telling me that I shouldn't worry, and he will protect us.

"Baby, you need to calm down. I have done many, many multiple births, mostly twins, you will be my tenth triplet case and I've done two quadruplets. You will have a sheet in front of you, that is so you don't see the surgery process, and yes, I will talk to you every step of the way. I will hold the babies over the sheet so you can see them, but it depends on them how long I can do it. Let's cross that bridge when it comes if they make their appearance before thirty-four weeks. I'm bringing my dad in to assist me, if that makes you feel better. I've asked him because he is the only other man I trust to help me with you. Also, if you want I can get a mirror in the operating room so you can see everything I am doing. I'm warning you, it isn't pretty to see your flesh being cut away. Are you squeamish?"

"I think I can handle that I want to see it all since this is my first and last time at it. Thank you for bringing in your dad. That means a lot to me."

My mind is racing with so many questions. Maybe I should write them down and we can discuss some more in depth.

"Elizabeth, can I ask you a question?"

"Sure."

"Why did you say that this is your last chance at a delivery?"

"You haven't read my file? Isn't my info in there?"

"I know these babies were conceived by IVF, but that is the bulk of your history in your file."

I slump in my chair, and lean my head against the cool window. It hurts to dig all these memories up, but I should tell Jacob. I softly start to tell him.

"Grant and I tried for years to get pregnant on our own. After our first year of marriage I went off birth control. Once our second anniversary came around I came and saw your father. He advised me to see Dr. Wilson, so we met with him and started IUI treatments. I was artificially inseminated six times and nothing happened. I never even got a positive on a pregnancy test."

I can feel the burn in my eyes; I tilt my head back hoping that they won't come out.

"It's okay, Elizabeth. You don't need to tell me if it will upset you. I understand."

"No, I'm not crying about Grant if that is what you are thinking. I'm crying because for another year I prayed for a positive pregnancy test even if I ended up miscarrying. At least then I would know that I could have gotten pregnant. Grant knew how desperately I wanted to get pregnant, so for a first attempt at IVF we dipped into our 401K fund and did the whole cycle. We did two embryos. I didn't get pregnant. Second time around Grant sold his car for another round of IVF. Another two embryos later and no luck. I kept pushing for it, I wanted to do it one more time. Grant wanted to wait till we were further into the new year, but I pushed him for one more try, and then we would start the New Year infertility treatment free. I begged him and he agreed one more time. I was called into Dr. Wilson's office on a Friday because my embryos weren't looking viable, so Ella took me and in a split second decision I asked to have all four put in. I couldn't flush two down the drain and I couldn't choose. I had my IVF treatment done on that Friday morning, by Saturday night I was watching my husband die from his motorcycle accident.

Jacob grips my hand, and is kissing it. I lean over to his side, hold his hand in both of mine and kiss his palm.

"So, if you remarry down the road, you don't think you will have another baby?" He quietly asks me.

"I don't know, my life plan hasn't really been going the way I thought it would. I would love more babies. I don't think I can get pregnant on my own. I really can't go through the emotional roller coaster of hell again with those treatments. I feel it killed Grant and I don't want to go through it again. If my new husband can accept my boys as his own, then that is all that matters…I think? I don't know why, but I can only hope that God has a better life plan for me then the one I had planned for myself," I softly mummer to him as my lips are still on his palm.

"Baby, I'm not a religious man, even though I know I should be. You know how my mother died from breast cancer when I was thirteen."

I nod and eye him to keep going. "Baby, I have to believe that there is a reason for everything. Even though we have no clue why it's happening now, we will get our answers one day. I have to believe that my mother guided Grant into heaven, because I feel that this," he points to him and me, "is the reason we are together and those two are your guiding angels for your babies. I believe Grant accepts us as a couple. I have to believe in some twisted way of life that it was planned for my mother to leave me when I was thirteen, so that I could honor her and become the best doctor I can be. It was planned for you to get pregnant as a widow and for us to meet. I HAVE TO BELIEVE THIS! I believe in God and that he does give miracles and I believe my miracle is you!"

I just stare at him, with tears running down my face. "That is the sweetest and most logical thing anyone has said to me in seven months." I sniffle out the words, and then I lift my hand and rub it along his stubble on his jaw line. He kisses my hands again, and I lean my head against the head rest. "OOWWW!"

"What, what's wrong?"

"Just my boys wrestling, here feel them." I grab his hand to where they are kicking me. He rubs his hand over my belly feeling every kung fu kick and punch. He just smiles while looking ahead and driving.

"Pretty amazing, huh?"

"Yes, it is, baby!"

We get to the beach parking lot. He helps me out of the truck. Once I'm out, he cages me with the door and his arms. "Beth, I know that the last seven months have been difficult for you, and I hope that I have been more help than bad. I know we both have loved with all our hearts before and we have lost our hearts as well. I'm a different chapter in your life now and I am not here to out shine or compete with what Grant gave you in your marriage and your life together. I just want to give you what you want and need now. Am I what you need now?"

I put my arms around his neck, while standing on my tip toes. I pull him down for a kiss. I kiss him hard with every fiber of strength in me. He sucked lightly on my bottom lip and I gladly opened my mouth eager to taste him again. Our tongues twist with each other. His kisses are beautiful, sending ripples of desire racing through my core. "Babe, you are exactly what I need. Please don't ever think different. You are the reason I am standing here, smiling and happy. There'll never be enough '*thank you's*' for what you have done for me."

"God, Elizabeth, you are an amazing woman. I can't tell you how bad I want to make love to you!"

I smile up at him, and kiss his chest. "Come on, let's get to the beach."

He pulls out his surfboard, and a chair with an umbrella attached to it. "Here can you get these," he hands me two water bottles.

"I sure can." I say back with a wink. Before we hit the boardwalk, I tell him I have to use the restroom. He waits patiently while I use the restroom. Once we finally make it to the beach, Jacob shows a different side of him, he looks like a child who is about to go on a roller coaster for the first time. He sets up my chair, with the umbrella and puts the water in the cup holders. He helps me sit down, then hands me his towel. He takes off his shirt, and I feel my eyeballs bulge out. Thank goodness for my sunglasses. He has the body of an Adonis. I don't think I have ever seen abs so ripped. I mean Grant was lean and firm but never abs this ripped. I want to touch them and feel their hardness. Holy mackerel he has that v shape groin. As he lifts his arms, the waist of his swim shorts drop just a little. He has golden hair that trails from his belly button down his happy trail. I have to lick my lips, to make sure I'm not drooling. He skin is so golden and smooth. I want his skin against mine so badly. When he turns slightly I notice he has a tattoo. He has a shark tattoo on his right shoulder. "I didn't know you had a tattoo?"

"You mean tattoos. I have two. Yeah, the shark I had done on spring break during college. We went to Hawaii and it's done in a tribal art form." I know who "we" is when he mentions it. He's talking about Rebecca, so I can see why he doesn't bring up a certain tattoo that has meaning, which you really don't want to remember.

"Then this one," he says while turning and facing away, "I did once I turned eighteen in honor of my mother." Oh my, it's so beautiful that I have to stand up and touch his back. It's a Celtic cross that starts at the base of his neck and stops right below his shoulder blades. Behind the cross are angel wings that spread across his shoulder blades. The cross has pink roses intertwined in it. Then at the bottom are three meaningful letters, which spell MOM. "Jacob, this is beautiful" I say as I am still tracing over the tattoo. I can feel he has goose bumps from my touch. "Did you draw this up?"

As he turns around, grabs me around the waist and pulls me close. Raise my sunglasses to my head so I can gaze into his eyes. "Baby, I had an idea of what I wanted. My mother was Irish and loved Celtic music. I remember her always listening to it when she cooked. The angel wings represent what she means to me. I know she is watching over me. Pink roses were her favorite and her birth flower. I told the artist what I wanted and this is what he came up with."

"It's beautiful. Your mother would love it." I say as I kiss his chest.

"Baby can you hold my sunglasses for me?"

"Of course."

"Do you need anything before I head out?"

"Nope, I am good…you know you better give me a good show out there. I don't sit and watch surfing for anyone, you know."

"I'll do my best, baby." He leans down and gives me another one of his amazing kisses.

I pull out the iPod and turn it on. He has downloaded so many songs. Songs and artist I have never heard of. I look at the playlist and read through the list of songs in alphabetical order:

3 Doors Down – Here Without You
Brad Paisley – She's Everything
Chris Daughtry – Life After You

Chris Daughtry – Lullaby
Christ Daughtry – Start of Something Good
Edwin McCain – I'll Be
Hinder – The Best Is Yet To Come
James Blunt – You're Beautiful
Joe Diffie – Pick Up Man
John Mayer – Your Body Is a Wonderland
Josh Groban – You Are Loved
Lady Antebellum – Need You Now
Nickelback – Far Away
Nickelback – Never Gonna Be Alone
Tim McGraw Feat. Faith Hill – I Need You

As I start to listen I explore the ocean and watch Jacob paddle through the waves. Words can't describe of how in awe of him I am. I see him straddle his board, glaring into the horizon for his perfect wave. A wave is coming up on him close, he lies down, his arms paddling and within seconds he jumps up and dances with the waves on his surfboard. It is pretty spectacular to watch. He has such a talent. He has so many incredible talents. This man keeps calling me amazing, but I think he has it backwards, he is amazing. The way he moves his body up and down the waves, twisting and turning with such grace is spectacular. I'm oblivious to the music that is going through my ears. I just stare at this man, knowing that I am falling hard for him, and fast. *Way too fast, Elizabeth!*

I listen to the music, I listen attentively to the wording. Jacob says that a few of these songs are songs of how he feels about me. I laugh when I hear Joe Diffie's song *"Pick Up Man."* It makes me think to the first time I saw him in his hot truck. The one that speaks to my heart is Josh Groban's song "*You Are Loved.*" How ironic is it that my brother gave me a Josh Groban song and now my favorite on this iPod is another Josh Groban song? Jacob has gotten me through the toughest time in my life. I honestly don't know where I would be without him. Maybe he is right, maybe this was my life plan all along. There is that saying my mother uses all the time, "The road of life can only reveal itself as it is traveled; each turn in the road reveals a surprise. Your future is hidden." Maybe, I was meant to experience grief and pain with Grant and now on this journey of life with Jacob I can experience joy and peace once again. Is it too much to say that I'm terrified, terrified to experience that kind of love, and then to have it ripped out of my soul? I can't imagine going through that again.

I stand up, stretch, and stare out in the ocean, watching him float over the water. I have to pee, again. So I wave to him, signaling that I am walking back to the restrooms. I slowly walk back, not realizing I am going uphill. Damn this is so hard, especially when you can't see your feet! I'm half way there, when I hear Jacob yelling my name. I turn around and see him sprinting for me.

"You didn't have to come after me. I just wanted to let you know that I'm going to the restroom."

"I don't want you going alone." He says out of breath.

"Alright, then you can help me. I feel like I am walking in quicksand."

I put my arm around his waist as we walk up to the restrooms. He's standing there gazing out over the ocean when I walk out. Being behind him I wrap my arms around his lean waist. Place my nose against the curve of his back and take in his smell. He smells of ocean and coconut sunscreen. "You are really talented! I liked watching you. Maybe one day, you can show me how to surf?"

"I would love to teach you and the boys when they get older. I was five when my dad taught me."

"I think that sounds like a great plan." I say, as I kiss along his spine.

He turns around, and kisses my hair. "Did you listen to your music?"

"Yes, and I am shocked to see you like so much country. I love them all, thank you."

"Baby, I'm born and raised Floridian. Of course I like country. I just love rock, more."

He winks at me, as we walk back down the boardwalk. "Wait here, I don't want you walking back down in the sand. Let me run and go grab our things and we will head for lunch."

I smile and watch him run back to get our things. Hot damn does he have a fine ass! We are back in the truck heading to lunch. We pick a seafood restaurant that is on the canal where the cruise ships port. We are sitting outside under the umbrella, talking about everything under the sun and moon. I tell him how I finally put the house up for sale. I don't think it will sell fast, because I want top dollar. I need every penny I can get, since I'm not working and I can only live off of Grant's life insurance for so long. Plus I have college times three to start planning for.

"Baby, I have a thought about this and I know it is really fast, but what if we move into a place together?"

"You mean, we buy a house together?"

"Yes! Let's buy a house together. I'll sell my condo and we can buy a house big enough for our dogs, the boys, guests, and us."

I stutter out of shock, "But, why? Why Jacob? We have only been seeing each other for a couple months and you want to buy a house. Babe, we haven't even had sex yet."

"I know I am in this relationship for the long haul. I know we are meant to be together, so why not? You want to start fresh in a new house. I would love to be in a house with my dog again. We can do it together, and build our own dreams."

"Wow, Jacob you just really know how to throw a curve ball at someone! I don't know, it just seems so fast. You haven't even stayed overnight with me. Hell, you might see me in the morning and run for the hills. Please, let's take baby steps here."

He grabs my hand from the table and holds it. "You see this finger?" He's pointing to my finger that still holds my wedding band to Grant.

"Yes, what about it? Are you upset that I haven't taken this off? I can't do it yet. I promised myself I will take it off once the boys are born. "

"Baby, one day this finger will have my ring and it will represent my feelings for you and how I will be with you the rest of my life. I don't need time to tell me that I want to be with you forever."

All I can say to him is …"Jacob, Jacob, Jacob …baby steps please."

We finish lunch watching ships and boats come in and out of the canal. He pays the bill and we head home. I don't know if it was the sun or what, but I am exhausted once we are in the truck I pass out. I wake up to feeling Jacob's hand on my belly. He's rubbing it, as his way of telling the boys and me he is here. I look over to him and with the back of my fingers rub it along his jaw line. "Sorry to fall asleep on you."

"Honey, its fine, you need your rest. We are almost to your house."

I sit up a little taller in the seat, and stare out the window and think of what we talked about over lunch. I need Ella and Kate. Jacob and I have been seeing each other so much lately I feel like I have pushed them to the back burner. Maybe dinner with my girls is just what I need after a day like this. I have no idea what I am doing. I'm tired of feeling scared. I was never a person to let fear consume me. Will I ever be free…free from this terrifying grip of death that is choking me?

We pull into the driveway, and Jacob helps me out of the truck. "Want to come in for a while?"

"Baby, I would love to. Let me grab my change of clothes." He kisses my forehead, and opens the back door for his bag of clothes. We head to the kitchen, where he drops his bag on the bar stool.

I go to him and wrap my arms around him. "I'm going to take a quick shower, help yourself. I'll be out soon."

"Take your time, baby."

In the middle of trying desperately to shave my legs is when I feel a sharp pain. It is running along the right side of my belly, and it is squeezing everything around it. I feel a shooting stabbing pain in my lower back then more stabbing pains into my butt. I freak out and lose it ... "JACOB!!! JACOB!!! COME QUICK!!!" I scream for him, while opening the door. Ouch, it's not going away.

Jacob runs in the bathroom, white as a ghost. "What? My God, What?"

Standing there with the door open, I try to inhale and exhale, but damn does it hurt. I sputter out.

"Pain, I have pain all around here and into my lower back and ass." The shower door is open and he sees me shake from the cold. He jumps in the shower with me. He places his hands all over my stomach. "I think you are having Braxton Hick Contractions. Hold on a sec." He jumps out and reaches across the bathroom sink and grabs a glass, he fills it up with cold water and brings it in the shower, "Here baby, drink this. I think you might be a little dehydrated. Braxton Hicks can come on fast when you are dehydrated."

I gulp down the water, with his hands on my hips. It hasn't even occurred to me that I am stark naked and he is in clothes. Once I am finished he takes the glass out of my hand and places it on the floor behind him. I cross my arms over my chest, I am so embarrassed of how he is seeing me for the first time.

"That really scared me. I didn't think they could be that strong. What the hell was stabbing in my ass?" I say while trying to catch my breath.

"The pain in your fine ass is probably your Sciatic nerve. That pain will come and go and just depends on how the babies are positioned on your lower back. Braxton Hicks will come and go, but shouldn't last too long. If they last too long and come frequent then we have other issues." He starts to rub his hands all over my body. He grabs my body wash from the shelf and squirts some onto his hands. "Turn around let me wash you since I'm in here."

"It's alright Jacob, I can handle washing myself. I'm just sorry that you had to jump in here with your clothes on."

Pulling my arms away from my breast, he stares at with me with pure lust in his eyes. "You are absolutely stunning, Elizabeth! Turn around, please. I want to wash you…I need to touch you." I turn around and he's on his knees. Squirting more body wash into his palm he washes my feet, then up my legs. With his hands on my butt, I can feel him kiss each cheek. Then hands on my hips he whispers for me to turn around. He kisses my protruding belly, washes my hips and belly. He stands up and grabs the bath wash and squirts more on his hands. He continues to wash my belly, and then his hands go from my wrist up my arms, down my collar bone and down to my breast. He rubs his hands all over my breast, with his thumb and forefinger he grabs my nipples and tugs on them gently. My nipples are pebbled and send shooting bolts of electricity to my nether regions. Pulling his hands around the nape of my neck, he bends down and we kiss. Our kiss is slow, and full of need. He gently bites my bottom lip, and I softly moan into him. Then our tongues entwine with one another and move with each other as our mouths were meant to be for each other. He pulls away from our long sensual kiss. He kisses my jaw line, then right under my ear lobe where more jolts of electricity are pulsating through my body. He whispers in my ear, "Elizabeth, you're fucking sexy as hell and you have no clue how bad I want to make love to you and worship this body." His hands glide all over my body and rest on my breast.

"I think I have a clue. I'm the one with raging hormones, remember."

"Baby, I know and I would whisk you out of this shower so fast, but I...don't know, I feel I should just wait. In due time I will have you and I will make love to you all night long."

I'm starting to prune, but I want to give Jacob the same shower treatment. "Here since you are in here, why don't you shower with me?" I say as I peel his white shirt off of his mighty fine broad shoulders. Once he pulls the rest of his shirt off and throws it on the shower floor, I trail my fingers down the ridges of his abs. Starting to untie his swim shorts, he grabs my wrist. "Baby, I'm dying here and I want to be inside of you, so damn bad. I don't think this is a good idea. I don't want it to lead to something that will jeopardize us.

"Jacob I know what I'm doing. I'm just going to wash you. I'll stop you if you get out of hand." He smashes his mouth on to mine and I feel the need in our kiss. He grabs my face, pulling me deeper in our kiss. His tongue is hot and soft as it dances with my tongue. I slowly suck on his tongue trying to show him what I would like to do to his cock. I pull away as I bite his lower lip.

"Let me get you clean," I say as I squirt body wash into my palm. Facing him I start with his broad shoulders, washing one arm at a time, and then I pull him into a hug while rubbing his back. I glide down to his tight ass and massage the soap into firm ass cheeks. I bring my hands around to hip lean hips and rub up and down along his abs. Coming back down, I'm inches away from his cock. He grabs my hands. "Don't go there, at least not yet. I don't want to come for you like this." I just nod. I bring my hands back up his chest and around his neck. I pull him towards me and study those sexy blue eyes of his. "I'm pruning and cold, let's get out and maybe continue this in the bedroom." I wink as I reach for the shower knob.

He jumps out of the shower first to grab us towels. After he wraps the towel around his waist and holds mine open for me to walk into. He swaddles me in the towel. Pulling another one out, he wraps my hair in the other one. "Let's get you dressed." He says as he guides me into my bedroom.

I put on a jersey shirt style dress. I tell him that I want to lie down for a while. He pulls on a pair of gym shorts and lies down in the bed next to me. "Is this alright?" He says looking at me knowing he is lying on the side that used to be Grant's.

"It's fine ..." I say as I yawn. "Can we talk for a while? I have questions that need to be answered?" We are laying on our sides facing each other. His hand is on my belly rubbing it in a soothing way. My hand is rubbing the bicep that is caressing my belly. He pulls me closer to him; my face is in the crook of his neck. This is better, because I don't know if I can see his face for what I'm about to say.

"The song choices were really good. I've never been a country fan, but I like the songs you gave me. I really like the Josh Groban song. What made you put that on there since it's not really country or rock?"

"My sister Olivia gave me his CD about five years ago when I was going through a hard time. She made me listen to that song over and over when she was around."

"What happened five years ago?"

"Life passing by," he says in a depressing tone. "I was going to weddings out the ass, everyone was getting married or having babies and I was just alone. I mean I've dated women, but never felt anything close to what I had with Rebecca, not until I met you. You are so much more than I felt with Rebecca."

I'm so glad we are not looking at each other. "So I take it then that you have had multiple women?"

"Elizabeth?" He tries to survey my face and I just bury it deeper in his neck. "I guess you can say I've had my share of women. I'm thirty-seven. I haven't been celibate, but I don't think I have been a man-whore either. I've only had sex with condoms, obviously Rebecca was the only one I didn't, and I was checked after I found out she cheated on me. Why?"

I'm such a twat! "Jacob, I've only had two lovers in my life. My high school boyfriend that I was with my senior year and then Grant."

"I think you are a fortunate one, baby. So, why the question about the song? We kind of got off track."

"No, it was that Grant's memorial video my brother made was set to a Josh Groban song. Since hearing it at his funeral, I have started to listen to more of his music." I say to him.

"Elizabeth, it's just another sign that we are meant to be. Both of our siblings gave us songs that have meaning to the situation we were in," he says as I nod into his neck.

Okay onto the major question that has been racking my brain.

"Jacob, I've picked out the boys' names. But, before I tell you, you need to know that these names are dear to me, they have meaning to me and my past. I need to know that if there is a future with me, if you will be alright with the boys being named after my past. Since, technically, they will always be half of my past as well."

He takes in a deep breath. Shit this is it, he can't handle this, and I knew it. "Beth, you can name them whatever you want. Hell, name them after the turtles as Kate suggested. I will like whatever name you pick, because like you said they hold meaning to you, just as any other parent picks out baby names. They hold some type of meaning. I will be okay with it."

I hesitantly respond, "So you will be okay if I name the first one born Grant?"

"Baby you can name all three Grant like George Foreman did with his sons. They're your sons, you name them." He says with his lips close to my forehead.

"Well, I've decided to name them after the three important men in my life; these are the men who got me to where I am now. I want the first to be named Grant, then the second one Evan, after my father. Finally, the third Cole, after my father in law. If it wasn't for him, I would have never become a lawyer."

"I think those are some mighty fine, strong boy names. They will grow up to become amazing men." He says to me as he pulls away to stare into my eyes. "I love the names, Elizabeth."

Silence surrounds us. I think that both of us are thinking of what to say next. I am so comfortable lying here next to this man, but my head is spinning with so many questions and concerns. I'm so scared.

"Elizabeth …I …um…I want you to know that I have some very strong feelings for you, stronger beyond like. I …I think I'm falling in love with you."

He just stares, finding a reaction and I have no idea what to say or do. I keep searching his eyes for a clue. "Jacob, I don't know what to say?"

"Say nothing; say nothing until you are ready. I wanted you to know that I fell head over heels the first time I saw you. Call it love at first sight or cupid's arrow, hell I don't know, all I know is I couldn't breathe around you. My heart was skipping beats, my pulse was racing. Between your inner beauty and your amazing body I was yours on that day. I have dreamt of you every night since that day. I dream of you as you are now, I dream of you in our future. You are my shining light in the dark that I have been in for a long time. You bring me hope for me and us. You and I together can finally have what we have always wanted."

I am in complete shock, what do I say to this man confessing all of his love and dreams for me? Sure, I care for him and I like him, but I can barely plan tomorrow, let alone the future.

"What do you want, Jacob?" I whisper. I don't mean to, but I'm scared to think I have just been an easy package.

"I want a wife, I want children, a home, and a life to come home to every night after work. I want to make memories with the ones I love."

WHOA!! I knew it! I scoot back so I can look at him further. "Did you pick me just because I showed up on your exam table as a pregnant widow? Can you love another man's children? Is this what I am hearing?"

He appears pained, like I just stabbed him in the heart. "Baby, I met you before you knew you were pregnant, remember. I was there the night Grant passed. Kate called me to come. Once I got there, Ella was the one that said you needed to relax before you lost the baby. That you couldn't lose the baby. So I went and got the sedative that would make you relax. My heart broke for you, for what you were going through. I knew what you were feeling, I was in that exact spot at one time in my life. But, I felt something the moment I held you in my arms, and it wasn't damn pity for you. I felt strong feelings for you, and hell I didn't even know you.

"Yes Elizabeth. I could love Grant's children, because they are a part of you. I've been on this journey with you and whether you want me to or not I have developed feelings for these boys, but I'm not asking to replace their father."

This is just moving way too fast for me, I can't comprehend everything he is saying now let alone what we have talked about all day. "Jacob, I don't mean to be a real bitch here, but you have to leave. I need to think about all of this. This is just going so fast, that I feel like I am in a choke hold. I like you so much, but today you have declared your love to me, asked me to move in with you, and be my children's surrogate father. I don't know what to say or do. Please just give me time."

He leans up and gives me a kiss on the lips. "I understand," is all he says. He walks to his bag on the floor and pulls out a shirt and puts it on. He stands by the doorway and says, "Call me if you need anything. Oh, and Elizabeth, please don't be mad at

Ella. She is a special woman who solely thought of your baby." With that he has walked away. I hear the front door shut and the sound of his truck pulling out of the driveway. I roll over to Grant's pillow and pull it into me. It doesn't smell of Grant anymore, it smells of Jacob and with his smell, the tears pool out of my eyes and onto the pillow. After a good cry I call Kate. "Kate, I am in a desperate need of girl talk. Can you and Ella come over tonight?"

"Bethy-baby, you okay?"

"Just stuck between a rock and a hard place."

"Let me see if my mom can watch the girls, I have news of my own to share with you two. I'll call Ella, too! I love you, hang in there!"

Chapter 13

Jacob
- Help Me, Dad -

It's Wednesday late afternoon and I just left Elizabeth's house. I'm so fucking pissed with myself for rushing her and spilling my feelings to her. I know I went way too fast, and I seriously need a good kick in the ass. Knowing who can do it and put some sense into me, I pick up my phone and dial his number. He knows what I want by the timing of my call. "What is it, son?" My father asks in his concerning tone.

"I've fucked up…help me dad! Help me make it better." I rarely get emotional with my dad and I can feel my chin start to quiver. I can't lose Elizabeth. She was just starting to come to me and now I open my fucking big mouth and have possibly lost her.

"I'm off work in an hour, you want to meet for dinner and we can talk about what is bothering you. Is it Elizabeth?" He goes quiet and I know this is his way of making me talk and he just listens. He has always been the father that makes us understand what we've done wrong.

"Dinner sounds great Dad. I'm going to go home and change and then I will meet you at our usual place."

"Sounds good, Jacob, see you shortly." With that he ends the call and I continue to drive home nervously tapping my thumbs against the steering wheel. I wonder what Elizabeth is doing. I just pray that I didn't leave her in tears. It pains me to see her cry, especially for the stupid shit I just handed her. Smashing my palms against the steering wheel, I reach over and crank up the radio louder.

Sitting at the high top booth, I am sipping my beer and waiting for my father to come. Peeling the label off the beer bottle I glance up to see my father walk into the restaurant. My father and I are built alike. I have his height and build, yet I inherited my mother's hair and eye color. My father has chestnut brown hair, speckled with gray hairs and hazel eyes. Walking towards our table I can already see the shit eating grin he is giving me. I know by the end of dinner he will have me be kicking my own ass and he will watch in enjoyment.

Standing up to greet him, he pulls me into a hug. I pat his back and pull apart from each other. "You look like shit, son. What the hell did you do to acquire a face like this?" He says as he gently taps my cheek.

"You want a drink, dad?" Trying to change the subject before he lets me have it.

"Sure." I get the attention of the waitress and order my father's beer. "So are you going to tell me or do I have to beat it out of you?" He says with a smirk.

"I just moved way to fast with Elizabeth today. We had a great day at the beach and along the way I told her that I wanted us to buy a house, that I was falling in love with her, and that I wanted to be a dad to her boys." I say sheepishly to him and bow my head. I know I fucked up, I just don't want him to say it.

"Why in the hell would you go and say that to a woman who is pregnant first of all. You know better than any male not to stir up any pregnant woman's emotions. Second, she buried her husband how long ago?" He says, waiting for me to fill in the missing pieces. Taking a sip of his beer he just watches at me and raises his eyebrows.

"Her husband died seven months ago." I mutter out the words.

"Jesus Christ son, what the fuck were you thinking? You know if some woman said all that shit to me seven months after I buried your mother I would have shown her the door and told her never to come back. She buried her husband, Jacob. She didn't end her marriage because she wanted to. He was taken from her, she didn't have a choice in the matter. You of all people should know this." He gives me the same look he gave me any time I did wrong as a teenager.

"Dad …God do I know. It's just I can feel it with her. I know that she is the one that I have searched and waited for. I want it all with her, now. She is the answers to my prayers. I want a home, Dad. I want a wife, and children. I want to start traditions with my family. I want the family vacations. I want the little league games with my kids. I want it all now, I'm thirty seven years old and I feel I have waited long enough. I'm tired of being alone. It's just that I know Elizabeth is the one. I just needed her to realize it first that she is the one. I jumped the gun, and told her too soon."

Taking my palms, I rub them against my face, then through my hair. I want to call her. I need to hear her voice and know that I didn't hurt her. I pull out my phone and start to dial her number. "What the …?" I say to my dad as he pulls the phone out my hand.

"Son, the only way she is going to realize anything is on her terms. Give her time, Jacob. Let her sort out her emotions along with the overwhelming hormones she has. Time, Jacob, is what she needs. She certainly doesn't need you up her ass. Be damn lucky that she has given you the last seven months. Most women wouldn't have given any man a hello let alone a relationship. She sounds like a very brave and strong woman. I would like to meet her one day. Only when she is ready, though!" He exclaims.

Taking the phone out of his hands, I place it back into my back pocket. I grab the waitress attention and tell her we would like to order. Looking into my father's intelligent eyes, I tell him he is right. "You know son, we all have been asses one time or another and one day you will have this talk with your son. Guarantee it!" He smiles to me and pats my back. Once our food has arrived we eat and chit chat about sports and work. When we are done eating, we walk towards our vehicles; I ask him the one thing that has been on my mind. "Dad, if that woman did come to you seven months after mom died and told you she believed you were the one, would you believe her and give her a chance?"

Leaning against the car, he stares at me and says, "Son, I really don't know. I can't tell you one way or another because what you are talking about is only felt here." With that he touches my chest where my heart beats desperately for Elizabeth. "So, if I felt it here for her, then sure I would believe her and give her a chance. But, only Elizabeth can decide that, no one else." He leans into me and gives me a hug. "Jacob, I'm truly sorry you are going through this, but I assure you with time, something good will come out of this."

I squeeze him harder and tell him. "I know, Dad …I know. Thanks for dinner and I will see you at the office."

Watching him get into his car, I know it will be a long time until I hear from Elizabeth. I will be the man she needs me to be and I will give her the time she needs. I won't like it, but if this process is what needs to happen for her to be mine, then I will get through it. Hopping into my truck, I drive home slow for I know it will be a long night.

Chapter 14

Confused and Scared

Around seven that night Ella and Kate come to my house with take out from our local bistro. We have salads and sandwiches. Kate and Ella chug the wine, like it is going out of style, while I pick at my food. I have no appetite.

"Okay, spill it girlfriend, what happened between you and Jacob?" Kate, says while pouring her third glass.

"Honey, you know I'm not driving your drunken ass's home." I point to Ella and Kate as they slowly becoming trashed.

"Beth, don't worry. I'm savoring every drop in this one glass, so I can take home the lush." Ella says as she raises her glass to Kate.

"Jacob and I had a great day. He took me to the beach. I saw him surf. He is an amazing surfer. Holy Shitballs! He has a body to die for. Then we had lunch at the port. Somewhere between lunch and this afternoon he told me he wanted to buy a house together. That he loves me. Oh, and that he wants to be my children's father." I say, as I pick apart my sandwich.

"He what?" Kate shouts to me in her buzzed state of mind.

"Beth, you knew this was coming. That man has clearly loved you since the beginning. Why wouldn't he want to be a part of the boys' lives, he's been there since day one?"

"I think I will have this conversation with Kate, I like the drunken stupor advice over your practical shit. Ella, do you realize what a clusterfuck my life has been in the last seven months?"

Ella gets pissed. She slams her wine glass down and pushes her chair back. She leans over the table, grabs my face with both of her hands. "LOOK at me and listen real hard. What I have to say is the best damn advice I will ever give you. You apparently have not been listening to Jacob or me. I don't know if it's due to being pregnant or just damn stupidity.

"Beth, NO ONE knows more of the hell you have been through in the last seven months than I do. I have been there every step of the way. Hell, I have been more connected with you these last seven months than my own husband. I am so God damn sorry that Grant was killed. But, there is not one damn thing anyone can do with it. You have mourned, grieved, and cried for him. You have got to move on."

I slap her hands away. "You are such a bitch! How can you say to move on, he was my fucking husband and the father of my children? Our children will never know him! Nine years Ella. I was with that man for nine years!"

"Beth, I know I am being a bitch right now, but if you let the best thing in your life right now walk away because you are hanging onto a ghost, you'll be considered the bitch. God took away your husband, but gave you multiple loves in return. He has given you three children and a man that is over the moon in love with you. A man that will do anything for you! A man that is willing to step up to the plate to raise and be a role model to your boys."

I peek at Kate and she is just nodding her head in agreement with Ella.

"What the hell is wrong with you two?" I ask in a whisper. "Yes, I like Jacob, I am happy with him and yes I can see a future with him, but way down the road. Things are moving too fast, I'm scared. I just want to do right. I want to do right by Grant, right by Jacob, and right by my sons. Right now I'm just confused and scared."

"Bethy-baby, Ella is right. I know the timing with everything has been fast, but you need to look at it this way. Would you accept everything Jacob has said and done for you if he appeared in your life five years from now?"

Wow, Kate is logical when she is buzzed. "I guess I would accept it, I would have been on my own for five years. Of course I would want to be with him. Grant has been gone for seven months. I kissed another man four months after he had died. I feel like I am being dishonest to him. Dishonest to the nine years we were together. As if none of it really mattered. I loved him and I'm scared to have those feelings for another man."

Ella grabs my face again. "Just like there in no magic parenting book, there is no magic time over loss book. Sometimes you know when it is the real thing. You know love when it slaps you in the face. It could take a moment, a day, or years to finally know love. Hell, I knew at sixteen who my love was. I knew Chris and I were in it forever, even though everyone thought different. Jacob knows you are the real deal, and I think you do, too. I think you are just scared."

Ella holds my face tighter. I think of Alexis and Brooke, and feel sorry for them when their mom gets stern with them. "Will you stop holding me down as if I was your child ...get your hands off my face!"

Watching her place her hands back in her lap, she looks at me with those big brown eyes of hers.

"Beth, I have told you since day one with Jacob take it slow. Don't shut him out. We don't want you to be alone, you don't deserve to be alone. Yes, it's not fair that Grant won't be there for his kids, but the boys do need a father figure and you are lucky you have a good man who wants to do it.

Buy a house with him if you want? You are going to need help and he wants to be a part of your life. This isn't an experiment for him. He is talking life long, even marriage." She grabs my left hand and slides her thumb over my wedding band.

"Honey, accept that Grant is gone. Cherish the years you had with that amazing man of yours. Be thankful that you had nine years with him and that you got your blessing of his children. Take this off," as she keeps sliding her thumb over the band. "Put it with the memories you have saved. Know that Grant is happy for you, that you have someone loving you and his sons. Know that one day you will see him again, and that he will meet his children. Wearing this band does nothing but keep your walls up to Jacob. Let him love you!"

I'm at a complete loss of words. I never would have thought that they felt this way about me or that I was doing wrong by Jacob. I know I have feelings for Jacob. I feel fire erupting under my skin when I'm with him and that he makes me smile. He makes me feel happy, content, and loved. He does love me, but I'm not sure I love him. It is still too soon.

"Bethy-baby, we love you so much and we just want you to be happy. Realize how lucky you are Beth. You get two great loves in your life. Most people only get one and here you get two men who love you more than life itself. We all can see that Jacob loves you. Know that we support you in any decision you make." I watch her get out of her chair and she slowly walks to me to give me a hug.

"I don't know what to say. You are right. I really don't want to bring the boys home to this house. It feels inappropriate, and will bring up to many emotions and memories. I know I need to move on, it's just so hard."

I stand up to hug my girls and thank them for this much needed talk. I have a lot of thinking to do along with packing.

"Wait, Kate what did you want to tell us? I completely forgot."

"Oh, it's nothing really. I am getting divorced."

"What?!" Ella and I say in unison.

"Yep! I caught Keith in a lie and found out that he is screwing some female police officer. I'm done, I can't accept or want to fix what he fucked up. So, he has moved out and we are in divorce proceedings. We'll split custody of the girls and he can go screw the rest of Orange County for all I care."

"Katie-bear, honey I am so sorry." I say as I walk to her and give her a hug.

"Beth, seriously I am okay with it. It was a long time coming. I'm mad that he didn't have the balls to tell me before he fucked this girl. Also, I feel for my girls, they love their daddy. Too bad they are too young to see what a fucking douche he really is!"

Ella and I just chuckle at her saying. We move to the couch and talk some more. Kate also informs us that her Granddaddy is close to retirement. She has been in contact with an Architect and Contractor to remodel the 1970s office that her Granddaddy is leaving her.

"That office is just gross, I can't stand it. I won't stand it, so I'm meeting with an Architect to remodel and expand. I just want the funky green and yellow laminate flooring and cabinetry to go. I want to make it fresh and new. I also want to remodel the stables."

"That's great Kate! I know this next chapter in your life is going to be better," I say to her.

Around ten o'clock the girls leave and I walk into my room. I walk into Grant's closest. I haven't been in here since the day I came home from the hospital.

I walk into the massive walk in closest. I slowly start to pull his clothes off the hanger. I place my face to his shirts, trying to remember his smell. I start to fold the shirts, pants, suits, ties, and undergarments. I save the clothing that means the most to me, mostly his Harley Davidson shirts and shirts that I remember important memories too. I save the polo he wore when he proposed. The tie he wore to our rehearsal. His flannel pajama bottoms that he lounged around in on the weekends. The Mickey Mouse shirt that he bought but never wore when we went to Disney years ago. I make a collection of the items I want to save, but have no idea what to do with them.

Before I know it, it's one in the morning. I've cleaned out Grant's closet. I have garbage bags of clothing that are ready to be given to the Salvation Army.

I take a hot shower. When I get into bed I stare at my phone and end up texting Jacob.

Me: Jacob, I'm sorry for this afternoon. Do you think we can talk tomorrow?

Jacob: I'm in the office tomorrow, we can meet for lunch or I can come over after work.

Me: After work is okay. I'll make you dinner. ☺

Jacob: Why are you up so late?

Me: I couldn't sleep. E and K left around 10p.m. and I ended up cleaning out Grant's closet.

Jacob: Are you okay?

Me: I'm good.

Jacob: I miss you and I can't wait to see you tomorrow night. Sweet dreams, love.

Me: I miss you, too. Goodnight babe.

Ugh! I put the phone on the nightstand, roll to my side and try to sleep.

Thursday night slowly approached. I spent most of the day packing. I asked Cole to come by on his lunch break to pick up the last of the files from Grants office. I told Cole to take whatever he or Anna would want. He grabbed most of his college and law school mementos. He even took the box that was still left in the garage from his office. He practically hijacked everything from his office, which was fine by me. I felt relief when he seized it all.

For dinner I made chicken pot pie. I hope Jacob likes it. He's at my house by six. When I open the door he seems hesitant to walk in. I grab his wrist and pull him in. "Please, babe come in." I say as I close the door behind him. He stands there looking around at the mess. I walk to him and with my entire strength stand on my toes, grab his shoulders to pull him to me for a kiss. Our kiss is sweet, slow, and soft. As if we are both remembering this kiss for the rest of our lives.

He pulls away and looks into my eyes. "You are so beautiful, Elizabeth. I missed you."

"You saw me a little over twenty-four hours ago, silly." He pulls me in for a hug, I cling to him. When we separate, he rubs his hands all over my belly, feeling the boys move around.

"You doing alright? How have they been?"

"The boys are in full wrestling mode. They don't ever stop which kind of scares me. I'm doing well." Gesturing towards the kitchen I tell him, "I made Chicken Pot Pie. I hope you like it."

"Sounds delicious, and yes I love some good southern cooking. Umm, Elizabeth what has happened to your house?"

I look over my shoulder as he stands agape at the mess that has consumed my house. He is looking at all the boxes, garbage bags and miscellaneous all over the place. He is still in his work clothes. Today he is wearing gray slacks with a black long sleeved shirt. He has rolled up his sleeves and unbuttoned a few buttons at the top of his shirt. He slips off his shoes, and walks behind me where he wraps his arms around my waist and rubs his hands along my belly.

"I guess I have a serious case of nesting. Last night I started to clean out Grant's closet and I just kept going this morning. I feel it's time to pack his things away. Cole came by this afternoon and took most of his work and college things."

"I would have helped you." He says as he helps me set the table.

"I know, but it was something I needed to do. I saved some things for the boys, so when they get older they will have some of his things. I put away the pictures of us together, and made piles for charity. I'm doing okay."

We start to eat and he is chowing down my pot pie. I need to remember this recipe for him. I don't eat as much; just don't have the appetite like I should. Once we are done, he stands up to do the dishes. "Jacob, you don't have to do that."

"You sit there and relax, I've got this covered."

"I have something to tell you." I mumble to him while rubbing my belly. He looks at me as if I ran over his puppy. He walks back over to me. He cautiously sits back down in the chair beside me.

"Alright, what is it?" He says while gazing out the window. As if what I have to say, just might bring him to his knees. I pull out my realtor's business card and slide it over to him. He appears to be puzzled.

Spitting the words out fast. "She's a really great realtor, and I figured you might want to call her if we are going to be buying a house together." I have a shit eating grin on my face, because I know this was not what he was expecting.

"You're shitting me? You want to move in together and buy a house?"

"Yes, I had some very wise friends help me realize that I need to live in the moment and that if you are dead serious on making this relationship stronger and helping me with my boys, then I should take you up on your offer."

He slides out of his chair onto his knees next to me. He grabs my neck and pulls me into a fierce kiss. He kisses with strength, pulling the breath from my lungs. I push back, trying to catch a breath. "God, Elizabeth, I love you so damn much! I promise you I will make you so happy. We will find the home of our dreams. I will give you everything you want."

He leans down to my belly; he pulls up my shirt and trails kisses all over it. It is the most paternal image, the kind I have only witnessed in my dreams. I feel the waterworks about to start, but then I freeze when I hear him whisper. "I love you Grant." He kisses my belly where baby A is. "I love you Evan." He kisses where baby B is. Finally he moves his lips over to where baby C is. "I love you Cole." He glances up to me with his beautiful smile and that chiseled jaw. "I love all of you!" He whispers to me. He rubs his fingers through my hair, pulls my lips back to him and kisses me. This kiss gives me the lighting force shocks through my veins. My core feels like a volcano, where I feel like I'm going to erupt at any minute. My clit is throbbing; I can feel my nipples harden. Jacob pulls away from our kiss. Pulling me to stand up, he holds my hand and pulls me to my bedroom. Once we are by the bed, he asks me to lie down. He lies down next to me. He pulls me into his arms, and kisses me fiercely and passionately. His hands are all over my body. Within minutes we are naked and skin to skin. He touches me in places where my skin starts to sweat, my body shakes, and stars start to form behind my eyes. I return the favor of touching him all over. He keeps true to his words and we never made love, but just being this close to me I knew that we were both falling in love. As the evening carries on, we finally fall asleep in each other's arms.

Waking up before dawn I stare at the ceiling fan and wonder. Why did my life have such a fork in the road? Is this really how it should go? How do I bury a past I never wanted buried? How do I go on when I have the past growing inside of me? I just had amazing night with the man I think I am in love with and I can't get my past out of my head.

I silently talk to Grant and ask for his approval. That he needs to give me a sign that he is alright with this. That he will accept Jacob as his sons' dad. That he isn't angry with me for never telling him he has three sons. I feel my jaw tightening and the tears run down my face. I am relieved that Jacob is asleep as I go through all these emotions. I know I want Jacob, I know that I am falling in love him, and I know that I want a future with him. I need to find my closure with my past first.

Chapter 15

My Sign

The first several days of May have been a tornado of events. Jacob's condo sold in four days. I knew my realtor was great, I just didn't think she was a damn genie. So I try to clear out my belongings along with my past at almost thirty one weeks pregnant. My present and my future are merging too fast. The remnants of Grant's office are cleared out. I placed photos of his office furniture on Craigslist and I have a buyer coming to pick it up this afternoon. I have another buyer, picking up my bedroom furniture tonight. I'm selling all my furniture, I just don't feel comfortable, having Jacob and I start our new life together on furniture that Grant and I bought. I look at every piece, and it holds a memory.

I'm doing laundry when I get a call from Cole. He tells me he has come across paperwork from Grant for me. He found it in one of the boxes that he finally cleaned out from Grant's work office. I tell him I am home all day and to swing by when he gets a chance.

Forty-five minutes later Cole is knocking at my door. Walking to the door I'm really concerned that he got here so quickly. I can only imagine what he needs to give me. All of his insurance policies, and other paper work have been taken care of. I open the door to see Cole's eyes bug out. "I can't believe how big the babies have gotten." He murmurs while trying to move his eyes from my enormous belly.

"Yep! They are really wearing me thin these days." I can tell he wants some connection so as I invite him in, I stand on my toes to give him a hug. Then I grab his hand. "Here is Grant." I say as I place his hand over where baby A is. I see his laugh lines appear as he gives me the biggest smile, which I haven't seen in many months. I grab his other hand and place it over baby C. "This is Cole." I say as I wink at him. He's dumbfounded, he didn't know I was naming two of the babies after Grant and him.

"What is the other one's name?" He says as he gently rubs my belly.

"Evan. They are all named after three very important men in my life." I whisper as I feel my words start to choke up.

"Thank you. I am honored, as I know your father and Grant would be. I can't wait to hold them all." He leans over and gives me another hug.

He pulls out an envelope out of his suit jacket. "Anna came across this as she was going through the boxes you told me to take. She apologizes for starting to read it, since it wasn't addressed to anyone. She never read the whole thing, but wanted to let you know that it is from Grant. It's a letter to you.

"What kind of letter? I already got everything we discussed together if something happened to one of us."

"It's a letter telling you to be happy with your new life. Here!" Cole, hands me the letter as I walk to the couch. "Beth, I'm going to get going. I need to be in court soon. Are you going to be alright?"

I look up to him with tears in my eyes. Cole is acknowledging my new life as he sees what is going on in my house. Cole leans down to kiss my head. "Beth, it's good to move on. We all just want you to be happy. Anna and I understand all of this." As he waves his hand at all the boxes and furniture all over the place. "We just want a small part in our grandsons' lives."

I kiss him on the cheek and say, "You have a huge part in your grandsons' lives, nothing small about it. Tell Anna I love her and thank you. I love you, too."

He stands up, and winks at me. "Let us know if you need anything."

I hold the envelope to my chest as I take in deep breaths. I slowly reopen the letter and see it's a hand written letter on his legal pad paper. I feel my throat close up and I try not to sob. It's dated January. Written ten months before his death. *I don't understand why he never told me about this?*

To my sweetheart, my love, and my heart Elizabeth,

Elizabeth, it's another year and I pray that this is the year we are finally parents. It breaks my heart a little more every time I see your dream come crashing down. I wish I could give you a baby so badly. I hate seeing you hurt for a child. Know that I think you will be an amazing mother when you finally become one. You have so much love to give, you are extremely patient kind, tenderhearted, smart, and care free. All these attributes are why I fell in love with you. I love you so much. Sometimes I wonder if you know that I am alive and breathing because of those three words you say to me every day. Do you even know how much I love you? Well, that is what I hope I get across in this letter. I know I say it to you and I show you when we make love, but I want it on paper so you know just how much I love you and how much you mean to me.

You know that I am dealing with a case where these parents lost their daughter due to texting and driving. Seeing these parents make me realize that life is just too damn short, that once we become parents we will have such huge responsibilities and love for a baby that is unconditional. Frankly it scares the shit out of me, but I want you and our future children to know how much you mean to me. God, if something ever happens to me Elizabeth, I want you to live. Live the life that you are blessed with. Live everyday as if it is your last. Live with all the love that you have and give that love to someone else who deserves your love. It kills me writing this and even picturing you with another man, but I can't tell you the amount of love your heart holds for people. I want you to go on and love another man and for that man to fill my role for our children. Our children will be so damn lucky to have your love. (Yes, I say children because I know we will have at least three beautiful babies.) Please, be happy if something happens to me. Please, smile that beautiful smile that makes my heart melt when you use it. I know if I die, I will die a very happy and blessed man because I lived a life where I woke up to you every day by my side. I had a life of your love, it might not have been a long life, but it was just enough to make me happy. I will never forget our wedding day. It was a day you made my dreams come true. Because you vowed to love me and having your love is all I ever wanted. I love you Elizabeth! Know that I will love you till the end of time, that even in heaven I will love you and will protect you and our children. Know that every day the sun rises and every night when the stars appear I am watching you and our children. I hope to God you will never read this letter, but if you are reading this now. I want you to smile, because I'm smiling back at you. Be happy sweetheart and love again!

I love you Elizabeth and I love my children.

Love Always,

Grant and Daddy

Oh God! I cry holding his letter to my stomach. He is finally giving me my sign. My sign to love Jacob and to go on with the life we are trying to make, or shall I say a life Jacob is trying to make. I'm the one digging my heels into the ground. Jolted out of the seat as the doorbell rings. I wipe the tears and open the door to people who are taking away my past.

Jacob comes home that night to see the house in an even bigger disaster as strangers made pathways to take the furniture away. Jacob brings flowers for me. I have no intention of telling him about Grant's letter. I folded it up and placed it in my box of memories of Grant for the boys. He smiles at me and kisses me breathless, he has exciting news. "I got a call from our realtor and she has a house for us to see. It's on a lake." He says to me in a sing song voice. "So go get ready, I'm taking you to look at the house and then feed you four." He smiles at me and pats my butt as I walk to change.

He takes me to a small gated neighborhood. There are only about twenty houses in this neighborhood. The odd thing to see is that all these houses are lined up around this huge lake. The lot sizes are big, close to two acres and the houses are even bigger. The house is beyond beautiful. It has a Tuscan feel to it. The stucco is an off white color, with red tile roofing and a huge, glass and wooden arched doors. The upstairs balconies have the iron rod railings. The house looks like something out of Hollywood with huge palm trees out front and next to the three car garage. Jacob is excited to show me the backyard. We walk around back through the iron rod gates to the cobblestone pathway. My draw drops when I see the backyard. The backyard has its own private boat dock. It has an enormous cobble stone patio, built in grill, fire pit, Jacuzzi and pool. A pergola is off to the side with a hanging swing. Jacob and I stand out here looking, knowing it is perfect for the boys and us. "We can't surf on that lake, but we can Jet Ski. Look at all this." He says as he waves his arm along the span of the backyard. "Look at that side of the yard. We could put a swing set and playhouse over there. Not only will the boys have room to run and play, but just think how happy the dogs will be. We could have some mind-blowing parties out here."

"I hope the inside is just as nice as out here." I say as I head into the house. Our realtor walks through the house with us. It is six bedroom and four baths with a huge loft that we can make into the boys' playroom. The kitchen is massive and opens into a huge eating area and a large family room. Jacob and I are quiet, but once we see the rooms we just smile to one another. My favorite is the laundry room, it's the size of a small room with two washing machines, two dryers, cabinets and an island in the middle to fold laundry. This room alone sold me. "So what do you think?" Our realtor ask to us.

"I think it is perfect, it's close to the hospital, the boys will go to good schools, and it's big enough for us five." I whisper into Jacob's side.

"Where do we sign?" Jacob laughs to the realtor.

"Jacob we didn't discuss price, or a budget?" I try to reason with him, but he doesn't care, he loves it and he knows I love it so that is all that matters.

"When can we move in?" I say as I showcase off my round belly. "As you can see, I'm due soon and would love to be moved in before the babies come."

"I am sure we can work something out" our realtor tells us. We sign all the papers needed to set a closing date. I walk to Jacob's truck with the biggest grin on my face. I can't believe we bought a house. I am so happy. I'm so in love.

After dinner we head home. I'm miserable, the babies have been moving up a storm. My ribs and back hurt. "Jacob, these boys are in such a mood, feel them." I say as I grab his hand and move his hand all over the place. Maybe it was dinner that is making them dance around.

"I have another surprise for you but it's not until tomorrow," he whispers to me while rubbing the babies to calm down. His hand finally lulls them to sleep. We finally are home, nothing like a hot shower and crisp sheets to pass out in. I awake in the early morning, with shooting pains to my lower back. I wake Jacob up as I toss and turn. "What's wrong baby?" He asks as he sits up in the bed. "I just have a pain in my lower back. I think I slept in a wrong position to long. He rubs my lower back, "If it happens again let me know, these can be contractions."

"Isn't it too early?" I ask him scared.

"Not too early for triplets. I'm not too concerned. Let me know if it happens again."

"Alright, well I am getting up and going to let the dogs outside. I need to walk around some."

By eight o'clock I am feeling better and haven't experienced any pains again. Jacob tells me to get ready and be dressed by nine thirty that he is taking me somewhere and I need to be somewhat dressed cute. Not sure, how I can dress cute, but I put on a light blue empire waist dress with a white ribbon that ties in the back. I wear my white ballet flats, and silver hoop earrings. I think I look cute. "Baby, you look beautiful." Jacob says as he twirls his finger in one of the loose curls that is framing my face. "Come lets go, I can't make you late." He pulls me towards his truck.

Once I see the direction we are going, I know where he is taking me. "Why are we going to Ella's?"

"Dammit, I knew I should have blind folded you!" He muttered with his deep laugh.

"Ella is having us over for brunch, she wanted to surprise you." He mutters while looking out the front window.

"You... Dr. Alexander are lying! I can tell because you can't look at me." I laugh as I watch him bite his lower lip.

"Just enjoy brunch." He mutters while still biting his lip. We pull up to her house and by now I see six cars that belong to people I know, including Anna's silver Mercedes. "It's a baby shower isn't it?" I smile at him.

"No, it's brunch!" He replies. "Baby, apparently I do this just –get- her- to-the-house-for-brunch- thing pretty shitty. So please go in there totally shocked. I hate to have the wrath of Ella if I ruined it." He groans.

"That is why I love you. You are so honest and truthful even if it is just a baby shower." I say sweetly to him. He gives me this shocked look, like I vomited all over him. "What?" I ask.

"Nothing, just taking in what you had said. You never said certain words before."

We are parked in Ella's driveway and he is about to get out, so he can help me out of the truck. I grab his wrist to pull him into me. He leans over and gives me a kiss. "Jacob, I love you." I whisper to him as he gives me his sweet and gentle kisses.

"I know." He says as he is still kissing me. "I love you, too. Thank you for saying it, I really do need to hear those words. But, you have shown me for months that you love me and I'm so very grateful for you and your love."

He jumps out of the truck and jogs around to open my door. "How did you know?" I ask.

"It's the way you talk to me, the way you touch me, the way you do things for me, and moving into our house. You wouldn't be doing all this if you didn't love me."

He pulls me into him for a hug. "Elizabeth, I know that those three words mean a great deal to you. I wasn't going to rush you to say them, I knew by your actions. I love you, madly!"

I grab my purse and pat his chest. "Thank you, babe!" I say as I start my walk up to Ella's house.

"Enjoy, brunch!" Jacob shouts to me. I turn around and wink at him. I ring the doorbell, knowing that the elephant is finally off my chest.

Ella swings open the door and I hear a room of women scream...."SURPRISE!!" I can't control my laughter. I'm embraced by hugs, belly rubs and kisses until I'm seated in my designated seat.

I'm totally shocked when I see my mom walk into the room from the kitchen. She walks over to me with tears streaming down her eyes. I mimic her as tears stream down my face. I can't believe she came. She leans over me and hugs me. We embrace each other for what seems like hours, but only seconds go by. "You are so beautiful, look at you. My baby is going to have three babies. I'm so proud of you!" She blubbers to me while I try to make sure my mascara is not running down my face.

Ella's family room looks like a baby store threw up. She has each corner stacked from floor to ceiling with presents. Each corner has the baby's name. The three walls are drenched in baby boy clothes on a clothes line. There are bunches and bunches of blue balloons. There is a three tier squared light blue cake with the words "Oh Boy!" written in white on each tier. We eat, mingle, and play the ridiculous baby shower games. I refused to have my belly measured, so instead we measured Ella and Kate together. I remember the games that I planned for them. Let me say karma is a bitch. I know around how big bellies get and mine is off the Richter scale.

Kate gives me the best gift. It is a blown up panoramic picture of me pregnant leaning against my Camaro. She had me pose before I turned over the keys to the dealership. It's all in black and white except for my red Camaro. I love it so much that I start to cry. Her card was cute, "Proof that you were once a hot mama. Save this for when the boys turn sixteen." She has me laughing so hard that I feel one of those pains in my lower back. I wince in pain, as Ella rushes to me with phone in hand. "Beth, you okay... tell me what's wrong? Should I call Jacob?"

"No, I'm good." As I take in a big breath and blow it out. "Every once in a while I get this pain in my lower back. I think I have sat too long, help me up so I can walk around."

"Okay, let me know if you get it again." She says.

"Geez, your boss teaches you well. He said the same thing earlier this morning."

"Well, we worry, and love you."

"Ella, thanks for all of this. This is beautiful. I hope the house we bought last night fits all of this?" I mutter to her hoping she catches on.

"Trust me, there is never enough room for .....what, you bought a house last night?"

I love her facial expression. I lean into her and tell her to lower her voice. I am not ready for Anna to hear that I have bought a house with my boyfriend/babies doctor. "Don't worry I will fill you and Kate in later."

As guests to start to leave, Ella informs everyone that there is one last thing to do. She wants to make a tribute to Grant for being a daddy. Even though he isn't here, he's with the babies in spirit. I start to cry, again knowing that just yesterday I read those words in a letter he gave to me. At the bottom of all the balloons is a piece of paper, where we all write something to Grant.

I take my balloon and go into the bathroom. I hold the pen and with shaking fingers I write: *I miss you so much! Thank you for the letter, thank you for watching over us. I look forward to the day I tell our boys what a wonderful man you were. I will always love you. You are my sunshine and stars. Your Sweetheart, Elizabeth.*

As, I walk out of the bathroom, Anna is in the hallway waiting for me. "I thought we could do this together." She says as she holds up her balloon.

"I would like that." I reply as I grab her arm and walk outside. On the count of three we all let go of our blue balloons with hidden messages to Grant. I don't know what others wrote, but I can see many smiles on the guest's faces. I hope that this was a way for everyone to say the goodbye that they always wanted to say. I know that I finally got to say what I needed for me to move on.

I'm up and walking around thanking everyone for coming and their gifts for the babies. I feel another pain come on, but I chit chat right on through it. It's too early for all of this. I am only thirty two weeks pregnant. I have at least two more weeks. Anna is the last to leave, her eyes are red and I know that this was a bittersweet occasion for her. "Know that Cole and I love you so much and we are so happy for you. I know that Cole said I didn't read the letter, but I did. I'm so sorry Beth, but I couldn't stop reading, I could hear him saying it to you. Grant is right, you deserve to be happy and move on with your life. I know you are seeing someone…" I interrupt her.

"His name is Jacob, Jacob Alexander."

She nods and continues. "Beth, I just want those boys to know who Grant was. I know that Jacob will do all the things that a daddy is supposed to do, the things that you and Grant planned for. But, I just want the boys to know who gave them life." I interrupt her again, by placing my hands on her arms.

"Anna, you and Cole have no worries when it comes to that. Jacob knows that Grant will always be a part of our lives. That these boys…" I grab her hands and place them on my belly. "They will know all about Grant, I will tell them, you will tell them, and Cole will tell them what an amazing man he was. I will always love Grant and I will always be forever thankful for the three miracles he has given us."

She throws her arms around me and cries into my shoulder. "Thank you." She cries into my shoulders.

I tell her, "Thank you for raising an incredible man, I hope I can only do as half as good as you did with Grant for these little guys. I love you."

I give her a kiss on the cheek and walk her out to her car. As she pulls away I smile up to the sunshine, as I know now Grant is smiling back at me. I blow a kiss up to the sky as I slowly walk back into the house. Once inside I plop myself on the couch. Kate shouts out to me that she already called Jacob to come and help pack up this baby stuff.

"He might need a moving van." I mutter as I try to find comfort on lying on my side. I'm so uncomfortable all of a sudden. Finally finding a position that I can tolerate, I start to doze off. When I awake, which seems minutes later, but once I look at the clock it's been an hour. Jacob is rubbing his hand on my hip.

"Hi, baby. Did these ladies wear you out?"

I huff, as I try to sit up. Jacob sees the strain in my face and helps me into a sitting position. "I just got tired all of a sudden, and I had another pain in my back. The boys are restless. I feel like a pumpkin and they are carving out my insides."

"Well, let's go home and you can rest some more. Your mom had to run a few errands and will meet us at the house later. Everything is loaded in the truck. I have no clue where we are going to put all of this." He says.

"Right, I said the same thing to Ella."

He pulls me up and grabs my purse for me. With his hand on my lower back we walk to the door to say goodbye to Ella and Kate. "Thank you so much for this, I love you both to pieces!"

With lots of hugs and kisses we finally part ways. Jacob helps me into the truck. We are on our way home where my bed is calling my name. I am consumed with exhaustion.

Chapter 16

Something is Wrong

"UGH!" I cry out. I have tossed and turned most of the night. I'm so uncomfortable. It hurts to breathe, and I feel like they are playing tug of war in there with my organs. Jacob is passed out cold. I know he has been working non-stop between his shifts at the hospital and packing up this house. I look at the clock and see that it is just before five o'clock. I roll over and get as close as I can to Jacob's back. I feel excruciating pain and warmth between my legs. *OH SHIT!* I slap Jacob's back to wake him up. "Jacob, something is wrong!" I cry to him. He jumps off the bed and is trying to comprehend what is going on. I throw the covers off of me to see what is coming out between my legs. It's dark, I just see dark and so does Jacob as he turns on the bedside lamp. Once the light has hit the sheets I see it. It is crimson red and pooling in between my legs. "Fuck" is all I hear come out of Jacob's mouth.

I am in shock I see and hear things, but my mind can't comprehend what is going on. *Please God, let everything be ok.* I chant over and over in my head. I see Jacob throw on clothes and has his phone to his ear. He is calling an ambulance. Fuck! This isn't good.

"Elizabeth, look at me." He calmly says to me. I look at him and I sob, I'm brought back to reality by looking into those gorgeous eyes of his. "Baby, the placenta is separating from your uterus, we have got to get you to the hospital and deliver these babies. I called an ambulance, and we will be on our way. I need you to slowly get up." He grabs my thighs to pull me to the side of the bed, but once he makes me close my legs I scream in agony. He pulls my legs apart and looks in between my legs. I see absolute fear in his eyes.

"Fuck! Elizabeth, what I'm about to do is going to hurt, and I'm so sorry but the baby's umbilical cord is prolapsing...its coming out first and it's not good." With his final words he grabs the cords and fists it up into my vagina. I buck off the bed and scream in pain. "Oh shit, baby I'm so, so sorry ...breathe baby just breathe!" I feel Jacob pushing harder and harder and I want to pass out, *just knock me out*! He keeps his hand there and with the other hand he grabs the phone off the bed. I hear him talking to the hospital, and telling to prep the OR and to alert the NICU that he has three, thirty two week gestation males coming in. I feel my body shake from crying so hard. Once he is off the phone he screams for my mother. "GRACE, GRACE come here!" He shouts about four times before my mother comes running in. My mother gasps when she sees what is going on. "I called an ambulance they will be here any minute, please let them in. The baby's cord is coming out and I can't move my hand." My mother nods and runs off for the front door. Minutes later the paramedics are in our room. I feel like I have tunnel vision that so much is going on around me. Yet all I see is complete darkness in front of me.

"Elizabeth, they are going to move you to the gurney, but, baby, my hand needs to stay here so the cord doesn't come back out. I'm so sorry, love, to put you through this, but once we get to the hospital it will be better." With that, I feel the men lift me onto the gurney and I cry out in pain. Once we are in the ambulance I see Jacob gets his cell phone with his other hand and call someone.

"Dad, hey it's time. Elizabeth has Placenta Abruption with a prolapsed cord. We are in the ambulance now. How soon can you be there? Good. See you soon." Once he is off the phone, he bends over and kisses me. "You are doing so good, baby. Hang in there. I love you."

"What's going to happen to the babies?" I sputter out the words.

"You all are going to be fine." He tells me way too calmly.

"Jacob, no doctor talk, you tell me the truth. Are they going to be alright?"

"The babies are early. There is no telling what the outcome will be with babies this small. You will be fine. I promise I will do my best with everything. Nothing bad is going to happen, I won't allow it. I'm getting my best people in the OR now."

"I'm so scared, Jacob. I can't lose any of them." He is practically laying on me with the position he is in. His hand has got to hurt. He just kisses me and whispers "I love you" over and over.

We are finally at the hospital. Getting out of the ambulance was another shouting episode. It hurt so bad, that Jacob hoped on the gurney and ended up straddling me with his hand still inside of me. "Elizabeth, you are doing so good, hang in there. I love you!" Jacob told the paramedics which floor to take us to and to take us straight to the OR doors. Jacob screamed for someone named Kathy. I see from my side Kathy running down the hallway to us.

"Elizabeth, this is Kathy, she will be by my side in the OR. I need to go scrub for surgery. I will be right back, Kathy is going to switch places with me until I can get in there and get the boys out. They are going to take you in to prep you for surgery, okay?"

I look into those eyes and those eyes aren't telling me the whole story. I realize that this is an emergency. I've read up on emergency cesareans. They put the woman under, most of the time.

"Jacob, you have to pu…put me under, don't you?" I stutter the words to him. I cry for the realization that I won't witness their birth. Their biological father won't witness their birth. I grab his hand and put all my faith and trust in him. "Do what you need to do to save them and keep them healthy. Tell them their Mommy loves them when you see them."

"Oh God Elizabeth, I wish I didn't have to. You can't sit in a sitting position for a spinal. I love you so much and I promise to keep them healthy and safe. I gotta run and get prepped."

He leans down to kiss me and I turn my head so he ends up kissing my temple. I gasp for small breaths, since the pain is excruciating from crying so hard. This wasn't part of the plan. *Oh, God, please keep my babies safe! Grant, please make sure our babies are safe!* I cry out agony again as Jacob pulls his hand out and Kathy places hers in, which is some relief considering her hands are smaller. Kathy straddles me since she is too short to walk and have her hand inside me. Once we are in the operating room she helps with her other hand by placing blue paper sheets all over me. I meet the Anesthesiologist, and as soon as I am prepped he gets to work with his equipment. Right before he puts the mask to my face I see Jacob at the window putting on his scrub hat, paper blue gown, and mask on. I have never felt such adoration and love for someone, yet I felt complete numbness and pain for what I am going through. As the mask is placed on me, I am told to take deep breaths in. Counting back from one hundred, I look over to see Jacob walking towards me. *One hundred, ninety nine, ninety eight, ninety seven* …I'm out before he says anything to me.

Awakening to the machine that I despise, the machine that beeps for every heartbeat. Slowly opening my eyes I squint, because it is too bright. I hear women talking around me, but don't see them. Rubbing my eyes, so I can see better. I see I'm in the recovery room. Alone, but I still hear the women behind the curtains. My mouth feels like I have swallowed cotton. I try to talk, but it hurts. I feel as if my tongue has doubled in size. My hands slide to what once was my protruding belly and there is nothing there. Feeling my ribs and pelvis, it's the weirdest sensation to know my hands were once propped by a protruding belly, only moments ago for me, and now I lay them on flatness. Pushing the covers to the side of the bed to see the difference. I see, white gauze below my belly button, spanning the width of my hips. I start to get emotional when I feel that they aren't inside of me. I mourn for not having more time with them inside of me. Grieving takes over because I didn't memorize their kicks and movement one final time. I cry, about the separation between my babies and me. Crying harder, since I'll never experience the miracle of life growing and kicking inside me again. I use the sheet to wipe my eyes. Clearing my throat I get the attention of a nurse. "Can I have some water, please?" I hoarsely say to her.

She brings me ice chips and tells me to take it slow. "Where is Dr. Alexander?" I ask.

"I've paged him, he asked me to page him once you woke. How is your pain? From one to ten what would you give it, with ten being the worst?" She cheerfully asks me.

I feel like asking this woman if she's seen my chart. I've just been gutted like a fish. I don't think there is a number for the pain I'm in, especially emotional pain. "My babies, when can I see my babies?" I mumble to her as I swish the ice chips around in my mouth. "Your babies are doing fine. Your pain level? Do you need more pain relief?"

"I'm around a six or seven, no I don't need pain meds. Can you sit me up please?" I ask the nurse who is jotting notes in my file. I feel so out of it. I finally see Jacob, in his scrubs and white jacket, running through the recovery room doors. Coming to my side, he leans over the bed rail and gives me a soft and gentle kiss.

"The babies are beautiful! They are doing well for their gestation. As soon as you can stand on your own we can go see the babies. How are you feeling?"

"Fine, tired, anxious. I want to see the boys. Are they healthy and breathing on their own?"

"They're all on CPAP machines, which is good. They are breathing on their own, they just need a little help."

"Jacob, how much longer till I can go see them? I'm dying to see them. How do they look?"

"Patience, love. Here I have these for you." He pulls out pictures of the babies and a CD. Suddenly his pager starts to go off. "Shit, I gotta run…another emergency. Your mom is in the waiting room I'll send her back." Leaning over he kisses me on the lips. "I love you," he says as he runs back out the double doors.

Minutes later my mom is by my side. She feeds me ice chips, as if I was a child. She is just as anxious to see the babies. We look at the pictures. They all have dark brown hair, like Grant. Their faces are all scrunched up, they have the cutest lips, and plump cheeks. I can't wait to see them, talk to them, and touch them. During the thirty-two weeks they were inside of me, they were protected and nurtured, now they're so far away from me. I pray that they're going to be healthy. "I'm so proud of you, Elizabeth. Those boys have the bravest mommy ever." She leans over and hugs me. When she pulls away I see tears sliding down her cheek. "What's with the waterworks?" I say as I wipe the tears away from her face. "I'm just so happy. You're going to be an amazing mom, and those precious boys are so blessed to have you. These are happy tears, baby girl." I just smile at her.

"I have to get going. I need to go back to the house, deal with the dogs, and go pick up your father. He's flying in this afternoon. We will come up this evening. Ella and Kate should be here soon. I love you." She gives me a kiss on the forehead, grabs her purse, and walks through the curtain.

Chapter 17

❧

Mommy

With my mom gone, I continue to stare at the snapshots of the boys. They have writing on the bottom. It's Jacob's handwriting as he wrote their timeline for me.

Baby A: Grant
Born at 6:20a.m.
3lbs. 12oz. 19in.

Baby B: Evan
Born at 6:21a.m.
3lbs. 14oz. 19in

Baby C: Cole
Born at 6:23a.m.
4lbs. 1oz. 19 ¼ in.

I look at my babies, they're the most beautiful babies I've ever seen. I look at the other pictures of Jacob cutting the cords, their feet stamped, being swaddled and placed in my arms. I can't believe it, the last picture is all three swaddled and in my arms, with a few extra hands in the picture. He knew how important catching all of these moments were for me that he took it upon himself and did it.

The curtains are thrown to the side and in walks Kate and Ella.

"Hot damn babe, look how skinny you are now!" Of course those would be Kate's exact words.

"Nice to see you too, Kate!" I mumble in a shitty tone to her.

"OUCH! Someone doesn't handle drugs very well."

"Kate, seriously? You're going to come in here and those are your first words to me. I'm dying to see my boys, and I can't which frustrates me. I'm handling the drugs just fine."

Kate plops down in the chair she looks like a scorned child. "Beth, how are the boys?" Ella says in her mothering tone.

"Jacob says that they are doing well for their gestation and that they all are on CPAP machines. I just want to see them!" I cry, I cry so hard that the sheet I am crying into is soaked.

Ella pulls out her laptop and places it on the table in front of me. "EL, what is this? What do you want me to do with a laptop now?" I ask her sarcastically.

"Nothing, I want you to watch. Then hopefully you will change that 'poor me' attitude of yours." She gives me the look that I shouldn't even reply to her comment.

She takes out the CD and puts it in the laptop. She sets it up to watch a video. Seconds later, I see Jacob over the surgical table. I'm covered in blue paper except for a small rectangle over my belly. *Oh shit, he had someone tape the births for me.* Jacob talks to me the whole time as if I was coherent. "Elizabeth, we're cutting now," seconds later he has his strong beautiful hands inside of me, pulling out my tiny baby boy. "This is baby A, Grant."

He holds him up to the camera and Grant is just screaming his little head off. I cry, because Jacob thought of this moment and captured it for me. Ella sits there and rubs my shoulders. Seconds later, he is pulling and tugging out Evan. "Here comes baby B, Evan." He holds up Evan to the camera and Evan has his blue green eyes wide open. He is very quiet, until he pees all over the place. He gets a few good laughs from the people in the OR.

"At least we know his bladder is working." I can tell it was Jacob's dad that said that. *His dad had shown up to help him.* "Alright, Elizabeth, this is going to hurt some baby, and I'm sorry. Cole has pushed himself up high." I'm watching him with his hand deep inside of me pulling and tugging. I see another pair of hands pushing on the top of my belly. "Poor Cole is comfortable in there." Jacob's father says as he is pushing Cole towards Jacob's hands.

"Here he comes, baby C. This is Cole. He's the biggest one." Jacob holds him up to the camera and holds him close to his body. With his hand he grabs Cole's little hand and waves to the camera. "Mommy, we are perfect. We love you!" Then Jacob passes him off to the nurse. Jacob turns back towards the camera and says, "Baby, you did awesome, all three are healthy. Apgar scores are good for all three. Grant is fine, the prolapse didn't hurt him. They're on their way to the NICU to get more tests done. I love you, baby!" With that he blows a kiss to the camera and then it goes black. I stare at the black screen and realize that somewhere between him scrubbing in and coming into the room he got someone to video tape their births so I wouldn't miss it. He went against the protocol not allowing video cameras in the room, he did it for me. *Because he loves us.*

"Jacob called you didn't he?" I say to Ella but I don't look at her. She is putting the laptop back in her bag.

"Beth, he did the best he could for the situation you were in. Most doctors wouldn't have done half the work he did for you. He loves you so much and it shows in how much he loves those boys. He did this video not only for you, but for them, too! And, yes he did call me when he was scrubbing in. He wanted me to come and video tape it, but I was nowhere ready to be up here in that short amount of time. I reminded him that the Lamaze class has video cameras for their mock labors. I'm assuming he had a tech or nurse run up and grab one for the births."

"I know he did, I just wish their births went to plan." I whisper to Ella.

"Honey, you know better than anyone, not all plans are followed through. Your boys had a mind of their own, they didn't want to follow your plan. Goes to show you, what strong-willed boys you already have." She says with a huge grin and wink.

Kate stands up and gives me a kiss. "You gonna be nice now?" She says as she picks up the pictures. "They're beautiful Mommy, you did well. They all look like Grant."

I smile at her, knowing that they do. "Listen, Beth, I know I'm the last one to say the right things, that's Ella's job. I know how upset you are, and if Ella or I could, we would switch places with you in a heartbeat, for you to have experienced a moment of that miracle when life is pulled out of you. But, Beth, when it's all said and done, isn't the whole reason to all of this is to be a mother? It doesn't matter how you got here, it only matters that you got here. You're a mommy, Beth. Look at these boys." As she holds up the photos of my babies. "You're a mom, and, honey, to be honest with you, the labor pains have just now started. And there is no epidural for motherhood, because if there was that shit would be surgically implanted into me."

I pull her down to me and hug her tight. I kiss her cheek and whisper. "I love you. Thank you." Once we break from our hug I look to Ella. "Ella, I want to go see them, please ask the nurse when I can go see them."

"As soon as you think you can move. Can you move your legs?" I nod telling her that I can. Once she sees that I can move my legs she walks to grab the nurse. The nurse comes to my side and holds my left arm. "Swing your legs over, and see how you do," the peppy nurse said. "Kate, go find a wheelchair." Ella instructs. Kate takes off bothering every nurse and worker for a wheelchair. I wasn't prepared for the pain that shot up through my whole body. Minutes later, Kate runs into the bed with the wheelchair. "Sorry, girlfriend!" I give her a groan and then they all help me into the chair. Once I'm in the chair, they escort me to the NICU floor. I am so anxious. My palms are sweating so much that I have to keep wiping my hands on the blanket. I just want to see them and touch them. I wonder if I can hold them.

I come to a door with an intercom. They ask the patients last name. I say Thomas. I am buzzed into the waiting room. The peppy nurse leaves me once another nurse comes around the desk and shows me what to do every time I come to visit. She gives me booties that I will put on once I start walking. Then shows me the sink of where I will wash my hands. She shows me how. Finally after hand washing I am buzzed through another door to a long hallway. There are many sliding doors along the hallway that hold 2-4 incubators. My boys are in room 303E. Once I am at the door, I'm nervous to go in. Ella puts her hands on my shoulders, and encourages me to go in. "Beth, they need to hear you and smell you.

Preemies thrive off of their senses. Go bond with your babies, you've waited so many years for this moment. Kate and I will go, call us later."

"Wait, don't go. I don't want to do this alone." I say as I turn my head and look at her.

"Ma'am, only parents can be in this level of the NICU." The nurse barks to me. I'm a little scared of this nurse. *Like I knew?*

"Beth, Jacob should be here with you. He would want to be here with you at this moment. This is what you both talked about wait for him to get here."

Dammit why does she have to be right all the damn time! Kate just looks at me and smiles her sweet grin at me. "Page him, babe!"

I ask them to wheel me back to the nurses' station. Once we get there I give the nurse Jacob's pager number and page him to meet me at the boys' room. She does what I ask, and then I am off to finally meet my boys.

The nurse wheels me inside the room. There is a huge floor to ceiling window view of downtown. The first thing I notice is the sun, the sun is shining bright into the room. I smile to myself, knowing that Grant is with me and his sons. The wall to my right has two incubators that says A and C on the front. To my left is another incubator with B on it. Next to B, is a glider chair and ottoman. Next to the door are cabinets, and a computer on top, with a counter height chair. In the middle of the room is a long island of cabinets and desks. I ask the nurse, to wheel me over to Grant and Cole's beds. I stare at them and I completely melt. These are my babies. They were just inside of me hours ago. They are a part of me, a part of Grant. I never knew love like this existed. Parked right in between both incubators I reach my hand through the little hole of their incubators and place my hand on their small heads. I whisper, "Mommy's here, my loves." With my left palm on Grant's head and my right on Cole's, I peek over my shoulder to Evan's incubator and my heart hurts for him, all alone on the other side of the room. Realizing that I can't do this alone. Tears start to pull in my eyes, and before the tears hit my cheek my savior walks in. Jacob gives me his big beautiful smile.

"I'm glad to see you in here." He says as he gives me a kiss on my hair. I pull my hands out of the little doors and close them. I turn towards him and pull him towards me. I kiss him hard. Kissing him with all the feeling I can muster. His lips are warm and soft. The smell of his coconut shampoo and sweat invade my senses. He brings his hands up to my face and deepens the kiss, tasting me. He pulls back, "I'm so sorry. I feel like I failed you. I wish I could take it back, but I did the best I could. I...." I put my fingers over his lips.

"Shh, you did everything perfect. I love you and thank you for helping me to bring these babies into the world. I wouldn't be here if it wasn't for you. So, you didn't fail. I failed, by not giving you a chance and listening to you. I'm sorry. Please forgive me!"

"I understand, baby." He kisses my head and diverts our attention to my boys. "They are beautiful, baby. You did well!" He stands behind me and rubs my shoulders. "They have your lips. I think they will have your eyes."

The nurse comes over and introduces herself as Nora, and their other daytime nurse is Shirley. Nora goes over protocol with me and how to take care of my boys. For now they are on a tube feeding until they can get their strength to suck. She advises me now to start pumping my milk. Breast milk will increase their growth. They will be on the CPAP machine for the first 24 hours, after that they will be tested to see if they need any help or if they can breathe on their own. She shows me how to touch my babies, preemies are sensitive to touch. They don't like to be rubbed or petted. They just need a firm hold. She pointed out where my hand is and called me a natural already. They have IV's in their arms. She told me that they have to be changed every two days and that preemies bruise easily, but heal just as fast. The waterworks start again, because I ache for my babies. Needles and procedures will be done to them and there isn't anything I can do.

"Why are their heels all wrapped up and elevated?" I ask Nora.

"We have to test their blood and do heel sticks for jaundice. So far they're good, but be warned that they might have to have light therapy. Every baby is different so that is why we have to do numerous blood work on them.

They have wires and tubes all around them. Nora showed me what I was watching for on the screen. She advised me that babies will have what she calls "Bradys," they are Bradycardias. Preemies will sometimes stop breathing, which is Apnea, but then once they stop breathing their heart rhythm slows down causing "Bradys." Nora also told me that they received their first dose of Surfactant, which is a steroid to open up their lungs. Preemies' lungs are small and their bronchioles are sometimes sticky, which makes it hard for them to breath. This is the reason why they need help from the CPAP. The best news was that this time tomorrow I can hold them.

Once I hear this news, I smile. Jacob leans down and kisses my head. I pull my hands away from Grant and Cole's incubators. I tell them that I love them. I will be back soon. I ask Jacob to wheel me over to Evan's bed. As I get close to Evan I'm amazed by how alert the little guy is. His blue green eyes are just opened as wide as they can be and he is looking around. He makes me laugh to myself, because I see so much of me in him. I slide my hand through his little door and place my hand on his head. I talk to him, telling him I love him and how beautiful he is. His eyes follow my voice, which catapults my heart into my throat. *My baby knows my voice!* Jacob says, "Hi, little buddy!" and I watch as Evan's eyes search for Jacob. My grin couldn't get any wider. Evan knows Jacob's voice, he is seeking for Jacob. I tell Jacob to bend down. I place Jacobs's huge hand into the door and tell him to hold him. Evan could fit in Jacob's palm. His little head is nestled against Jacob's palm and Evan closes his eyes as he content to be close to Jacob. Jacob turns to me and smiles. He gives me a huge smile and in his blue eyes I see Jacob's love for my boys.

We sit for a while and talk to Evan. I suddenly feel lightheaded and ask for Jacob to take me to my room. He obliges and we are off to my room. I tell Nora to call my room if she needs me. She asks me to get with a lactation consultant as soon as possible so that they can start to eat. I tell her I will get on it once we get to my room.

Jacob is pushing me and is very quiet. I ask, "Shouldn't you be at work by now?" He kisses the top of my head and says, "No, baby. I switched with the doctor on call. He is doing office visits. I will stay here as long as possible."

"Jacob, you can't do that to your patients, they will expect to see you."

"You and those boys are my number one priority, everything else can wait."

"But, you don't have to. We all will be ok. I have Ella and Kate, and oh shit…where is my mother? I need to call Grant's parents. Tell them what has happened."

"Your mom went to the airport to pick up your father. They will be by as soon as they can. Obviously, I didn't call Grant's parents."

I laugh and lean my head back for him to kiss me. "Thank you, love! You are truly wonderful. I don't know where I would be without you."

We entered my room and when I think he will scoot me in farther next to my bed. He stops the wheelchair, walks around in front of me and squats down so we are eye to eye. "Elizabeth, I love you. I think I have been in love with you since the moment you fell in my arms. We have come so far in this journey, and every day I love you a little more. Every day, I wonder if this is the day that my heart will explode from the overabundance of love I feel for you. Everything I say and do is for you. I thought I knew what love was, I thought I understood how to love. But, then I meet you and you change all my beliefs and way of thinking, living and doing. When I am around you, my breathing changes, my pulse quickens, hell my body temperature rises and it makes me so damn crazy in love with you. Even though I love you this much, the love I feel for those boys is magnified by a million times." He pauses and stares at me as if he is carefully picking his words. "I know I am not their father, but hell, I love them as if they are my own. Being with you on this journey has made me develop feelings for them that I didn't think I would have. Seeing them take their first breath, made me take my own as I held my breath through every procedure. I, as a doctor, have never been terrified in all my life. I understand you have a ton of emotions going through you now, but I just wanted you know what I feel for you and those boys. Being with you just now, was an amazing experience and I will always remember that moment." He stands up and leans down. Putting his fingers on my face, he pulls me in for a kiss that makes me melt. He gently sucks on my lower lip, and then pulls it just so that I open my mouth. Once my mouth is open his tongue invades my tongue and they dance as if it was their last dance. He slows the kiss, and pulls back. He kisses my nose, "Baby, you and those boys are my life, my everything, and I want to be with you and them forever." He looks into my eyes where his ocean eyes are filled with tears.

"I love you, so much Jacob. We both wanted forever with our other loves and we both never got forever so for now, let's take it a day at a time. Love me today!"

"I love you, today and always." He replies as he stands up and picks me up out of the chair. "Let's lie down and then I want to look at your incision."

I lie down in the bed, and he gently pulls my hospital gown up. I have on these hideous white netting underwear with a diaper size pad on, and then gauze pads all at the start of my pubic bone. He softly pulls the gauze back and sees that I haven't opened anywhere, or bleeding. He calls me a very good patient.

"Have I ever told you, that you look so damn sexy in your scrubs?"

He gives me his panty dropping smile and laughs. "Once my doctor gives the okay to have sex, we might have to act out the doctor and patient role. Because you sir, are making all my wildest fantasies come true standing their all hot as shit!"

"Baby, I would be more than happy to make all your fantasies come true."

I lie down in the bed, and make room for Jacob to join me. He lies next to me. I scoot into his body, and lay my head in the crook of his neck. He tenderly strokes his thumb across my jaw line. "I love you, Elizabeth." He whispers to me.

"I love you too." I reply.

Chapter 18

Holding Miracles

The next morning I wake up with the terrible urge to pee. Seeing Jacob is no longer in bed with me, I slowly roll onto my side, grabbing the hospital bed rails and pull myself into a sitting position. *Who the hell knew you use your core for everything? This pain sucks!* I notice on my bedside table that Jacob has left me a note scribbled on my styrofoam water pitcher.

> Baby, I had to go into surgery. I'm not sure how long I will be considering I have other patients to see. I love you! See you soon. Call me if you need me and kiss the boys for me. Love, Jacob.

I smile at the little note. Picking up my phone to see the time. It's five o'clock in the morning. I call my nurse and ask if she can take me to the NICU. Slowly pulling myself out of the bed I walk to the closet and I grab another hospital gown and put it on like a robe. I need to ask my mom to bring me some clothes, this get up looks ridiculous. My nurse strolls in with a wheelchair. I grab my phone and carefully sit down in the chair.

My nurse wheels me to the famous scrub sink. She gives me these hideous green socks with these white rubber stickers on the bottom. "Until you can walk better, wear these socks in there for now." I give her a nod obliging to her statement. She places the socks over my white cotton socks and helps me out of the chair. I scrub my hands, then I am buzzed in to see my boys.

Walking into my boys' room I see that the nurse is taking Evan's temperature. I stand next to her, in complete wonder of how her hands move around my tiny son. "Don't worry honey, they look small and fragile. I promise they won't break." She tells me in her southern drawl.

"What are you doing?" I ask her quizzically.

"I'm taking their temperature to make sure their beds are at the right temp. I have to check their temp every four hours. If their body temp goes up or down they can have some negative effects to them. We will cross that bridge if we get to it. For now Evan is right where he should be," she says as she is placing new leads on his chest. I can hear him whimper a little and it starts to bring tears to my eyes.

"How did you know his name, yesterday he was still Baby B?" I whisper to her for the fear she will see me start to cry.

"Dr. Alexander made up these signs and placed them on their incubators." She raises the side of the incubator to show me. My jaw drops, then I turn around and see Grant and Cole's name on their bed, too.

"Wh..when did he give this to you?" I stutter to her.

"A couple hours before you came in. He said that they have names and we shouldn't refer them to Baby A, B or C." She says as she wraps Evan up like a little burrito. She pulls him out of the bed and cradles him in her arms. "Well, mama would you like to hold your son?" She says as nodding to me to sit in the rocking chair.

I sit and she places him in my arms. I feel my chin start to quiver. I've waited for this moment for so many years. I finally have my baby in my arms. I pull him to my lips and feel his heavy breathing. "I love you so much, my sweet baby boy." I say as I kiss his little head.

"Evan is in heaven, just look at his stats." Nora says as pointing to the numbers on the screen. She asks if I want to hold all of them.

I smile exuberantly at her. "Yes, I would love that," I mumble to her trying to hold back the happy tears. I am finally crying happy tears. She calls the other nurse and they work together bringing Grant over to me, with wires and all. Within a few minutes I have my three sons in my arms. An experience I will always cherish for as long as I will live. To feel them inside one moment and then to see, feel, and smell them in my arms is truly an epic moment. I start to over think, which I told myself I wouldn't. My babies are nestled in my arms and against my chest. I stare out the huge window and see the stars. Tears slide down my cheek and I silently talk to Grant.

"We did it, Grant! We made these beautiful babies. Please watch over them. I miss you! I hope I'm doing right by what you have asked in your letter. Grant, I'm finally happy. It took me awhile, but I'm happy now that I have our sons in my arms. Thank you Grant, I will be forever grateful for what you gave me…us!"

I look down at my sons and see so much of Grant in them. I thank God for giving me three boys that will remind me every day the life I had with Grant. He was part of my life plan, a life plan that went almost perfect for nine years with him. I sit for hours with my little guys in my arms. "Nora?" I mumble for her trying not to startle the boys.

"Yes, hun?"

"Could you take a picture of the boys and me with my phone?" I ask her.

"Of course, honey!" She captures a couple of pictures of the boys and me. She is about to walk away when I tell her. "My arms are going to sleep and I'm afraid to move with all three of them."

"No problem, honey. It's almost their feeding time anyways."

"I think one of them peed on me, my chest is all wet."

Nora looks down at me as she holds Grant and gives a little chuckle to herself. I give her a facial expression as to ask, 'what the hell is wrong'?

"Honey, they didn't pee on you. Your milk has come in!" She says as she passes off Grant to the next nurse.

"What do I do?" I question her, since I have never experienced this before.

"Honey, you sit right there, I'm going to have Shirley get you the pump and you can start pumping milk for your boys," she answers to me while doing her business with the boys.

Minutes go by and my sons are bundled in their new blankets and tucked in their beds. Shirley shows me how to pump. I place the cups under my wet gown and let the machine do its job. Fifteen minutes later and I have milk for my babies. I want to high five myself for doing something for my sons. I give the milk to Nora in a stored container with an orange lid. She instructs me how to label my milk and to place it in the freezer when I make a drop off. I'm officially now the milk maid. She gives me a new gown, which I change into in the bathroom. I go back to sit in the rocking chair and just stare out the window. What an incredible morning that I have had. It is amazing what a difference 24 hours can do. I look at the pictures and send a text to Jacob.

> **Me:** Had the best morning. I got to hold the boys, and my milk came in. They'll have their first official meal shortly.

I pull my legs up on the ottoman and slowly start to rock myself. Shortly I receive Jacob's text.

> **Jacob:** Baby, I am so happy for you. I wish I was there with you to see your beautiful smile. I'll call you when I can come by and see you. I love you. XO to the boys for me.

I send the picture to my parents, Ethan, Kate, Ella, Cole and Anna: Introducing Grant, Evan and Cole Thomas. I'm officially a mommy!

One after one I get a text back. They all can't wait to see them. I can't wait for my little guys to know how much they are loved. Once the texts stop, I lay my head back listening to the beeping noises of the boy's monitors. I stare out the window and think. Realization hits me so hard in the chest. I close my eyes harder trying to control my breathing. My palms are sweating, and I can feel the pulse in my temple pulsate harder. Reality just threw me a curve ball. How the hell am I going to do this once I leave this place? It's easy right now. I have nurses to help me, there are machines that are feeding them, beds to keep them warm, and machines letting me know if they stop breathing. How can I do this once I leave this place?

I silently talk to myself. *Get a grip Elizabeth, its only day 2. Things will get easier.* I wipe my palms on my gown. Gradually I start to rock myself, taking in slow deep breaths, and focus on my new plan. It is crazy how one moment I was with family and friends having a beautiful baby shower and then the next I'm having one of the scariest events take over me. I should still be pregnant, at home packing and preparing for these little guys' arrivals. I shouldn't be sitting here…well I shouldn't be a widow at thirty either.

What in the hell do you do when higher power, the universe or LIFE totally fucks up your life plan? My life plan was going the way it should've been going. Going down the list and checking it off as I accomplished each life goal. Now, I sit here in this plastic rocking chair staring out the window looking out over the city. A city filled with people who will start to wake up and get on with their daily lives. I sit here in this chair and have no idea when my life will restart. All I hear are the monitors' beep and the alarms that go off. Wavy lines go in zigzag motions, lines on the screen that I have no idea what they mean. I listen as the nurses speak in whisper tones.

All I can do is just stare out the window and think back of how my life plan got so off track just seven months ago. Seven months ago my life came to a screeching halt, my world, my life, my soul, and my heart all disappeared in an instant. Then life hands me three reasons to hang onto hope. Three reasons that I need to wake up, put on my big girl panties, and start a new life plan. I gaze out the window, thinking of what the hell am I going to do. The nurse's whispers become louder. Then, I feel a slight rub on my shoulder, as I turn around I see Ella, my best friend, my rock.

"What are you doing here this early? How did you get past the nurses' station?" I say.

Ella responds, "I called up to your room and then I called the nurses' station. They said you've been in here since five a.m. Nora and I have bonded…she snuck me in. I decided I would come see if you needed anything before I went into work. You alright?"

"Ella, I need a new plan, and I have no idea how to go about it?" She looks around the room at my boys.

"Honey, with what you have, you can't have a plan. All you can do is live each day to the fullest and do your best. Day by day, moment by moment is how you will live your new life."

"Ella, I am so scared, literally scarred shitless. Look at all of this" as I wave my hand and guide her to what I am staring at. "I have no clue what to do. This was nowhere near my plan. You don't even have three children so how in the hell am I going to raise three?"

"Beth, if you can handle one you can handle a hundred. It's the same with each no matter what."

I sit in the chair, I find myself rocking harder with agitation, when I feel someone pull the back of the chair as their way of telling me to slow down. I look up and see Nora. "Beth, your nurse just called and said that Dr. Alexander is on his way up to your room to check on you."

"Thanks, Nora. Will you call me if you need me?"

"Of course, dear" she whispers quietly back to me.

Ella helps me out of the chair. She grabs my right elbow. She helps me walk, or more so watches me shuffle in my bright green socks with the rubber stickers on the bottom. We walk down the hall, and all I can think is how depressing hospitals are. No matter the occasion, it has such a sad feel to it. We enter the elevator, and I can tell she wants to say something, but doesn't have the heart. I nudge her hip, "alright spill it, what is on your mind?'

"Seeing you with your babies, it kinda makes me want to have another, who knows maybe try for a boy. Do you think I'm crazy?"

"Ella, hello you're talking to crazy. I think that is wonderful news." I wrap my arm around her waist and lean my head against her shoulder. "We seriously know how to put the FUN in dysfunctional, huh?"

Chapter 19

Good News

My babies are three days old, and doing well for their gestation. Evan has had a few apnea setbacks, but it's to be expected. I'm progressing well in my recovery. I'm not letting this surgery hold me down. I need to be there for my sons.

Today is my discharge day, a day that I have been dreading. I really do not want to go home to the house that Grant and I planned on bringing our babies home. Except that I will be the only one going home. Jacob and my relationship has been a revolving door these past few days. I barely see him and when I do it is when he is sleeping in my bed. He hasn't been to the house either. He says it feels strange to be there alone without me. He's working non-stop, not sure if that is a good thing or a bad thing.

I've packed my bag. Dressed in one of my maternity dresses, I can't believe how big I really was. It's really nice to be able to see my toes again. I am sitting here waiting for Jacob to come and discharge me. Twenty minutes later Jacob is walking in the door.

"Hey, beautiful, how are you doing?" He says as he walks over and gives me a kiss. He sits next to me on the small love seat and grabs my hands. He has a devilish smile on his face and his eyes are glistening.

"What gives, Jacob? What are you hiding behind that smile of yours?"

He leans over and gives me an incredible kiss. He pulls back and places the manila folder on the side table.

"I have good news, then I have great news. What order do you want it?" He tilts his head and smiles. I give him the goofiest laugh because he looks like a child on Christmas morning.

"Alright, give it to me any way you want." I say as I wiggle my eyebrows at him.

"Baby, the good news is I'm not discharging you. I'm going to keep you here for three more days. Because …." he opens the manila folder and places it in my lap. "These are our closing papers."

My jaw drops to the floor. We weren't supposed to close for another three weeks. I scan through the papers and everything is legit.

"Babe, how did you pull this off so fast, we just saw the house less than a week ago? The sellers weren't ready to move so quickly."

"Money does a lot of talking. I gave them a few thousand more on their asking price to be moved out in forty-eight hours. I told them we had a family emergency and we needed the house as soon as possible. They agreed all we do is sign and we have a house to bring the boys home too."

"How much is a few thousand, Jacob?" Glaring at him and knowing I'm slowly becoming his buzz kill. I grab his hand and with my thumb I start to rub his knuckles.

"Baby, it's not a big deal, we need this house. I know how you feel about going back to your house. This had to be done."

I squeeze his hand and whisper "How much more?"

With his clouded blue eyes looking at the floor his quietly mumbles. "Twenty five thousand."

I gasp and throw the folder on the floor. The house was so over budget as it was and he goes and throws in another twenty five thousand. My breathing starts to quicken. I feel hot all of a sudden.

"Baby, you are so pale, calm down, please. Let me explain."

"Please, explain Jacob. Because I want to know how in the hell are we going to afford a mortgage on that kind of house when you threw away an extra twenty five thousand out the window. Our budget was for your salary, adding an extra twenty five thousand goes over our budget. I don't want to go back to work right away. I want to stay home and raise my children. With our mortgage and my loans I will have to go back to work. God Dammit, Jacob, why didn't you think of talking to me about this?"

"Beth will you chill for a second and listen. You don't need to go back to work. I will take care of you and everything else. I have the money for this. I should have told you ...I have more money than you originally thought.

He pulls me into him and now I am leaning across his chest and my head is under her chin. He pushes my hair behind my ear and traces my jaw line with his thumb.

"Beth, my mother left me a trust fund. Her parents left her a massive amount of money when they died. She had no use for it so she left it in a trust fund for us. I was granted half at eighteen and the other half at twenty five. Let's just say that this fund paid for all my schooling and I am still in good hands. Then when Rebecca died I was received her life insurance. We are financially well off, Baby. You can stay home with the boys for as long as you want. I promised you that I'd take care of you and I mean it. No worries from you. I have this covered."

Pushing myself off his chest and grab his face with my hands. I quietly say, "Jacob, I do worry. I have so much to worry about now. We're still newly dating and rushing into so much at a rapid speed. I worry that once we finally get comfortable, you won't want this life that has been thrown at your feet. You have no commitments here. You can walk away whenever you want. I worry about this, hell it consumes me. I'm scared out of my fucking mind." I barely get the last sentence out before my voice cracks and I start to cry. Jacob scoops me up into his arms, careful of my incision.

He kisses the corner of my mouth, and then softly kisses my lips. He looks into my eyes, as if they were windows to my soul. I look away, as his gaze into me sets my body of fire. *God, I truly love this man.* "Elizabeth, look at me."

I melt gazing into those clear blue turquoise eyes of his. "I love you more than life itself. I love our boys more than life, more than my own life. I swear to you that I will take care of you. If you want I will write a contract stating that if anything does happen in our relationship you will be granted the house, all yours no questions asked. I'm telling you I'm not going anywhere. You and the boys have me for life."

"You said our … our boys?"

"Baby, they are our boys. I consider them my sons. I've been there since the beginning. Is it alright if I think of them as my sons?"

"I just didn't think you felt like that. These boys are a massive responsibility. Are you really up to being a dad?"

"Baby, I want nothing more than to be a dad, to our sons."

"I love you, Jacob."

"I love you so damn much. I promise you will be so very happy."

"Now hand me those papers, I want to sign so we have a home to bring our boys home to."

He kisses me with such force that I feel lightheaded by his kiss. He cradles me in his arms, where I feel safe and content. I feel his love pour out of him and into me with the ferocity of his kiss. He looks at me and whispers, "Forever baby, you're mine forever."

I look into his beautiful eyes and smile.

The next three days staying in the hospital were busy to say the least. Jacob finally got to hold the boys. What an amazing sight to see this big man, hold these tiny babies in his arm. It was so touching and heartwarming to see his love pour out for these tiny little human beings. He honestly does love my boys. To see him talk to them, and kiss them, was a moment that will be forever engrained in my memory. He helped me give the boys a bath, he praised me when I finally got to nurse them, and he even changed a few diapers. To see him go from Jacob to dad was mind boggling. He made the transformation so much more lucid than I did. I had months to plan, and I didn't transition as easily as he did. My favorite time with him and the boys would be when we sat together. We got to hold the boys in the "kangaroo style" where the boys were skin to skin. Jacob would take two babies and they would be placed on his golden soft skin. Then he and the boys would be wrapped up in a blanket. I would have the other baby skin to skin and wrapped up. Jacob and I would sit in the rocking chairs side by side and quietly talk or even nap. It was the most relaxing and emotional part of my days, still I loved to look forward to that time together.

Grant, Evan, and Cole were developing well for being a few weeks early. Days were long with them in the hospital, but I had great nurses who were teaching me everything I needed to know about preemies. When I wasn't with them in their room, I was either in the pump room expressing milk for them or in the cafeteria reading, sending pictures and emails to family about the babies' development, and trying to see Jacob here and there. The hospital was my new home for now.

During my three day stay in the hospital Jacob hired a moving crew. Along with the help of my mother and father, they packed up my entire house. Anything of Grant's or his and mine together was packed up and sent to a storage unit for me to go through when I was ready to deal with it. Jacob didn't feel it was right to bring anything of Grant's into "our" home which I agreed too. Jacob has been to the new house and to oversee the placement of furniture and belongings. I haven't been to the new house yet but I want to go. I'm anxious to do something other than what I've been doing, but in all actuality I'm nervous. We still don't have a buyer for my house, so it sits empty. Just as I have grieved and said my goodbyes to Grant and our past, I know I need to go say goodbye to the house one last time. I'm sure it is the first thing I'll do once I'm ready to leave the hospital.....another check mark on my life plan.

Chapter 20

Father's Day

June

Oh where do I begin? We are a couple weeks into June and if I thought my life was a rollercoaster before, I was dead wrong. I'm in a category five hurricane, with nothing to hang on to. Ten days after we signed for the new house, I had the courage to go to my old house and say goodbye. I went alone with an air mattress in tow and decided to stay the night. I had a good cry, and the solitude did me some good. I thought a lot of the past and the memories the house held. I slept on the living room floor, but spent many moments sitting in each room. I believe I did more talking to Grant in that one night than I have in the past nine months. Locking the door to that house, I walked down the driveway one last time. Once I got into my truck I stared at the front of the house and said my final goodbye to my past with Grant. I pulled out my phone and took one last picture of the house. With the house in view and the sun was starting to rise over the roof top, I burst out in laughter. Knowing that Grant was giving me another sign. He was saying his goodbye with me.

That morning I met Jacob at our new home. I wanted to see the progress that was being made. He and my parents have done so much. My parents are still here, they have made the small "in-law" suite above the garage their new living quarters, for the time being while they are here visiting. My mother surprised me with presents for the boys. I sat on the couch as I watched her bring out three boxes.

"Elizabeth, here you go. I made these for the boys and I hope you don't mind that I went ahead and did it."

I give her this perplexed look of confusion.

"What are you talking about, mom?"

"I went through Grant's things and made something for the boys. I thought this would mean more than his items sitting in a box."

She sits next to me with her hand on my knee. I slowly start to unwrap the present that says Evan's name. Opening the box and I inhale air into my lungs, but my body has somewhat forgot to exhale.

"Breathe, baby girl, it's alright. If it's too much pack it up and give it to them when they're older."

I pull out the handmade blanket made with Grant's clothing. My mother has made a patch work quilt of Grants clothing. In the center of the blanket is a picture of Grant on his Harley. She even has patch worked motorcycles, in between his clothing. At the top she hand stitched Evan's name and date of birth. I pull it to my chest and bury my face in the quilt.

My mother's hand is rubbing my back, waiting patiently for a response from me. I pull my face out of the quilt, and fall into her for a hug. I whisper in her ear, "This is the most beautiful, treasured gift ever. Words can't describe how thankful I am for these blankets for my boys. I love you."

"I love you too, baby girl. I'm so glad you love it. I was terrified you would be so upset with me about what I did to his clothing."

"I could never be upset. You gave them the best gift ever of their father."

I open up Grant and Cole's blanket. They are somewhat similar, but with different patterns to them. My mother must have worked night and day to make these. I wrap them up and place them back in the box. I don't think I want the boys to use them now, but when they do ask about their father, I will have something to pull out and show them.

I don't stay at the new house long. It feels awkward not having the boys or the dogs there yet. It doesn't feel like home. So in the meantime, I have taken up residence up at the Ronald McDonald house. It is across the street from the boys. So I can come and be with them whenever I want. It works out great, because I see more of Jacob, too.

I'm informed that the boys will be going home on Sunday, depending on if they pass their car seat test. They have been in the hospital for 4 weeks, and I can't wait to bring them home. I walk into their room, and see them all in a crib sleeping with one another. Once they were able to keep their body temp in check the nurse put them back together. She informed me that multiples want to be bundled together. They do much better that way. On top of their crib is a 5x7 card stock paper with the boys' foot print, and a sweet Father's Day poem, about one day filling their daddy's shoes and walking in his footsteps. I feel wetness forming behind my eyes. The boys will be coming home on Jacob's first Father's Day. I take the card stock paper off their crib and place it in my purse. I want to surprise Jacob with these poems. I have an idea in my head of what to get Jacob. I don't know if I can out do my gift that he gave me for Mother's day, but I hope its close. For Mother's day he got me a mother's ring with three emeralds in a platinum setting. It is the most beautiful stone ring I have ever seen.

Sunday morning arrives, Father's day. Jacob and I are lying in bed talking about what we are going to do. We are embracing each other and I don't want to move from this bed. I know after today our lives are forever changed. We have only a few hours to think of ourselves. Our plan is not to leave until the hospital calls and tells us when the babies will be discharged.

Jacob rolls onto his side. I can feel he is hard for me. We kiss. I moan into his mouth at his amazing kisses. I am so turned out right now. Jacob's lips part leaving my mouth, trailing over my chin, down the line of my throat. I arch my neck, offering him better access. While his tongue flicks and teases, I slowly slide my hand down his rock hard abs to his shaft. I slowly clench and stroke his cock. He moans into my neck. I can hear his breathing change. He pushes me onto my back and cups my breast. My beaded nipples press into his hot palms and when he caresses, shock waves of desire shoot straight to my core.

His mouth moves back up, his lips lightly kissing me, "I need you Elizabeth, I'm going to devour and consume you. I am not leaving this bed until I have touched, licked, and kissed every inch of your body. You are so fucking amazing, you blow me away!"

I can't talk, my brain has become unresponsive, and I can't say anything. I'm thinking that this is too soon. I need to wait for a couple more weeks, like most women. Then again he is my doctor and should know what he is doing. I've waited for this moment for a very long time. I've waited to make love to him, his skin to my skin. I've imagined this moment many times, and I am going to embrace it for how it comes. I pull his neck towards me and kiss him. "You make me so happy. I love you."

"Beth, I love you!"

He slides his hand down my side across my hip and then pushes his fingers into me. I whimpered as he slowly and methodically moved his fingers into me. With him moving his finger in and out of me. I keep moving my hand up and down his shaft to the speed of his fingers. "Baby, please stop. I will be done in no time of you keep doing that. I want to come inside of you, not on your hand."

I let go as he repositions himself over me and slides down me. His mouth is over my nipple and he starts to suck on it gently. I am in heaven. This man does things to my body where I see stars. From my nipple down to my hip bone he kisses and licks my skin. He grasps my hips, and with his forearms held my thighs down to the bed. He gives my thighs soft sweet kisses, then all of a sudden his tongue impales me.   Licking and tormenting my clit, my thighs started shaking, and my core was quivering.

"Let go, Elizabeth. Come for me, I want to taste you."

With that I bite my bottom lip to hold back the scream. I grab the sheets for dear life as I come, my body trembling fiercely, sensitive muscles constricting frantically around his merciless licking. His groan vibrates through me. I start to move, thinking he has stopped. "Don't move, I'm not done with you. I want more!"

He returns to my clit and sucks softly, tirelessly until I climax again. I'm sweating and shaking, slowly falling back to earth. "Baby, you taste heavenly," he whispers to me as he moves his body up. He mouth caresses my mouth.

"I can taste myself on your lips." I mumbled to him.

"You taste good, huh?"

I nod my head as we kiss. I could spend the rest of my life just kissing this man. His palms stroke up and down my abdomen. It felt rejuvenating knowing he was feeling just me. I felt the tip of his hardening length probing intimately while his mouth continues to devour mine. Jacob is gentle, but demanding, considerate but firm. His right hand slides along my waist and hip, than he cups my ass and lifts me.

He stretches himself on top of me, placing his left forearm to the side of my head. His fingers combing through my hair, our gazes are riveted with the love we feel for one another. His eyes are dark blue and I could see his love for me trying to escape his gaze on me. "Baby, I love you so fucking much." He mumbles to me as I feel his harden length slowly enter my slick folds. I arch my chest into him as he was filling me. Stroke after stroke the tension was building fast. "Christ …baby, you feel amazing." I could start to feel the pleasure ripple through my core.

"Jacob …I love you." I whisper the words as I feel my muscles start to clench down on him. He buries his face in my neck and holds me as he plunges hard and fast. Within seconds we are coming together. We cry out each other's names and fall into one another. We're sweating and gasping for air. We can't talk, but words don't need to be said, we feel it. My body pulses and tingles. His face was still in the side of my neck. We can't move, it feels like hours we stay in this position.

"Wow, that was …incredible." I finally say to break the silence.

"Baby, I don't want to leave this bed. I want to be inside of you all day and night." With that he rises up and looks at me. "My God, you are beautiful and so fucking sexy. I'm completely and madly in love with you."

I smile at him. "You're the sexy one." He just laughs and rolls over.

"Let's shower I want round two to be hot and wet."

"You are Mr. Insatiable, now."

"Baby, do you know how long I waited for this? You haven't seen anything yet. We have so much to make up for."

With that he was on top of me, kissing and touching. "Alright, hot stuff, let's get you hot and wet." I say as I slide off the bed and shake my ass in front of him as I walk to the bathroom. Seconds later, I hear him running after me. I squeal as his picks me up and spins me around.

"I love to see you smile and to hear you laugh. You are beautiful, Elizabeth."

Round two, hot, heavy, primal wet sex, took place in the shower. We are finally clean, dressed, and ready for a late breakfast. While at breakfast, we're called by the boys' nurse saying that they are ready for discharge. I hang up the phone and smile to Jacob. "We can bring our boys home." I say, as I place the phone back in my purse. I pull out his present and place it in front of him. "Happy Father's Day! I had no clue what to get since this was my first time shopping, but I promise to make it better next year. Thank you for taking on such a huge roll and being there for our boys. They are so lucky to have you as their daddy."

For once Jacob is shocked. I can see the complete confusion and utter loss for words on his face. "I don't know what to say, baby. You know I love those boys as if they are my blood. I would do anything for them and I promise to be the best daddy I can be." He blows me a kiss and starts to open his gift. He opens it and the biggest smile spreads across his face. "This is the best gift ever. I'll put it on my desk at work. Thank you, baby, I love it!" He keeps staring at the 5x7 picture frame that has surfboards on one side and palm trees on the other. In the middle is a picture of the boys. I got onesies for the boys, each with a different surf saying. Grant is wearing a light blue one that says, 'I'd rather be surfing' and Evan has on a white one that says 'Daddy's Lil Surfer' and Cole has a mint green one that says 'Crawl, Walk, Surf in that order'.

The waitress brings us the check and Jacob holds up the picture frame. "See my sons, aren't they beautiful?"

The waitress looks at the picture. "Triplet boys, wow, you are one lucky daddy. Happy Father's Day, sir."

He turns around and exclaims "I love you!"

Seeing his priceless smile, I hand him the poems that the nurses made with the boys foot prints. He just smiles. He stands up and walks to pull me out of my chair.

"How will I ever thank you for giving me the most precious gift ever? I'm a father because you gave me a chance. You took a chance on the love I have for you. Thank you, Elizabeth, from the bottom of my heart."

"I think we both are thankful for what we've been given." I say as I rise on my tip toes and give him a kiss. We walk towards the truck and ready to bring our sons home.

I feel like I couldn't get to the NICU fast enough. Jacob is trying to keep up with me. We enter their room with excitement. They were already in their car seats lined up. They still had their monitors attached. Evan still has bouts of Apnea, so he will be coming home on an Apnea monitor. Jacob and I had to take a quick course on Apnea and how to use the machine. I had to take a CPR class. The small back pack holding the monitor is terrifying, but the nurses encourage me that I will be fine with it.

Shirley is at her desk. "Well, hello Mommy and Daddy, Happy Father's Day to you. This is some special day." With her clipboard in hand we walk to the boys' car seats. They all passed their test. Of course, Evan passed with the machine on. "Until they are stronger in the neck it is best to have them lying on their backs rather in a sitting position."

I nod as she goes through the checklist. I think it was more ironic that Jacob had so many questions when he's the doctor. During the conversation between Shirley and Jacob, my sweet and determined Evan started to scream. I recognized his cry and immediately go and unbuckle him. I carry him along with the wires and back pack to the rocking chair. Unbuttoning my shirt I hold him to my breast to feed. For a while it is just Evan and me. I stare into his stunning eyes. He doesn't lose his focus on me. I slowly start to rock and sing, "You are my sunshine."

Jacob comes to my side and kisses the top of my head. He walks in front of me and squats. "Baby, do you know how amazing you are to watch. I watched you do all of that with such fluidity. You know exactly what each of them need. You, my love are something else."

I just smile at him and murmur "I love you" to him. He stands up and whispers that he is going to get their things together and take it to the car. Of course, what I do for one, I have to do to the others. I sat in the rocking chair a little longer than anticipated, because once I placed Evan in his seat, Grant and Cole woke up to eat. I have a feeling that they will show their true colors once we get home and alone.

Driving home with the three boys in their car seats I was on cloud nine. This mental image is everything I envisioned from the moment I was told I was having three babies. The ride home is quiet. Jacob and I don't talk much. We just listen to the babies snoring and deep breathing. We finally pull into the driveway of our new house. I grab Jacob's wrist to stop him. "Let's sit here a second. I want to remember this moment forever. Us, finally walking into our house as a family, finally able to live in our home as a family. I just want these next few minutes to be engrained in my memory."

He leans in and gives me a kiss on my temple. "I want nothing more. But, once we are in, I have a surprise for you."

Now, I am curious and anxious. I smile and give him a laugh as I say. "Okay, I'm ready."

He honks the horn, within moments the front door opens and family and friends come pouring out of the house. Our dogs come prancing to the door. It is the biggest and best welcome home bash I have ever seen. Children are running amuck with the dogs in the front yard. I look at Jacob who is watching me for my reaction to all of this commotion. I laugh and give him a wink. He smiles back, as we both open a back door. He hands off one car seat to his father, then the other to my father. My brother Ethan is behind me waiting to help me with the car seat. I pass the car seat to him, leaning in to give him a kiss on the cheek.

"So good to see you like this, Elizabeth. You make some beautiful babies!"

"Damn straight I do!"

He grabs my arm and pulls me to the side. "Before you go in there I just want to warn you that Cole and Anna are inside. Jacob asked mom to invite them. They came, but I don't think they were expecting Jacob's family here. They seem uncomfortable, but I know they are doing this for the babies."

My cloud walking has suddenly taken a fall. It breaks my heart all over again for them. To know that if Grant were alive this would be such a different homecoming. "Ethan, can you take baby Cole and Grant's parents to the patio? I think it will be best to visit with them out there for a while. I'll bring the other two out with me in a minute."

Ethan takes off for the house. I tell Jacob what Ethan has told me that I want to give Cole and Anna some time alone with the babies, since they really haven't bonded with them. Jacob rallies everyone into the house, where my mother and Jacob's sister Olivia go into the kitchen to start making an early dinner. Jacob helps me with getting the boys out of their car seats. He places Evan in my arms and drapes the backpack on my back. Then he places Grant in my other arm. "Are you sure you don't want any help out there?"

"I think it's best if I did this alone." I kiss him on the cheek and head for the patio.

As I walk to the table and chairs I hear them laughing and sniffling. I know they both are crying. It is a bittersweet moment. I experienced this moment once I held them, too.

"Hi guys, would you like to meet two more handsome boys?" I ask as I place Grant in Anna's arms, and I pull the chair closer so they can see Evan in my lap. "Anna meet Grant, and this little one is Evan." I hold him up to show her. Grant just grunts and pulls his long legs into his chest. She pulls him into the crook of her neck and cries. "He's just like his daddy, isn't he? It's funny how even being so small they have such personalities already. Cole is more like me, laid back and takes things as they come. Little Evan here is feisty and stubborn. I think he has the two worst attributes of Grant and me together. Poor boy!"

"Or he is just like his Grandpa." She smiles then looks terrified all of a sudden.

"Anna, are you alright?" I ask quietly.

"Beth, can we be called Grandma and Grandpa?"

"Anna, don't be silly you can be called whatever you want them to call you. No one has really given me their take on what to be called, so you two get dibs first."

She smiles and looks to Cole. "Then Grandma and Grandpa it is."

Kate comes out with her camera. "I thought that these boys need official pictures taken with their grandparents."

"With their Grandma and Grandpa!" I correct her. I stand up and place Evan in Anna's arms and the monitor on the floor. Kate takes some pictures, than instructs me to get in the picture. As soon as I do, the sun gets brighter than it has all day. "Crap, hold on a sec." She's digging in her bag for a different lens. I just smile, holding my face into the sun and absorb the heat on my face. She takes a few snapshots, then tells me that I am needed inside. I leave the boys with Cole and Anna and go in the house.

Jacob is at the door. "I want to show you your surprise." He pulls me upstairs.

"You know that now is not the time to run to our room as we have a house full of guests."

He laughs and pulls me to his side, "As much as I would love to sweep you off to our room, I have an even bigger surprise."

He guides me to one of the biggest bedrooms. He has his hand on the door knob and his other hand on my waist. "Close your eyes." He says. I look at him a little longer than he would like, because I have no clue why we are at this bedroom. We haven't discussed which rooms would be what. "Close your eyes!" He says as he kisses both eyelids. I hear him turn the door knob. He pulls me into the middle of the room. I can feel him standing behind me as his wraps his arms around my waist. "Open your eyes, baby!" He whispers into my ears.

I open my eyes and gasp, and cover my mouth with both hands. My eyes are open wide as I take in the magical transformation of this room. Somehow Jacob has made our boys a nursery. All I can stammer out is, "how.....how did you do this? When did you do this?"

"Olivia did most of it, I told her what you liked, gave her a little of what I liked, and she put it all together."

"Jacob, did she do that?" I point with my shaky finger to the most beautiful mural on the wall.

"Yes, baby she did it all!" He whispers in my ear, while peppering kisses along my cheek.

I am staring at the most amazing sunrise in my sons' room. She has painted this incredible beach scene on the wall, with a huge sun rising out of the sea. There are three surfboards stuck in the sand, with each of their names. The sky is so blue, as if she picked the blue out of Jacob's eyes. She even painted an airplane flying over the sun, tagging along one of those banners. In the banner she painted the lyrics to the song I sing to the boys 'You are my sunshine'. The ceiling is painted the same blue as the wall with fluffy white clouds. I notice stars in the ceiling.

"She placed glow in the dark star stickers up there. She says that the boys will like them once they get older. Max has them in his room." He informs me that his nephew Max picked out these certain stars.

The other three walls are painted a soft tan color. My babies have their own crib. They are walnut color and they each have a different crib. "These cribs convert to bigger beds once they get older, I figured they would want their own style." He points to each style of the cribs. Two cribs were together on one wall, and the third was right next to the middle crib by the corner wall. On the wall next to the walk in closet was a long eight drawer dresser with a changing table on top. Above the dresser were three surf board shelves and just above that was the picture of me next to my Camaro that Kate photographed.

"I wanted that picture in my office, but Olivia said that it was better in here…for now. I am sure the boys won't want to be looking at their momma like that…forever." He says while pulling me to him for a kiss.

I kiss him with such force that he had to stabilize himself to keep us from falling. Grabbing me by my waist he picks me up. I wrap my legs around his waist. Pulling his mouth towards mine I give him a gentle kiss. "I love you, Jacob Alexander, and I can't thank you enough for giving our boys such a beautiful room to grow into." I whisper into his lips. He and I are eye to eye and I take in those beautiful eyes. "Geez, you have the most incredible eyes, Love. I love how these eyes" as I take my fingers a brush over his eyelids "look at me with so much love and affection."

"Baby, you are beautiful and easy to love no question about that."

He slowly places me back on my feet, so I can take more in of the room. The boys' bedding is in a patchwork quilt, made of a gingham plaid print of reds, blues, and tans. There are picture of surfboards, fish, waves and palm trees. It is the perfect bedding, something I would pick out. Under the window are shelves with wicker baskets for storage. In the middle of the painted mural wall and are two khaki colored rockers with a matching ottoman. Between to the rockers is a small table with a light on it. I walk over to see the picture of the boy in the frame. I pick it up and give a small chuckle. "Is this you?" I hold the frame up to show Jacob.

"Yes, it's me when I was five. It was my first surfing lesson. Olivia thought that one day the boys would get a kick out of it."

I stare at the blonde haired boy and his eyes are as bright as the sea behind him. He had a beautiful smile; even back then toothless and all. As I start to take in the room and picture, tears start to fall down my cheek. I place the frame on the table and stare at the mural on the wall. I don't want to, but with all the emotions of the day I just lose it.

"Baby, you don't have to keep the picture in here. Olivia got carried away with the whole beach and surfboard theme. Why are you crying? You aren't sad are you?"

I wipe my tears and glance up at him. "I'm not that sad, it's just so much to take in. I never told you that Grant had written me a letter a couple years ago, when we were trying for a baby. It was about being responsible and how being a parent was going to change us. He went on to tell me that if anything were to happen to him, he would want me to be happy and to find a father figure for our children. He said that whenever I needed him he would be in the sun and the stars looking down on us. To see this mural and those stars it just made me think of him watching his babies. Then I see this" as I hold the frame to him "and it saddens me to know that I will never have blond hair blue eye children with you. Are you really okay with not having biological children with me? Because there is a chance we won't have children together."

He kneels in front of me and places his hands on my face. His thumbs wipe away the few tear drops on my cheek. "Like I said to you before you even gave us a chance. I love those boys because they are a part of you. You are my whole world, Elizabeth. You're the reason that this is still beating." He places my hand over his heart. "It beats for you and those boys. You have my whole heart and soul. Biology doesn't make me less of a dad. They will have all of this," as he places his hand over my hand that is still on his chest. "They will receive the same amount of love and devotion as if they did carry my genes. So to answer your question, I'm really okay with what we have now. Because you and the boys are the greatest gifts ever given to me and I love you four more than anything."

He kisses me deeply. We're interrupted by a knock on the door and Olivia walks in. I get up and give her the biggest hug possible. "This is beautiful, thank you so much!" I tear up as I look into her deep blue eyes, like Jacob's, but a shade darker.

"It was an honor to do this. I'm just glad you like it." With another hug she starts to laugh. "Does this mean I'm officially the best aunt ever?" She exclaims while grinning towards Jacob.

"What's up?" Jacob asks her.

"Umm Elizabeth is needed, Grant is crying and so is Cole. Are they due for a feeding?"

Jacob looks at his watch and tells her that they are. He tells me to sit and that he will bring them to me. I sit in the rocker and stare at this magnificent room. It looks like something out of a catalog. I'm so very blessed to have so many people love the boys and me.

The evening comes to an end with Kate taking so many pictures of the boys. She included the grandparents, aunt, uncles, and children. My mother takes Kate's camera and gets a mommy picture of Ella, Kate, and me with the boys and girls. I finally feel like a mom posing with them. For so many years I have been the one behind the camera. Then as she is about to leave, Kate takes a picture of Jacob, the boys and me. She smiles as she scrolls back and looks at the pictures. I can't wait to see what she does with them. As the last person leaves, Jacob and I sigh in relief.   It is nice to have some peace ….finally.

Chapter 21

Running

October

Being a mom to triplets is close to being the ring master of a circus. I feel like my life has turned into a circus, and there are days I am a clown juggling a lot more than flaming torches. I think flaming torches would be tranquil compared to the last five months.

The past five months have been hectic, but I wouldn't change the circus life we lead. Jacob has merged his office with another group of OB/GYN's, so he is only on rotation at the hospital one to two nights a week compared to the four or five he was doing. This helped out a tremendously, and my mother was finally able to go back home.

I have spent the last five months getting into a routine. The boys still see many doctors. Evan is finally off the Apnea monitor, but we still have monthly visits with the Pulmonologist for the boys' Synagis shots that will prevent RSV. We have seen numerous doctors to make sure that they are developing at a healthy and normal rate. For being born at thirty two weeks they are considered very healthy and normal. The boys are around the fifteen pound mark and are finally getting those cute chubby rolls.

Jacob was concerned that my baby blues were turning into something more along the lines of postpartum depression. He thought it would be good for me to get out of the house more. It was a difficult decision to make, but last month I ended up going back to work. I only work two days a week in the office. It gets me out and socializing with adults again. It works out well because those days I have Anna watch the boys and those are days that Cole takes longer lunch breaks at work. I also got a personal trainer and meet him three times a week. I am feeling more like myself these days. The boys are eating solid foods, and are on formula. I still nurse when I can, but not as much as I was doing.

Jacob and I have talked about marriage, he brings it up more than I do. I feel like it's still so soon. The last year has been a tornado of events. I try to change the subject when it comes up.

Looking at Jacob and the boys my heart palpitates out of my chest filled with so much love for them. I didn't think I could love like this. Jacob is lying on the floor with the boys. They are rolling all over the place now. He is blowing raspberries on their bare bellies. Grant is laughing up a storm. Evan is giving him his don't mess with me look, and Cole is just watching the three of them act like monkeys. Grant stops laughing and babbles "dadadadada". I stop doing the dishes and listen to see if what I thought he said was correct. Jacob sits up tall, and does the same thing I am doing, WAITING for him to say it. I come to the floor and smile at my baby boy. He gives me his own version of raspberries, then looks to Jacob and says "dadadada". I fall to me knees, not knowing if this is a good thing or not. I mean I know that this would happen.

Jacob is over the moon, he is laughing and holding Grant to his chest, shouting "that's my boy" and he said "dada before mama." I just stare at the floor. Hating myself for going back into the past and thinking of my dead husband.

Later that night while Jacob and I are getting ready for bed, he hits me with another blow.

"Baby, I've been doing a lot of thinking and today just clarified it even more..."

I cut him off by my rudeness. "I don't want to talk about marriage, if this is where the conversation is going."

He gives me the look that says I'm being a total bitch and what just spewed out of my mouth was not appreciated.

"What I was trying to say, is that I would like to adopt the boys." He doesn't even look at me.

"What? Why?"

"Are you shitting me? Why? Well, for one, I'm their daddy and have been since I gave you the fucking results that you were pregnant. Two, because they still have the last name of Thomas and I think as their dad they should have my last name."

I know this is going to get ugly. "I still have the last name Thomas and I'm not changing it. They will have my name. I want them to still have a part of their real father."

Ouch, I know that was a nasty blow, and it's even worse by seeing the blue in Jacob's eyes turn black. His hands are clenched into fists and his breathing is getting faster and faster.

"So you are telling me that even when we get married you are going to keep your dead husband's last name. You aren't changing the boys' last name due to the fact that their father, a God damn sperm donor's last name is Thomas. Elizabeth, when the hell are you going to see that Grant was a sperm donor? He NEVER FUCKING KNEW you were pregnant! He never knew he was going to be a dad. But you know who the hell has been with your through it all, is me. I'm their father through and through and if you are going to throw DNA in my face, then we have a whole shit load of other problems."

"I'm not ready for all of this." I mutter to him.

"Well, when you are fucking ready please let me know, so I can step in and be a father to those boys and a husband to you. In the mean time I hope their ghost of a father does a damn good job."

He picks up his phone off the table, grabs his pants on the way out of the room. He slams the bedroom door and I know that I will not be getting a good night sleep. A few minutes after he slammed the door, I knew he left as I heard his truck peel out of the drive way. He did leave me a text saying he was going into the hospital. That he didn't know when he would be home.

I can't sleep, so I head to my laptop, and do something I know I will regret. I run. I book three seats on a flight to my parents. I pack a large suitcase for all of us and load up the SUV. I call my mom and let her know we're flying in the morning.

Once we land at the Asheville Airport we're greeted with my parents, Ethan and his girlfriend Megan. My father bolts for us as I am trying to push a stroller with three babies and drag a suitcase. My mother is giving me this look, like "why are you here?"

"Elizabeth." Is all she says to me? Suddenly I feel like an eight year old being scolded for lying.

"Mother, please not now." I say as I brush past her and go hug my brother.

"Hey sis, you okay? " He whispers, as he gives me a hug.

"No, not really, but nothing a little time away can't help clear the mind." I reply as we walk to the car.

My mother and father are in pure bliss with the boys. My father even built a swing set. He spends the mornings pushing them in their bright blue seats.

I'm in pure hell. I know I have done the worst thing ever to Jacob. But, he pissed me off and I let my stubbornness take over. I ran, thinking we needed to cool off, although it just led me to be consumed by more frustration. He should adopt the boys, they might not have his genes, but he has been a father since day one. Everything he told me six nights ago was true. Grant ended up getting me pregnant, but Jacob has done everything a father should do.

We haven't talked. We've only have exchanged a few short texts to one another. I know he is giving me time to get my act together. He is highly pissed I left without telling him, which on my end was another bitchy thing to do considering his wife did this to him. I know that the timing of all of this is a huge factor. Today marks the one year anniversary that Grant was killed in his motorcycle accident. If baby Grant never called Jacob Dada and Jacob never brought up adoption, then I know I would still be home. I'm in such a state of pissed off frustration. So much has happened in a year, some really wonderful things. I became a mom, I fell in love, and I can see where my future is going, where this time last year I couldn't get out of bed. Why is it so damn hard to let go off a *perfect* past? My life was going somewhat to plan. Struggling with infertility was just the tip of the iceberg. Then my life did a complete one eighty without any notice.

Now I have to plan for my sons. I want to make sure I am doing the right thing. Will they be pleased or pissed about the decisions I am about to make. I just want them to be happy. Boy do I pray I am doing this right. I head for my lap top to finish up some work. While on, I get a ding from my incoming mail. I click on it to see it is an email from Jacob. He never writes emails.

Elizabeth,

Words can't describe the pain I'm going through right now. I miss you and the boys terribly. The house is way too quiet with you all gone. Please, please come home. I am so sorry for rushing you and talking about adoption.

I won't bring it up again. I don't care about their last name I just want you all home safe and sound.

I'm so upset that you felt the need to run. I wish you would have talked to me. I know I can be a hot head sometimes, but if I knew you would've taken off, I would have come back to talk to you. I love you. I knew I loved you the moment you fell in my arms this time a year ago. When I looked at your face, my heart bled for you. I held you in my arms for hours. I couldn't let you go. I wanted to protect you from the hurt and the pain that you were falling into. I wanted to give you hope, and I wanted to show you how much I loved you. You are the most beautiful, amazing, intelligent, and fun spirited woman I have ever met. As much as it pains me to know that the only way you entered my life was by a death of a loved one, I will be forever grateful of Grant's death. His death gave me a life I only prayed for. His death gave me the love of a beautiful woman. His death gave me three perfect sons. His death gave me a home. His death gave me a future, where dreams could come true. So as much as I hate to be thankful of someone's death, look at what has happened. How can I not be grateful for his death? I apologize deeply for calling him a sperm donor. I was mad at you for throwing the boys genetics in my face and I said something completely out of line. You and I both know that he wasn't a sperm donor. I know he was a good man and that he loved you. So, I will be right by your side whenever you want to tell our boys about their biological father.

But, you need to do something for me. Stop throwing his god damn DNA in my face. He might have gotten you pregnant, but I carried you through your pregnancy. I was there when I took that blood sample. I was there when I held Ella as she cried tears of joy for you. I was there when you were scared of miscarrying only to give you news that it was triplets. I was there to tell you that you were expecting boys. I was there when baby Grant almost died. I am the reason he is alive. I was there when they took their first breath. I cut their umbilical cords. I WAS THERE!! I AM THEIR FATHER!! I am no different than if you adopted these children yourself. I am in love with those boys, unconditionally. I would die for them, give them my last breath. So please don't throw biology and DNA at me ever again.

I love you Elizabeth. You are where I belong and right now you need to be here, home. So please, I beg of you. Just come back home and let me love you.

Love Always,

Jacob

UGH!! I stare at the computer screen. I want to throw the laptop across the room. I'm so mad at myself. I can't believe I did this to him. I couldn't agree more with everything he has said. So I reply back that I will be home soon and I will let him know when my flight would be arriving. While finishing up some more work, my mother is at the door with Cole in her arms. She has her pinky in his mouth and he is not a happy camper.

"I think this little guy is hungry. I made a bottle, but he wants nothing to do with me." She passes Cole over to me. His chubby cheeks and heart shaped lips make me smile.

I lean back in my chair and pull the side of my shirt up getting him situated to nurse. My mom sits on the edge of the bed. "Have you talked to Jacob?" She asks while looking around the room.

"I just read a lengthy email he sent me. Everything he wrote is true. I know I shouldn't have left the way I did, but I was just pissed more so with life and timing."

"So, what are your plans now?" She says with her motherly stare.

"You know, that is one saying I will never say to my boys. I hate that saying mom. I have no clue what my plans are. But, what I am going to do is go back home. I will look for a flight home tomorrow. "

"Well, I'm sorry for asking, but you need to plan. If not life hands you lemons and then ..." I cut her off before she goes through the whole analogy.

"No offense, mom, but that analogy is shit. I planned and life brought me death. So, I don't get to sit back and sip the lemonade that life handed me. I buried my husband. UGH!! Why can't you for once just talk to me instead of giving me these stupid age old analogies?"

I say to her as I see the tears billow up in her eyes. Cole can feel my tension as he starts stirring in my arms. I pull my legs into me and hold him a little tighter.

"Shit, mom, I'm sorry. I've just been dealt a hard hand to deal with. It's taken me sometime to figure out how to play this game." I whisper to her as I give her a wink. Like Mother like daughter.

"For a daughter who says she refuses to mother like her mother she just threw her parenting style in her mother's face." She winks back.

I start to laugh because I swore to myself I wouldn't do these crazy ass things my mother did, yet here I am reciting lines she would say to me as a child. God help my sons!

"Elizabeth, listen we all travel down this road. Sometimes our road is smooth, sometimes it is loaded with pot holes, or sometimes it's a dirt road we travel. Yet, we adjust our lives to the road we travel, then somewhere out of the blue there is a bend in the road that we never saw coming. We hate that we had to steer our lives around this bend and continue on the road of life, but just down the road a little more is another bend with no warning sign.

"So what I am saying in this crazy analogy is that honey, you are living a great life, and life will have bends on smooth, pot holed, and dirt roads. The only thing important is who is traveling with you on these roads.

"And my darling, you had Grant to travel on your smooth road of life, and then you hit that bend with the pot holes in it and found yourself traveling alone. Then Jacob came along and is trying so hard to join you on your travels with your boys. He loves you *so* much."

I wipe the tears that are coming down my face. For once my mother gives me an analogy that I like, and do learn from. I know what I need to do.

"Thanks Mom. I know Jacob loves me and the boys. I'll never run again, and I'm looking forward to our travels on the many roads we will endure."

My mother gets up and walks over to kiss my forehead. She bends over and kisses Cole's soft dark brown hair and walks out. I finish feeding Cole, then head downstairs.

That evening during dinner I inform my parents and brother that I am leaving tomorrow afternoon to head home. I tell them that I made an ass out of myself, to which they all laughed and said I do it gracefully. Each adult held a baby in their arms, which left me to clear the table and do the dishes. As I am standing at the sink, I notice a car flying up my parent's driveway. I ask my parents if they know this person. My dad walks to the window and says that it's Ella. I go to the door and I open it to the wrath of Ella. *Oh Shit!*

She storms past me. "Hey Grace, Evan, and Ethan. Hi, baby boys." She says as she walks over and kisses each one on the cheek.

"Umm ...Ella, what brings you to North Carolina?" I mutter to her as I load the dishwasher.

"Your sorry ass is what brings me. If you don't mind, Grace, I need a very long word with Elizabeth, outside."

She gives my mother another kiss and then stomps herself towards me. She grabs my elbow and pulls me out the side door to the porch swing. She has her legs crossed and het foot is shaking a mile a minute. I know she is upset with me.

"Beth, what the hell were you thinking? Jacob is a complete mess. I know that today is a hard day, which is why I came, to remind you of what you have gained in comparison to what you have lost."

"Ella, you wasted your time and your sky miles. I'm coming home tomorrow. Jacob sent me an email and it clarified and made me realize everything he has said is true. I even liked the analogies my mother gave me during her talks."

"What did Jacob say to you? He's a walking zombie, I don't think he has slept since you have been gone, and he misses his boys terribly. He told me that Grant called him Dada and that night he brought up adoption. Then you went bat shit crazy on him and the next day he realized you were gone."

"He basically said that Grant was a sperm donor since he never knew I was pregnant. Jacob said that he has been the father since he confirmed my pregnancy. I just never looked at it that way. Grant and I had so many dreams together and we accomplished so many as well. It's just hard to know that my sons will never know or get a glimpse of the kind of man he was. Although, I know if I could have any other man to be a father for my boys it would be Jacob. Something about him that makes him so remarkable and I know that our boys are so lucky to have him."

"Beth, you can't run anymore, you're a mother now. You can't pull temper tantrums like this. Stop being so hard headed and open up your heart."

"Ella, I'm just so scared. What if I love this man with all my heart, then in a few good years he is taken away from me? My heart can't handle another loss like I experienced with Grant. I just can't."

She turns sideways and grabs my hands. "Honey, stop with the 'what if' shit. You are wasting time drudging up scenarios that don't mean shit. You of all people know that life is too damn short and you shouldn't be wasting it on thinking about something that might happen or not. Grant is your past, Jacob and those boys are your future. Focus on today and tomorrow. You can only go ahead, you've already wasted days away because you were scared. Life is scary, life is a battle. It's a scary uphill battle. So put on your running shoes and run with it."

"Not you too!" I shout to her. "I swear to God, I hope your Grace-isms aren't from being around my mother. I get it, and I am going home to my new love and we are going to plan for a happy and full-filled future."

"That's my girl!" She exclaims as she pulls me into a hug. We swing in peace on the porch for a while before I am beckoned to feed my babies.

Chapter 22

Jacob
- Falling to Pieces -

Today is the one year anniversary of Grant's death. Today is day seven since I haven't formally spoken with Elizabeth. I sit in my office and I type out an email for her. I know I was wrong and I said some really shitty things to her, but I can't stand that she throws genetics in my face. I've always believed that any man can be a father. But, it takes a real man to be a dad. I don't care that those boys have none of my genetic make-up. They are a part of Elizabeth and that is all that matters to me. I love those babies, they are my heart and soul.

I'm so thankful that the office is slow today. Ella informed me she needed the rest of the week off. I know why, she is so easy to read. I know she is going to North Carolina to get Elizabeth. Sitting here staring at the screen, I'm struggling for the right words to come out. I just want her and the boys' home. I want her in bed, next to me. I miss her smell, her touch, the sound of her voice when she is in pure bliss. I miss the look on her face when she is about to come. I miss every God damn thing about her. I'm going fucking crazy here!

I miss my baby boys. I finally hear the words that melted my heart, and not even a day later they are nowhere in my sight. Finishing up the email and I hear my cell phone vibrating. I reach for it quickly thinking it will be Elizabeth. It's not, it's my sister. "Hey Jake, how are you?" She cheerfully chirps into my ears. "I've seen better days Liv. What's up?"

"Not much…Listen Mike is taking the kids to the movies tonight. I was wondering if my baby brother was up for dinner tonight."

"Liv, I don't think I will be much company. Wait? Have you talked to Dad?" I hear nothing on her end and I know her, she is trying to find a way to soften the blow between Dad and me. "Liv….you know, don't you?"

"Jake, Dad is concerned. He says he has never seen you so distraught. He says he can't fix this and asked if I could help."

"Liv, I don't mean to be an ass, but no one can fix this except Elizabeth and me. I'm not a child and I don't need my father and big sister rescuing me. I'm fine, I just miss my family!"

Pacing my office, I know I am not fine. I'm falling to pieces here…slowly crumbling to the ground and the first thing shattering is my heart.

"Jake, we both got to eat so can we still meet up for dinner?"

"Sure, I'll swing by after work and pick you up. Be ready by 5:30p.m."

"Thanks, Jake, and see you later."

I throw my cell phone on my desk. Running my fingers through my hair and trying to compose myself for my next patient.

My afternoon drags. The days seem to get longer and longer without Elizabeth around. I go home to feed and let the dogs out. Once I am back in the truck and before I leave the driveway I send Elizabeth a text.

I miss you! Please, come home. I love you!

Pulling into Olivia's driveway I get a pictured text. It's the boys in a backyard swing giving the camera their big toothless smile. At the bottom, the text reads.

Love you Daddy. Coming home soon.

Coming home soon…what the hell, how soon? Why is she being so uncommunicative towards me? Did I make things worse sending the email? I need to call Ella, see if she got there and find out how Elizabeth is. I'm not in the mood to sit down with my sister and talk over dinner. I know what I need to do. Olivia is walking out of her door by the time I get to it. I give her a hug and walk her to her side of the truck.

"Can you wait for dinner? There is something I want to do first."

"Uh, sure I guess. I'm hungry so when we do it, don't complain that our meal is too expensive." She laughs at me.

"Liv, you asked me to dinner, so you are buying." She is just laughing away. "Little brother you are the high paying doctor and I am your wonderful sister so you are treating me."

We drive in silence for a while as I get onto the expressway and head towards downtown. She looks over to me with her big blue eyes and long wavy chestnut brown hair. She looks just like our mom, with the exception of her brown hair. "Where are we going, Jake?" She quietly asks.

"You, big sis, are going to help me pick out an engagement ring for Elizabeth. I'm not planning to ask her right away, but I want it when the opportunity arises."

She pats my arm and smiles. "I think this is a great plan, Jake. She will be lucky to marry you. You are pretty amazing!" She says as she winks to me.

We drive to the jewelers and scan the glass cabinets of rings. I have an idea of what I want. I finally find it. It's beautiful and speaks exactly what she means to me. I have Olivia try it on. I think they might be around the same size, maybe Elizabeth is a little smaller. I go a size smaller just to be safe. Once this ring goes on her finger, it will never come off.

Later on I treat Liv to a huge dinner where I hear all the creative ways to propose to Elizabeth. Little does Olivia know, I am taking her advice. She is a Pinterest freak and I know she has seen a few dozen ways to propose. I take a mental note of what she is describing, so I can give Elizabeth the special proposal she deserves.

Chapter 23

Coming Home

Flying home with the boys was hard and I was so relieved to have Ella with me. If she wasn't there, I think I might have jumped out of the plane.

My boys cried the whole time. Being on the other end of screaming babies I have come to the conclusion that it is so much harder on the parents than the other passengers.

Ella helps me to the SUV once we have landed in Orlando. I give her a hug and thank her for her love and patience with me.

"Beth, he loves you that's all that matters."

"I know Ella, and I promise I will make this right."

The boys finally pass out when we are half way home. I bring in the babies one by one in their car seats. I know Jacob is home because his truck in the driveway, but he doesn't greet us at the door. Once the last baby is brought into the house, I keep them bundled in their seats. I placed the baby monitor on the coffee table and go in search of Jacob.

I'm halfway up the stairs when I hear the shower. I quickly sneak in the bedroom and strip naked. I will give him one surprise home coming he'll likely remember. I quietly enter the bathroom. He is under the shower head with his head down, and eyes closed. Seeing the pain in his face hits me in the chest. I feel like the wind has been knocked out of me. I place the monitor on the counter and walk to the glass door of the shower. I open the door and wait for the cool air to hit him.

Feeling the cool air he straightens up and sees me standing there in my birthday suit.

"Elizabeth." He whispers.

"Hi handsome, is there room for me?" I quietly ask.

"Baby, you don't have to ask." He grabs my arm and pulls me into the shower. Once the door is shut, he pulls me into him and holds me tight as if I just might slip from his arms.

"Damn, Beth, I missed you so much. Don't ever leave me again. I don't think my heart could take it. Where are the boys?"

"You have me forever, I'm not going anywhere. The boys are finally asleep in their car seats. We'll hear them if they get up." As I nod my head towards the monitor on the counter.

I pull his neck towards me to bring his soft lips to mine. I kiss him slowly and gently, in between each kiss I beg for forgiveness. "Babe, please forgive me." Kiss. "I'm so sorry for running." Kiss. "I love you." Kiss. He doesn't say anything he pulls me tighter. His hands are roaming through my wet hair, and his tongue is dancing with my tongue. I hear him moan as I feel his hard length prod my abdomen. I slide my hand up and down his aroused length.

"Baby, you are MINE forever, until my last dying breath. Understand?" He growls the words at me as he places palms on my jaw, his eyes are burning with lust. I capture his mouth again, sucking his tongue, causing him to moan more into my mouth. Once I could hear his breath escalate. I push him against the wall. I licked the water droplets off his neck, gliding my tongue down his chest, and over the hard ridges in his stomach. I licked his happy trail from below his belly button to the base of his cock. I move my tongue up and down his hard shaft. I could hear his breath get deeper and faster. His hands were twisting and pulling in my hair. I was on my knees, with the warm water enveloping my body. I pull his cock into my mouth and suck. Moving my tongue around his shaft while sucking was pure ecstasy for Jacob. I felt empowered to bring him this kind of pleasure. Just when I could feel his release about to pour out of him. He pulls me off of him.

"The view of your tits shaking back and forth makes me want to be inside you so damn bad. Matter of fact ...I'm taking you now."

Without warning he picks me up. I wrap my legs around his waist and I have just enough time to turn the shower off. He doesn't even grab towels. He walks us towards the bed soaking wet. He throws me down in the middle and stares at me. "Damn, baby, you are so fucking sexy!"

He doesn't waste any more time on foreplay, he went right at it. He slides his cock back and forth over my clit, picking up speed. I could feel my body release more of my juices. I'm so close to orgasm when Jacob stops and impales me with his cock. I throw my neck back into the pillow as I scream from the slight pain and pleasure. He pounds into me, back and forth. In a matter of minutes I can feel my body start to quiver. Scrapping my nails up and down his back I yell out his name as my body releases a mind blowing orgasm. He pulls my legs up and presses my knees against my chest. I can feel him go deeper and deeper. His cock starts to twitch and I feel his warmth erupt inside me. He kisses my neck and rolls us onto our sides.

"I love you. I want this connection between us to never go away. You are mine forever and I promise you, you will have the last name Alexander."

We kiss some more when from the bathroom I can hear crying coming over the monitor. "Great timing Dr. Alexander. Duty calls …I'm sure you have some dirty diapers to catch up on."

He slaps my ass as he climbs out of bed. "Gladly! I missed my boys. Do you need to feed them or can I give them a bottle?"

"Babe, be my guest, they are all yours. After my flight with them, I'm in need of a hot bath."

With that I walk back to the bathroom, turn the baby monitor off and start my bath.

I've been home for three days now. Three days where Jacob has consumed and devoured me at every chance we can get. He has professed his love to me and the boys in more ways than one. Today, I finally am getting the chance to show him how much I love him and how much our boys and I need him. I am meeting up with Kate and Ella for lunch and then I also have to run into my office to pick up some much needed paper work, before I meet with them.

Pulling the SUV into the valet section of the restaurant I see Ella and Kate waiting for me in the lobby. I walk in wearing jeans, pink tank top with a black cardigan sweater and black heels.

"Whoa, look at you hot mama!" Exclaims Kate. I do a little curtsy as I walk up to them and give each hugs and kisses.

"Beth, you look amazing. I can't believe you are already back to pre-baby shape and your boobs are huge! Did Jacob see you leave looking like this?" Says Ella.

"Why thank you, and yes ladies, he did see me, which is why I'm late." I say as I wiggle my eyebrows to them. Kate gives us her cackle of a laugh.

Ella just smirks at me. "No wonder you are glowing, you two are like fucking rabbits. Those poor boys first sentences are going to be "Oh God Jacob ....more ...more!" Kate cackles some more. I slap her as we walking towards are table. Stranger's eyes are glaring at me.

We sit down to our lunch and our conversation flows. We talk about everything under the sun, mostly about Jacob and me. "Oh, before I forget, my dear. These are for you." I hand Kate her finalized divorce papers. I can't believe I helped her with her divorce when it seems like yesterday we were at the court house for her impromptu wedding. She looks a little distraught and bites her bottom lip. Shit, I didn't want to upset her. "Kate, I didn't mean to upset you. I just didn't want to forget, I know you want this over with."

She looks up to me with her huge blue eyes and sticks out her tongue. "I'm not upset, I'm more relieved and can't believe it is here. I just want him to stop being my responsibility. Let his new slut deal with all his shit. I just want peace for my girls and me." She says as she raises her glass. Ella and I follow and raise ours. "To the best damn girlfriends a girl could have. Love you biotches!"

We clink our glasses and finish up our lunches as we make room for cheesecake. "Oh, I want to show you what I got Jacob for Christmas." I say as I dig it out of my purse.

"You got him a Christmas gift already? It's not even Thanksgiving yet." Ella replies.

"It's still in the works, but I wanted your input on it because it will change us forever." With that I pull it out and place it in the middle of the two of them.

"Oh wow Beth, are you really going to give him this?" says Ella.

"I think it's the best gift ever, he will love it!" Mumbles Kate while her head is still down looking at his gift.

We gawk and talk some more about his gift. Once they are done I place it gently back in my purse. "So what are we going to do for your thirty first birthday?" Kate says while licking her fork clean from the chocolate and peanut butter cheesecake we all inhaled.

"Something big, last year was monumental learning I was having three babies. This year I want to celebrate and definitely have a drink!" I utter as best as I can while swallowing the peanut butter.

I can't believe how much my life has changed in a matter of twelve months. I'm very happy with how things have turned out. In a way, I couldn't have planned it better.

Chapter 24

Surprise ... Surprise

December

It's Christmas Eve. We've just said goodnight to Ella, Chris, their girls, Kate and her girls, Olivia, Mike, and their two kids Sophia and Max. It has been my tradition with Kate and Ella to do dinner on Christmas Eve. We ordered in pizza and wings....nothing fancy. The kids open gifts, while we watch Christmas movies. This year it was even bigger as Jacob, our babies, along with Jacob's sister and her family joined in. Seeing Jacob play with his niece, Sophia, and nephew, Max, along with the girls and our boys brought tears to my eyes and so much joy to my heart. It solidifies my gift for him even more. I can't wait for him to see it tomorrow.

We hug and kiss our family goodbye, and Jacob helps carry out gifts. As Jacob is helping everyone to their car I grab one baby at a time and take them upstairs to get them ready for their baths and bedtime. Tonight it's a quick sponge bath. As I am working on the final sponge bath I hear Jacob slowly coming up the stairs. He leans against the door jam, holding two bottles and watching me put Cole into his Christmas PJs.

"Did you have a good night?" He says in his oh sexy voice.

"Yes, handsome, I had a great time, did you?"

"I had a blast. I hope we do this every year. I especially can't wait for our boys to be older and to understand Santa and open their own gifts."

"Me too!" I say as I pass baby Grant to him, and then Evan. I grab Cole and we walk into our bedroom to feed the boys their milk. "Which one gets the boob and which two get these." He says while holding the bottles to me.

"Cole gets me and you get those two." I sit on the bed and start feeding Cole, as I watch Jacob lay the babies on the bed and then scoop them both up. He sits himself up against the headboard and bends his legs. He lays both boys propped up against his muscled legs. It amazes me how he picks up our boys with such strength and grace. Sitting here staring at the loves of my life, I realize how lucky I am. I've had some amazing love in my life.

It's Christmas morning. We wake up to the jibber jabber of voices over the baby monitor. I'm like a kid on Christmas morning and hop out of bed. Jacob beats me to the door. "You get coffee going, I'll get the babies. Oh and don't forget the camera!"

I give him a kiss and watch him walk to the boys' room. I run down the stairs to start a pot of coffee and make sure the camera has batteries in it.

My first snapshot is Jacob carrying all three in his chiseled arms like they were a sack of potatoes. The boys are giggling and smiling. Jacob's smile is to die for. He is so happy. Seeing his face, I hope it doesn't change when I present him with his gift.

The boys have watched us 'ooh and aah' over us as we unwrap their gifts. They were more interested in the wrapping paper. Jacob is about to get up off the floor when I tell him to hold it, that I want to give him his gift. I run into the kitchen pantry and pull it off the shelf.

"You put my gift in the pantry? Is it going to spoil?" He laughs at me.

"No, it's not going to spoil. I had to put it where you couldn't find it." I say as I place the shirt box on his lap.

He looks at me with curious eyes. He lifts it up and shakes it. "You got me a shirt?" He says in such a smart ass tone.

"No, it's not a shirt. I just had to find a specific box for it." He slowly tears off the paper and hands the boys' pieces of the paper. I reach down and pull the paper out of their mouths. I scoop the three and place them in my lap as I sit down on the floor with them. He pulls the lid off the box. He withdraws the tissue paper and stares blankly at the box. "Open it," I tell him as he hasn't even looked at the present yet. He pulls out the manila file folder out of the box. He opens the file and all I see are his bright blue eyes read over the writing of the papers. I see tears in those sea blue eyes of his and my heart melts for him. "Merry Christmas, Jacob!" I whisper to him. His lips fly into my lips so fast that I wasn't prepared for the impact he gave us. I held onto the boys.

He sits back on his heels. "Are you for real, is this fucking real?" He mumbles.

"Yes, babe, it's real." I wink at him as he reopens the file folder and stares at what is lying in it.

"So what do you think? It's what you asked for, do you still want it?" I ask to him.

"Elizabeth, this is the best gift ever. I've wanted this for so long. I promise you I will show you that this was the best decision you have ever made. Now hand me over my boys…Grant, Evan, and Cole Alexander. It has a nice ring to it…all we need is Elizabeth Alexander and we are set…right boys?" He is indicating to me, but talking to the boys.

"In due time Jacob …let's focus on your gift."

He keeps looking at the adoption petition forms. I think he sees that not only will they get the last name Alexander, that I also changed their middle names to Thomas. They all will have a part of their biological father with them forever. It works out better and I love that they will share the name with each other.

"I like their new middle names." He says and then smiles. "But, I didn't give you your gift yet?" He says. I lean over to him and kiss him with all the love I can possibly have for this man. Once I pull back I look into those dreamy eyes of his and tell him, "Being the father to my boys is the best damn gift ever, and I get it every day, not just today. I don't need anything else." I get up and walk into the kitchen to prepare breakfast. I stand back and just watch Jacob talk to the boys while he reads over his

Petition for Adoption that I filed for. We go to court after the New Year. I walk to the stove smiling, knowing I did give him the best gift ever.

Breakfast consisted of telling the boys not to feed the dogs their French toast, and Jacob non-stop talking about his gift from me. He wanted to know the how's, the when's and why's of it all. I told him how I started the paperwork once I got back from my parents back in October. I reassured him that he was completely right about the whole topic, and that I was the stubborn mule of it all. Once we cleaned up breakfast and the kitchen Jacob told me to go get a shower. He said, he needed to get my present ready.

"What do you need to get ready?" I ask him curiously.

"I need to prepare a few things before I give you my gift." He tells me while putting the boys in their pac-n-play, not wanting his eyes to meet mine.

"What do you have up your sleeve Dr.?" I ask walking towards him. I place my arms around his waist and kiss his chest. "Please, I really don't need anything and I don't want you to go through any trouble. I'm really happy and content with what I have."

He kisses my head and pushes me back some so he can look into my eyes. "See, Elizabeth that is where you are wrong. I need you and I'm not completely content with everything I have."

"Geez you are so greedy. If it makes you happy then by all means go prepare. I'm going to take a shower." I give him a kiss and walk upstairs to shower.

I'm in our room getting dressed when I hear Jacob call for me. "Elizabeth, I'm in the boys' room when you are done."

Pulling my shirt over my head I shout back. "Be there in a minute." I pull my wet hair back in a messy bun, pull my jeans on and head for the boys' room. I walk in to see Jacob hunched over Grant's crib.

"Hey there, you needed me?" I quietly say as I walk into the room.

Jacob turns around and he is acting strange and kind of jittery. "Yeah, I need you for a second, the boys have something to say."

I look at him as if he has lost it. I walk towards the crib to where I hear babbling and coos. When I look down at the boys my heart stops beating and my breath vanishes. I stare at what the boys' shirts say. He has aligned the boys shoulder to shoulder in the crib and they have on white shirts with one word across their shirt. Grant's say's "MOMMY" and Evan's says "MARRY" and Cole's say's "DADDY". "MOMMY MARRY DADDY" are the words I keep repeating in my head. I stand there just staring at the shirts so long, that when I muster up the strength to turn around I find Jacob on one knee. All I can whisper is, "Jacob?"

He grabs my wrist to pull me closer to him. I am standing in front of him with tears rolling down my face. "Baby, don't cry." He reaches up with his thumb to wipe away the tears. "Elizabeth, I have loved you from the moment you fell into my arms. You sent a shock wave of electric volts to my system the moment I held you. My heart started to beat to a different rhythm the second you entered my life. My heart has been yours ever since that day. My heart became theirs the moment they took their first breath. Elizabeth Ann, I love you more than the air I breathe. I want to spend eternity with you by my side. I can't promise you sunshine and roses all the time, but I will do my best to make you smile every damn day. I love you, Elizabeth. Please marry me and spend the rest of your life with me?"

I sob out tears of joy. I grab his face with my hands and bend so our foreheads are touching one another. "Yes, I will marry you." I whisper to him as I am trying to control my sobs. I fall to my knees in front of him and kiss him hard.

"Baby, I still have another step to do" as he is trying to pull away from our kiss. I sit back on my heels and watch as he pulls the most gorgeous ring out of his pocket. Sliding the huge princess cut diamond with two smaller diamonds on each side in a platinum setting, I gasp by it beauty. "The diamond in the middle reminds me of you and the four smaller ones are the boys and I, how you hold us all together. You are an amazing woman, baby, and I am so lucky to have found you." He stands up and pulls me into him.

"I love you, Jacob! Thank you for making me so happy."

"It's my pleasure to make you happy. I love you, baby and thank you for legally making me a dad.

Those three boys are the best gift you could have ever given me, I'll always cherish you for it."

Looking into those blue eyes of his and then looking at my babies. It was then that I knew that my life was perfect.

Epilogue

Fireworks

4th of July

"Beth, for the love of God, stop…just stop. This is your day and you are stressing me out. Everything you have planned up until now will go to plan. If not then it wasn't meant to be." Ella says as I am trying to find pins for boutonnieres.

"I just want to make sure there are extra incase a few get lost."

"Beth, we need to get you into your dress." Kate sings songs to me.

"Yes, let's get you dressed before I have to sedate you again." Ella says to me with a quiet laugh.

I walk to the door where my dress is hanging and smile. It is beautiful and simple. Jacob and I didn't want a huge wedding. We both did that with our first marriage. This time it was just about us. We are getting married on the beach in the late afternoon, where we will eat and party until the grand finale of fireworks.

Kate slides my dress off the hanger and unzips it for me to slide into. It's an off white, A-line Charmeuse gown with a beaded sweetheart neck-line.

The back is what caught my eye and is stunning. It is held together in the back by three slim beaded straps running across my shoulder blades and down my back. My hair is pulled into a low bun in the back and I have three baby pink roses in my hair.

"Kate, freeze, focus, stop dancing, and help me," I say as I'm standing in my blue thong panties, my something blue from Kate. She is dancing to music off her iPhone, which is playing "*Catch My Breath*".

"It seems fitting, Bethy, huh? Dance with me." Once Ella slides the zipper up, we three start to dance. Kate and Ella dance in their pale pink strapless sweetheart A-line dresses. Once we finish our little dance, I turn around for the mirror. "Bethy-babe you are drop dead gorgeous…and look at those sexy arms of yours. I told you those car seats would tone you up." She winks at me. I do look stunning, I haven't felt this cherished or beautiful in a long time.

My mother walks into the hotel room. "Elizabeth, they are all ready for you girls ….are you ready?" She says while watching me through the mirror. I turn around and hear her catch her breath. "Oh, baby girl, you are breathtaking."

"Thanks Mom, I hope Jacob thinks the same thing. Do you have the boys?"

"Yes, they are in our room with your father and Jacob's father Jeff. They look adorable in their outfits." I wanted simple and didn't want to blow a fortune on a wedding when all Jacob and I wanted was to get married. The men and boys are wearing Khaki pants with a white button down shirt. Jacob is in a tan tie and the other men and our boys are wearing pink ties. My favorite part is we are all going shoeless. Ella hands me my bouquet of pink roses. They are wrapped in the handkerchief that Jacob's mom had with her on her wedding day to his father. The pink roses are also in honor of his mother.

Ella, Kate, my mom and I walk out of the hotel room and head for the elevators. I am greeted in the lobby by my boys' squeals and laughter. "Hi, handsome boys!"

"Momma …momma ….momma!" My father and soon to be father-in-law picked them up so I could lean in and give them kisses. "We are ready to start this party…Jacob and the men are already down there with the pastor," Jeff says as he gives kisses to Cole's chubby cheek.

"I'm so ready…let's go!"

I leave the hotel pool deck and head for the beach. Our parents walked down the man-made aisle with our boys. I laugh as I hear our wedding march song, Chris Daughtry's *"Start of Something Good."* He wanted to pick the music, which I happily gave him that honor. It reminds me of our first date at the concert when he leaned into me and whispered into my ear that we had something good starting. Boy was he ever right! I watch as my best friends walk down to the beach. Kate turns around and blows me a kiss. I blow her a kiss back, and it's in that moment that these women are my rock and saving grace. I wouldn't be here today, walking towards my happy ending with my love if it wasn't for them. Once they were passed the sand dunes, I start to make my walk.

I walked by myself this time. I didn't think I needed my father to give me away a second time.

Finally, I am past the sand dunes and staring right into my man's sea blue eyes. I watch as I see his smile get wider. He places his right hand over his heart, as if I have stopped his heart. I walk towards him with thoughts of our future. I look forward to tonight when I give him his wedding present. I've surprised him twice, and I'm hoping that the third time is a charm. I look to our family and friends, who are standing waiting for my arrival into my husband-to-be's arms. I look at our sweet baby boys with their dark hair blowing in the wind and their sparkling green eyes watching their momma walk towards their daddy. I blow them kisses and smile at our parents who are trying to keep our boys still.

When I get to Jacob he grabs hold of my hand and pulls me close to him. He kisses my forehead. "My God, baby, you are absolutely stunning." He whispers into my ear. He makes my skin tingle by the simplest words. We stick with a simple ceremony. We say our vows, our I Do's, exchange the rings, and then he kisses me and sweeps me off my feet. My favorite part of the ceremony was when we were introduced as Dr. and Mrs. Alexander. We walk hand in hand back up to the hotel lobby.

After our beautiful pictures on the beach we are ready to start our reception. We walk into the hoots and hollers of our guests as they reintroduce us Dr. and Mrs. Alexander. With his arm wrapped around my waist he guides us to the dance floor.

One of my surprises is our wedding dance song. "I hope you like our song, baby. I thought it completely tells our story. I love you." With his ending words I hear the music start. He pulls me into his body, and his hands drop to the small of my back.

We start to dance to Rascal Flatts "*Bless the Broken Road.*" I lean my head against his chest, with the beating of his heart I listen to the words of our song. I feel my cheeks get moist from the tears that run down my face. We are dancing to the most beautiful song I have ever heard. He's right too. This song does speak about us. I totally believe that the path I had been on is the path that led me to Jacob. I loved my other path of life, and where it brought me, only this path, gave me all my new dreams and desires. Jacob is the new love of my life. Kate was right, I'm extremely lucky to have two loves of my life. My path way with Grant was what I had planned; my path with Jacob is what life had planned. My only plan is to take this path slower.

After our dance we eat dinner, then we dance some more. We cut the cake and feed each other a few bites, which turned me on so much. I could tell that he was turned on just as much as I was, when I sucked the icing off his finger. The DJ wanted to do the garter and tossing the bouquet. Which was a really sad sight to see considering most of the females at our wedding were either married or in committed relationships. So it was a no brainer when Kate walked onto the floor with Megan, Ethan's girlfriend and Sophia Jacob's eight year old niece. Kate is a sore loser and she wasn't going down. With a few pushes between her and Megan she did catch the bouquet. God, I love that girl!

The garter was a sight to see. I could only imagine what the guests were thinking while Jacob was under my dress for so long. I know what I was thinking...that I wanted to take this man up to our suite and have hot and heavy sex with him. I could feel his warm tongue lick up my thigh. I could feel my panties melt. After what seemed like hours he finally came up for air with the garter in his mouth. My brother ended up catching the garter and Kate was more than happy to let Megan do the honors of sitting in the chair. "Kate, that was so sweet of you. Now, I wonder who will get married next you or Ethan."

"Ethan."

"What makes you think Ethan?"

"Beth, I've already been down that road, plus who is going to want a single mom who works her tail off? I don't have time, and my time is what made Keith leave."

"Katie-bear, you are preaching to the choir here. Who was the one that pushed me to see Jacob for what he is. I didn't think he could love or want a woman pregnant with triplets. You are beautiful, and your next chapter is out there. So, I'm betting it will be you next."

"I love you, Beth, and I'm so happy for you."

"I love you more than you'll ever know, Kate. How will I ever thank you for all of that?" As I point to the table where Jacob is sitting with my parents, his father and our boys.

We had a half an hour before the fireworks went off. I pulled Jacob to the side and told him I wanted to give him his present. It worked out great because my mother came up to me with a sleeping Evan in her arms. Jacob and I decided to take the boys up to my parent's room and asked them to be up there in twenty minutes. I grab Evan from my mother and Jacob grabs Grant and Cole. By the time we reach my parents' room, all three are passed out. We undress them quickly and place them in their pac n plays. I walk over to the boys' diaper bag and pull out the little silver bag that is holding his gift.

"Here, handsome, this is for you." He pulls out the flat item and un-wraps the tissue paper. He stares and within seconds his jaw drops. I'm smiling from ear to ear.

"Is this…?" He stammers out the question.

"YES!" I squeal in pure happiness.

"But, how…you said it couldn't happen."

"Why, Jacob? You are the doctor; you should be telling me the answer." He holds the silver 4x6 picture frame that says "On Our Wedding Day" but it's the picture that has him captivated. He is staring at my eight week ultrasound picture of our baby. "Are you happy Jacob? Because I am over the moon thrilled. I wanted to tell you as soon as I knew, but I wanted to surprise you. I just found out three weeks ago."

He walks over to me and places his hands on my belly. "Baby, you blow me away with your surprises, but I am so damn happy. We made a baby...holy shit...wait...you're...eleven weeks? Who did this ultrasound? It's from my office. You're due in January?

He can't stop his rambling, which means he's happy. "Yes, babe, we made a baby. I'm eleven weeks and so far everything is going well. As you can see, I'm a lot smaller with one than I was with three. Ella took the ultrasound. She squeezed me in when you were off to a lunch meeting. Your dad knows, once the ultrasound confirmed it, I called him. I'm sorry to be sneaky, but what do I get the man that has everything? I thought that this would be the best surprise."

"Oh God...Love, I am not upset, and I'm just surprised that's all. We just never planned this. Holy Shit...I can't believe it, you are carrying my baby. I love you so damn much."

"If there is anything I have learned in the short amount of time that we have been together is that the best things in life are the things we never plan for. We can plan as much as we want, but then life turns it over and gives us the perfect plan."

"I love you, Mrs. Alexander."

"I love you, Dr. Alexander."

"Now let's go watch those fireworks with our guests. After that show, I'm bringing you back up here and creating our own firework show," Jacob says as he brings me to my knees in a panty dropping kiss.

"I like that plan!" I whisper during our kiss.

THE END

A Letter from Sarah

Dear Reader,

I can't thank you enough for reading this story. I apologize for the amount of tissues you had to use for this book. Writing this book put me through the ringer as well. My first intention when writing this book was for my personal use and healing. See, what you don't know is that many the experiences that Beth endured to have a baby I struggled with. When I started out on this journey, I told Beth's story from my experience. This book was many years in the making and during this time I witnessed the heartache that my friends and family endured to even conceive a baby. The scene with Ella and Beth, yep I experienced that with a friend. There are no words to say to a loved one, when they yearn for a baby that isn't even real yet. Yet, too many woman carry the guilt and heartache around for that dream of being a mom. I never had the issue of getting pregnant, my issue was I couldn't stay pregnant for long.

All three of my babies were born too soon. My first born was born at thirty five weeks. He was small, but overall healthy. You say that isn't bad. But, for a young twenty something mom in perfect health. I wanted answers. How does my water break just like that at thirty five weeks? When I was pregnant with my second son, I was in pure heaven bliss with my pregnancies. I was the lucky one who didn't have all those symptoms, until the backaches started. I was tested to make sure another pre-term birth wouldn't happen. Doctors called my first born a fluke and even linked it to him being breeched. I was on cloud nine that I was finally going to have my 'normal' planned pregnancy. At thirty one weeks while sleeping my water broke. As a mom for my toddler in the next room and for my unborn child, I can't even express or tell you in words the fear that went through me. I was hospitalized for five days. (I didn't know at the time, but as long as you don't dilate you can stay pregnant.) After five days, my body gave up and went into labor. My son was born at thirty two weeks weighing in at 3lbs. 14 oz. Today he is a healthy nine year old boy, with the few exceptions of respiratory issues.

My husband and I thought we were done, but I was approaching thirty and thought I knew my body better and that maybe the first two pre-mature births were flukes. I mourned terribly the last two months of my pregnancy. I will never know what it's like to be completely huge, I will never know the anticipation of going to the doctor every week. Seeing family and friends give birth and then go home with their baby was the real kicker. So, with thirty creeping up, we tried one more time, maybe for a little girl. Two months later I was pregnant and I was due one day after my thirtieth birthday. Couldn't have been planned any better, right? Nope, my third pregnancy was the hardest. I went for weekly ultrasounds, I was put on progesterone shots...those hurt like a bitch! I was on bi-weekly blood tests. Our third baby was another boy. I was having night terrors. Finally at twenty eight weeks I broke down telling my doctor that I have a feeling something is wrong. He did multiple test and assured me, that I will get my full term. With a forced smile I left his office, still worried. Call it mother's intuition, sixth sense or freaky-ness. But five days later on Easter Sunday, I stood in the lobby of my church with water trickling down. Full blown panic. With back and forth testing, I was indeed in pre-mature labor. Luckily my cervix was my saving grace and I stayed in a hospital bed for twenty two days till I hit thirty two weeks and my placenta abrupted. You've read my experience with my third child. I gave it to Beth. I just didn't have the hot doctor. Damn!

You're wondering why I'm telling you this. I want you all to know that ten percent of women in the United States will experience infertility issues. That one in eight babies in the United States are born before thirty seven weeks. That the rise of infertility and pre-mature births keep going up. For me, the doctors never knew why I had PROM (Pre-rupture of the membranes) every test under the moon came back inconclusive for whatever they were looking for. So, just like an infertility woman searching for answers of why she can't get pregnant, I was searching for a reason of why my body couldn't keep my babies in longer. Why machines, drugs, and hospitals had to help them grow their last month and I couldn't. I can't tell you the guilt I carried. I carried it for years. I wanted to write a story for me, for me to find my answer in a fictional sense. I was pushed to publish this book, and now I want women to know that you aren't alone in any endeavor you face to be a mom. I want to connect with that one reader, and let them know that they aren't alone. I'm here.

Today, I'm a mom to three amazing boys. They were my proof that life is never planned or how life never goes the way you want it to go. They are my reason, to turn every obstacle into a journey to learn from. They are my reason to be better.

I thank you for reading Life's Perfect Plan and I can only hope you will enjoy more to come in the Life Series.

Love,

Sarah

Acknowledgements

I wouldn't have written this book if it wasn't for life giving me unplanned experience. This book was four years in the making. Four years of celebrations and uphill battles. I wouldn't have succeeded if it wasn't for so many people in my life.

To my husband, thank you for being my rock through our marriage and writing this book. I don't know where I would be if it wasn't for you. Your support, strength, and love is what got me through so many obstacles. Thank you, love!

To my handsome and miracle boys. You are living proof that life has its own way of doing things on its own time. You three have shown me more strength, determination, stubbornness, strong willed, strong minded, and fearfulness in your short lives than I have in my lifetime. You three will never know how much these characteristics have changed me forever as a woman and a mother. Face life head on and always find the positive in the negative. You are my sunshine and I love you to the moon and back!

To my mother, if it wasn't for catching the stomach bug while visiting you, this story would never had happened. You were determined to keep me away from my boys so they wouldn't get sick and for me to start typing away at my book. Thank you for your help and pushing me to write.

To my very own Ella and Kate. Kristan, we have been though many, many years together. You have found humor in any situation we have experienced throughout our friendship, marriage, motherhood and life. It's because of you that I created a book. Throughout, you always said, "This needs to be in your book!" And as you can see through "Life's Perfect Plan", many have made it. Including the VICKS scene, I will never forget that experience and neither will our children. To Erica, you are more than a rock you are my mountain. You are the strongest and bravest woman I know. I can hope that throughout our friendship I gain a quarter of your strength, determination, and fight for life. You have shown me that life is a gift and to live each day minute by minute. I am so blessed that you are a part of my life.

To my editor Rae with word play 77 peaches. Thank you for your help, your talent, input, advice, feedback and opinions with this book. I couldn't be happier with this story.

To Robin with Wicked by Design, who created my book cover. You knew exactly what I wanted to have in a cover. You created a cover for me that I truly love. I look forward to working with you again.

To Tami with Integrity Formatting, you saved my sanity when it came to formatting. Thank you for your help and hard work.

To my Beta readers…Amanda, who read the book in bits and pieces. Your texts would push me to write one more paragraph or page. You loved where the story was going and I can't thank you enough for excitement in the story line. Michele, who read the worst rough draft ever of my book and who also read the final. Thank you for reading my book twice, thank you for being my personal cheerleader. I can't thank you enough for being my biggest fan. To Lucinda, Kerri, Chrissy, Stephanie, Jennifer, Corinne and Darla thank you for taking the time to read my story. Your advice, feedback, and opinions are what made my story better. Most of you wanted more Jacob, so with your advice I created Jacob's point of view. You will never know how much you truly helped me be a better writer.

To the amazing authors I have talked with through Facebook, Twitter, and Goodreads. Stepping into your territory is terrifying, yet you all scooped me up and placed me under your wings and helped me along the way. To Author L.B. Simmons, I truly love your books and your writing technique. When I expressed this to you, you were so helpful and didn't hesitate to steer me in the right direction. Thank you for helping me out and recommending some talented people into my life. To Author Janice Baker, I cannot give you enough Thank You's for what you have done. Your messages and texts always brought me peace. You didn't sugar coat the experience for me, you told me what would be hard and boy were those moments hard. Thank you for not only being a great author but a friend as well.

To the many bloggers that helped me to get my name and book out there. Thank you, Melanie with Nerd Girl, Tiffany with This Redhead Loves Books, Jessica and Sheraka with Crazy, Chaotic Book Babes, For the Love of Books, Booked on Romance, One More Chapter, and The Romance Cover. It's because of you all that I am where I am. You all did the hard work putting my book out there and I can't thank you enough.

Finally to my readers, thank you for taking a chance on me and reading my story. You will never know how humble and honored I am because of you. I can only hope that you will give me more chances and like the other stories that I want to bring to you. I hope "Life Series" touches you as it does for me.

Read Kate's Story next in "*Life's Next Chapter*" book 2 in the Life Series. Coming in Fall 2013

About the Author

Sarah Goodman was born and raised in Central Florida. She grew a love for the beach and reading. Sarah married her high school sweetheart and was blessed with three sons.

Sarah has taught off and on for 16 years teaching four and five year olds. The other time she is a stay at home mom to her boys. Life consists of baseball, music lessons, soccer, and car pooling. When she isn't too busy or tired she writes.

Learn more about Sarah Goodman at:

www.authorsarahgoodman.weebly.com

www.facebook.com/sarahgoodmanauthor

www.twitter.com/sarahgood

www.pinterest.com/sarahgood1215

sarah630goodman@gmail.com

Made in the USA
Middletown, DE
21 June 2024

56134774R00166